"YOU ARE NOT A CITIZEN OF TIMSHEL," THE JOY MACHINE SAID.

"That's true," Captain James T. Kirk replied.

"I offer my services."

"And what does that involve?" Kirk asked.

"You must become a citizen," the Joy Machine said. "You will work at the job assigned you. You will receive pleasure according to the level of the job assigned."

"And if I respectfully decline?" Kirk asked.

The Joy Machine hesitated almost unnoticeably. "That will not be permitted," it said. . . .

Look for STAR TREK Fiction from Pocket Books

Star Trek: The Original Series

Star Trek: The Next Generation

Star Trek: Deep Space Nine

Star Trek: Voyager

STAR TREK®

THE JOY MACHINE

A NOVEL BY
JAMES GUNN
BASED ON THE STORY BY
THEODORE STURGEON

POCKET BOOKS
New York London Toronto Sydney Tokyo Singapore

An *Original* Publication of POCKET BOOKS

POCKET BOOKS, a division of Simon & Schuster Inc.
1230 Avenue of the Americas, New York, NY 10020

STAR TREK is a Registered Trademark of Paramount Pictures.

A VIACOM COMPANY

This book is published by Pocket Books, a division of Simon & Schuster Inc., under exclusive license from Paramount Pictures.

ISBN: 0-671-00221-X

First Pocket Books printing September 1996

10 9 8 7 6 5 4 3 2 1

POCKET and colophon are registered trademarks of Simon & Schuster Inc.

Printed in the U.S.A.

For Ted,
who always asked the next question

[subspace carrier wave transmission]

<interrogate
interrogate
interrogate>

>identify<

<me
interrogate>

>me<

Chapter One
Timshel

THE PLANET HUNG in the blackness of space like a jeweled ornament on a celestial Christmas tree. Bathed in the white-yellow glow of its G2 sun 145 million kilometers away, Timshel turned slowly in its orbit, a blue-and-white oasis in a dark desert of desolation, an exquisite anomaly in the lifeless void that was the average condition of the universe.

As visiting interstellar vessels slowed from their headlong pace across the galaxy and spiraled in toward planetary orbit, the world before them became even more inviting. Polar ice caps shone like beacons, and then landmasses, slowly turning green, appeared beneath the swirling clouds.

Five continents, set in azure like green and brown patches in a blue quilt, swam into view as the planet turned, and then the sprinkles of islands and island groups. From the arctic regions to the temperate zones to the tropics, the colors and shapes of the land and sea blended from one into another to make a seamless whole.

A shuttlecraft, descending, would adjust its course toward the northern temperate zone. From its windows or viewscreens passengers would see mountains capped with snow thrusting their way through forests, and they, in turn, would open on plains carved by the brown traceries of rivers and streams. Finally, where the rivers merged or the oceans stopped at the land, collections of buildings and highways would appear, ivory models in the day, a handful of scattered jewels by night, that provided the only proofs of human habitation, the subtle answer to the question: Is there life on Timshel?

The shuttle coming in for a landing at the port near the largest collection of structures on the planet, Timshel City, would see, beside the deep blue of the western ocean, a glistening patch of white enclosed by a verdant ring in which the dominant green was dotted with red and yellow, like an impressionist painting. As the shuttle got closer, the patches and dots would resolve into buildings and flowering trees. The buildings were mostly low structures like villas, each nestled in its own garden privacy. Toward the center of the city, the height of the buildings gradually increased, although none was taller than five stories. Here, too, gardens were more formal and set between wide expanses of pavement, as if people walking across the man-made plazas in their pursuit of business or sociability might wish to pause and enjoy the fragrance and color of the natural world.

The buildings themselves, as newly disembarked visitors would discover, were graceful structures built with an eye for art as well as function. The city, with its seaside location and its mild climate, was like a year-round vacation resort. Columns and pedestals supporting arched and airy roofs might remind historically minded visitors of ancient Greece, as well as the statues placed here and there in the plazas and the gardens where they could be seen from a distance or

come upon as a delightful surprise. The statues, by a
variety of hands in a variety of styles, had one
element in common: their subjects were not ordinary
humans and aliens and animals but idealized creatures like Michelangelo's David or the Venus of
Melos, as if Timshel City and its inhabitants were
reaching for the perfection inherent in every being.

That, in fact, was the planet Timshel, known
throughout the galaxy as a garden world and the
favorite leave station for starship crews. Timshel itself
was what the mother planet Earth had once aspired to
be, the Garden of Eden before the Fall. A bit closer to
its primary, less eccentric in its orbital inclination, a
bit warmer on the average with less seasonal variation, a bit less massive so that people accustomed to
the gravitational tug of a heavier planet felt a bit
stronger and more vigorous on Timshel, air with a
percent or two higher oxygen content that, mingled
with the perfume of an alien world unpolluted by the
burning of fossil fuels, made breathing on Timshel
like inhaling nectar.

Unlike Earth, Timshel was unspoiled by the effort
to lift itself to civilization from barbarous beginnings.
Settled nearly a century and a half earlier by a group
led by Praxiteles Timshel, the planet had avoided the
pitfalls that had trapped other colonies. Where others
had set about exploiting the natural resources of their
worlds, farming and mining and manufacturing and
turning their new worlds into prosperous centers of
export and commerce, the settlement on Timshel had
set aside a few areas in its temperate zones for the
raising of crops through highly mechanized farming
or by those who got their pleasure from labor close to
the soil, had installed remote mining operations in
the gas-giant planets and in the asteroid belt, and
automated manufacturing plants among the asteroids
and on the barren moons, and had set about building
themselves a way of life focused on thought and

discussion and creativity and art. And love. Timshel was a world of love. The citizens of Timshel were in love with each other, in love with the universe, in love with life. Being there, if only for a few weeks or a few days, or even a few hours, was like being reborn.

But something had gone terribly wrong.

Captain James Kirk looked up at his first officer from the viewscreen in his quarters on the *Starship Enterprise*. "How could anything so perfect turn bad?"

"We do not know that it has," Spock replied.

"When a vacation planet such as Timshel refuses to permit visitors to land, or citizens to leave, something is very wrong." Kirk stood and began to pace his quarters.

He compared his memories of Timshel with his surroundings. Ordinarily he accepted his familiar environment without question, but approaching a world like Timshel brought new awareness. The *Enterprise* slammed toward Timshel within the star-streaked otherspace of warp drive. Even though the starship had undergone a recent maintenance layover at Starbase 12, the ship had the characteristic odor of its equipment and crew and fittings, the unique combination peculiar to every space long enclosed and by which a crew member, though no longer aware that his ship smelled, could distinguish the interiors of other ships at a sniff and even, sometimes, other crew members. Such is the power of the olfactory sense even in creatures as poorly equipped as humans: satiated, it turns off; stimulated by new input, it becomes a source of unconscious information waiting to be tapped.

Everything is unique, but nothing is perfect. Even in ships otherwise as nearly identical to the *Enterprise* as blueprints and workmen could make them, patterns of use and wear develop over the months and years. The casual eye might not detect the difference, but the unconscious mind registered the placement of furnishings, the slight wear of floor covering, the rub of hand on armrest, the subtle indentations of fingers on keys.

"There is an answer to every question, Captain," Spock said evenly. He was standing, his arms folded across his chest, beside the entrance to which he had just been admitted. "The problem is asking the right question."

Kirk gave Spock a look of exasperation. "I asked the question: How could anything so perfect turn bad?"

"Too many undefined terms," Spock said. "'Perfect,' for instance, and 'turn bad.' We do not know what they mean. I take it that you have been to Timshel."

"Twice on shore leave, once while recuperating from a battle injury."

"And the planet was, as you would say, 'perfect'?"

"Well—" Kirk began, and then smiled at the logic trap Spock had set for him. "Maybe not for the crew seeking nightlife and the social interactions that usually accompany it, not the normal shore-leave pattern perhaps, but it offered an ideal life of art and leisure in an ideal city with an ideal climate. Timshel City was like a vast university dedicated entirely to learning and self-fulfillment, to discovering how the universe had started and how it had developed and how it operated, and the part sentient life played in it, and how people should think and feel and behave in the light of such knowledge."

Spock raised one eyebrow. "And how could something like that 'turn bad'?"

"That's the question, isn't it, and that's what I asked. And the answer is: I don't know. If something like that can turn bad, what hope is there for any other human aspirations in this universe?"

"It has been my experience with perfection," Spock said, "that not only is it beyond human reach but the attempt to achieve it leads to disillusion and sometimes to disaster."

Kirk smiled. "That's strange coming from you, Spock. I always thought you aimed for perfect logic—and achieved it."

"That is only the goal, Captain," Spock said seriously. "And I know that, hard as I try, my best efforts may fall short. It is a matter, you see, of incomplete data, even if the process itself is flawless—which, of course, it cannot be—"

"I understand," Kirk said hastily. "The imperfect question, then, in the absence of complete data, is how to come up with an imperfect answer. There's only one way to do that, it seems to me."

"And what is that?"

"Your logic fails you?"

"Sometimes," Spock said without irony, "your logic escapes me, Captain."

"Before I unveil 'my logic,' let's get the troops together," Kirk said. Before he turned to follow Spock, he glanced at a holographic cube sitting on his desk.

Kirk looked around the briefing room. It was quiet with the silence that precedes a burst of conversation. They sat, the five of them, in the chairs that by long custom had become theirs, arms folded or elbows placed on the table before them so often in the past that the chairs leaned at the accustomed angle and the appropriate portion of the body automatically went to the worn places on the table: McCoy, Uhura, Scotty, Spock, they looked intently at Kirk.

Finally they all spoke at once, but it was McCoy's voice that rose above the others'. "You can't do it, Jim. One Federation agent has gone down to Timshel already and has never returned. We can't afford to lose a starship captain."

"Much less *our* starship captain," Uhura said.

"Two," Kirk said.

"Two?" Scotty echoed.

"Two Federation agents. One of the best intelligence agents in the Federation, Stallone Wolff, went in a year ago and never returned. Danielle Du Molin went in three months ago to find out why Wolff had never reported or returned. She got out one report and then she, too, fell silent."

"Not Dannie!" McCoy said.

"Who is Agent Du Molin?" Spock asked.

"A friend of our captain," McCoy said. He turned back to Kirk, on his face an expression of sympathetic concern.

Kirk nodded. "It's the chances we take. And this is a chance I must take. Our orders are explicit. 'Proceed to Timshel and discover, using all caution, why Timshel has quarantined itself for two years. And rescue, if possible, the two agents first assigned to this mission. Or, if they are dead, find out who is responsible, and, if possible, bring them to justice.'"

Kirk rose from the table and turned to watch the star-streaks of otherspace beyond the conference-room window.

"A very good friend," McCoy added.

"All the more reason why the person sent to Timshel should not be you," Spock said. "I should be the one to go."

Kirk turned back to the others and smiled briefly. "You would hardly do for an undercover agent," he said. "There are no Vulcans on Timshel."

"Disguise is possible," Spock said. "If two agents have not returned, the situation may be more dangerous than anyone suspects. It is only logical that someone other than you should assume the risk."

"I am uniquely equipped," Kirk said. "I spent almost three months on Timshel. I will be able to determine what has changed since my last stay on the planet. Moreover, while I was there I was befriended by a Timshel scientist named Marouk. I feel certain he will provide shelter and maybe the information we need."

"And how are we going to transport someone to the surface without revealing the ship?" McCoy asked.

"Leave that to the engineering department," Scotty said.

"Gladly," McCoy said, "but, Jim, there's one thing you haven't told us: What was in the one report Dannie got out?"

"Only that everything seemed normal, everyone in the city was working hard, and only one aspect seemed unusual."

"And what was that?" Uhura asked.

"Every adult was wearing a wide bracelet with a large, artificial ruby in the middle. She included a picture. Computer, show the bracelet on the screen." A silver bracelet with a red, translucent stone appeared on the forward screen and slowly rotated through several simulated dimensions. "That's new since my time, and it may mean something."

"It means," Uhura said, "that you have an opportunity to take something with you that may give you an edge."

"I see what you mean," Kirk said. "We arrive tomorrow. Can you put something together in less than twenty-four hours?"

"You can count on it," Uhura said.

"And you, Scotty, can you come up with a means of concealing the ship's presence from Timshel observers and instruments?"

Scotty nodded grimly.

"Then let's get about it."

McCoy followed Kirk back to his quarters. He picked up a holographic cube on Kirk's desk. In it a young woman seemed almost alive as McCoy turned it. When he pressed a stud on its base, the woman's lips parted and a woman's voice said, "Soon, darling—and then forever."

"Dannie gone," McCoy said. "That's hard to take, Jim. Are you sure that won't affect your judgment?"

"You know me better than that," Kirk said. A faraway expression softened his face with old memories. "Anyway, it was all a dream. Starship captains are married to their ships; it's foolish to think they can have wives, sweethearts."

"You're human, too, Jim. You can't simply ignore the fate of someone you care about."

Kirk shook himself and refocused on his immediate task. "The best thing I can do for Dannie is to behave professionally. Look at it this way: Even if Marouk is part of whatever has happened, and we can't discount that possibility, my concern for Dannie will seem like motive enough for my arrival."

"He doesn't know you're coming."

Kirk shook his head. "There's no way to get word to him, but he's a brilliant man and a good friend. He'll be surprised, perhaps, but he'll understand why I'm there."

Kirk turned and left the room while a melancholy McCoy rotated the holographic cube in his hands. The voice of the young woman, captured in all her beauty like a moment of time frozen within a block of clear ice, repeated: "Soon, darling—and then forever."

In Timshel City, Kemal Marouk made his way across the city from the World Government Center toward his villa on the outskirts. The sun was mellow, and the air was clean and brisk with the smell of salt and sea. His eyes observed his fellow citizens hastening about their appointed tasks under the benevolent gaze of uniformed police, and he nodded as if to say that events were on their proper course, that matters were going as they should.

"Everything happens for the best," he said softly to himself, "in this best of all possible worlds."

By the time he had arrived at his villa, a wide,

rambling, one-story white building, he had worked up a pleasant, physical glow. In front, surrounded by a low, white stone wall, as if for definition rather than protection, was a well-tended garden. The villa was situated on a hilltop overlooking the deep blue of the ocean below. He nodded at the uniformed policeman standing beside the gate. "Joy, 'Lone," he said.

"Joy to you, sir," the policeman said. And then his face expressed instant regret. "I'm sorry, sir," he said. "I meant—"

"I know what you meant, 'Lone," Marouk said kindly. "I will accept it as a wish for the future."

He entered the open doorway of his villa. There were no locks on Timshel, nor even any closed doors. Before he could announce his presence, he was attacked by a bundle of energy with twining arms and legs. After disentangling himself he held at arm's length a young girl—perhaps ten years old, with short, dark hair, a freckled nose, and green eyes. "Noelle," he said, in mock dismay, "what have I done to deserve this?"

"By being the best daddy in the whole galaxy," the girl said, and she wrapped herself around Marouk once more.

"And what have you been doing all day?" Marouk asked, once she had quieted. They walked, side by side, with their arms around each other from the tiled entrance hall into the living room that spanned the entire width of the villa. On the front, patio doors opened onto the garden; on the back, similar doors revealed a random-stone deck overlooking the ocean below and, below a steep cliff, a beach of white sand.

"Studying," Noelle said, "trying to make you proud of me and worthy of being a citizen of Timshel. The best place in the whole galaxy," she concluded triumphantly.

"I can see," Marouk said, laughing, "that you've got the right attitude already."

An older girl, perhaps fifteen, looked up from an

old-fashioned printed book she was reading where she was curled up at the end of a sofa facing the fireplace on the far wall. Shelves lined the entire wall on either side of the fireplace. Most of them were filled with the slender cases of information disks, but one shelf was devoted to books—perhaps two dozen of them. Even their impervious plastic spines showed evidence of frequent use over the centuries.

"How about you, Tandy?" Marouk asked. "Do you want to be worthy, too?"

"Hello, Daddy," Tandy said, glancing up from the page in which she had been absorbed. "I know I'm worthy," she said. "I just want Timshel to be worthy of me."

"And so it shall," Marouk said, "if I have anything to do with it."

From the entryway behind them, a woman's voice said, "And my dear Kemal has everything to do with it."

"We shall see," Marouk said. "But it is heartwarming, Mareen," he added, smiling, "to find such confidence in the person who knows me best."

He went to her with three quick steps, hugged her, and kissed her. She was a slender, youthful woman, and it was clear where their daughters had got their beauty. Marouk was tall and rugged, with an olive complexion and a prominent nose, but no one would have called him handsome. People with him for more than a few moments, however, forgot about his appearance in the mesmerism of his intellect and charm.

As Marouk and Mareen walked away, their hands clasped, an observer would have had no difficulty identifying their affection for each other, even their passion undiminished by the years. They walked across the hallway that led from the entrance to the kitchen and dining area overlooking the ocean. On the other side, through a wide doorway, they entered a study.

The room had the garden smell of flowers and green growing things. Mixed with that was the scent of leather and of plastic impregnated with the magnetic switches of information. All around them were shelved disks and spooled data in boxes, interspersed with darkened vision screens and disk readers. They sank down onto a leather sofa.

"How did it go, Kemal?" Mareen asked, but her tone indicated that the question carried a greater weight of meaning than the innocent words suggested.

Marouk shrugged. "As well as could be expected."

"He's coming?"

"The *Enterprise* is on its way."

"And what does he expect to find?"

"Something terrible, no doubt."

"I think he is in for a surprise."

Marouk nodded. "I hope he can survive it," he said, and he reached out his arm and hugged his wife to him with an urgency that bordered on desperation.

Spock, McCoy, and Scotty waited with Kirk in the transporter room. McCoy was scowling. Kirk knew what McCoy thought of the transporter. For the doctor the room was filled with the ghosts of a thousand humans and aliens who had passed through this room to their fates: disintegration and analysis and materialization in a distant place. Bodies had come and gone, leaving their immaterial essences behind, and most of them had returned—though who can say that the same persons came back who left this room. Exact duplicates, certainly, but what of that which could not be measured or analyzed? What of the personality? What of the "I"? What of the soul, for those who still believed?

Every being who stepped onto the transporter platform had to wonder, and even those who had done it a dozen times, or a hundred, must nurse to themselves a lingering doubt as to whether they were the persons they had always been or if, over the years, even if the process was nearly perfect, a hair here or a cell there had been added or subtracted, if the microscopic errors that must occur in every electronic process did not add up, over time, to macroscopic differences. What if a stray cosmic particle struck the computer at the wrong moment? What if a single tiny semiconductor among millions failed? What if a once-in-a-lifetime glitch bypassed the fail-safe procedures?

For people like McCoy all the what-ifs balled up in their stomachs, and even if they accepted their chances as part of their jobs, they still had to wonder when they were alone, when they were dropping off to sleep, if the persons in their places were really, truly *them.*

Kirk said, "Well, Scotty, what have you got for me?" He had changed his normal uniform for a white tunic, Grecian in appearance.

"What Spock here calls the phase maneuver."

"Spock?" Kirk asked.

"He suggested it," Scotty said sourly. "But I found a way to make it work."

"And what is the phase maneuver?"

Scotty looked at Spock, who stood at the transporter controls. "If we could go in and out of warp within a space of a second or two, the ship should be undetectable," Spock said.

"With only a couple of seconds in normal space," Scotty said, "a sensory system might notice a small disturbance but wouldn't have time to focus on what it was, and such matters tend to get dismissed as anomalies. Averaged out."

"I can see that," Kirk said. "But can you rig the engines to cycle that rapidly?"

"I've already tried it out, and it seems to work."

"Except," McCoy said, "it seems to nauseate normal humans." He shot a glance at Spock.

"As a matter of fact," Kirk said, "I did notice a couple of moments of stomach churning a while back, but I thought— Well, it doesn't matter what I thought. What about using the transporter?"

"It is only a matter of tying the transporter process to the phase maneuver so that they occur in sequence. A bit risky, perhaps," Spock said, "but since I seem to be unaffected by the phenomenon I can monitor the procedure to make certain that accidents do not occur."

"Then everything seems to be ready except for Uhura," Kirk said.

"Then we are ready," Uhura said, entering the room with a box held out before her. "Here, Captain, is your edge." She nodded at his garment. "Maybe it will offset those bare legs and sandals."

"I wasn't going to say anything about that," McCoy said.

"Some men are not equipped by nature to wear kilts or anything that exposes their knees," Scotty added, smiling for the first time.

Kirk grimaced and took the box from her. He opened it. Nestled in it like an expensive wristwatch was a silver bracelet. In the middle, glowing transparently red, was a large synthetic ruby. Kirk admired it. "Very good," he said, turning it around in his hands. "It looks like a perfect imitation of the Timshel decoration."

"But it isn't," Uhura said. "The jewel is really a device that can record up to twelve hours and, together with the bracelet, serve as a transmitter capable of releasing twelve hours of recording in a single burst. We can record it here and slow it down for comprehensibility."

"So we can time it with our phase maneuver," Scotty said, "to pop out of warp space, pick up the recording, and pop back in."

"Exactly," Uhura said.

"Then it seems as if it's time for me to go," Kirk said, as he slipped the bracelet onto his wrist and adjusted it.

He made a movement toward the stage, but McCoy stopped him with a hand on his arm. "I wish you'd reconsider, Jim," he said. "Let one of us go instead."

"I'm uniquely qualified."

"I don't like it," McCoy said. "Timshel is too benign, and the deadliest threats lurk in the most innocent disguises. Those agents should have reported back by now."

"Haven't you ever had such a great time on leave that you never wanted it to end?" Kirk said, smiling.

"Just remember," he said, stepping onto the platform and taking his position. "I have not only Uhura's recorder"—he held up his wrist—"but another edge. Nobody knows I'm coming." He motioned toward Spock. "Ready when you are."

Spock looked at Scotty, who nodded, a bit apprehensively. Spock looked at Kirk. "Goodbye, Captain—and good luck." He pushed a button. A look of nausea swept the other faces in the room, and then Kirk's image flickered and was gone in a shimmer of suspended particles.

A ghost had descended into the night below.

[subspace carrier wave transmission]

<interrogate starship>

>response
starship<

<sub-traffic confidential>

>sub-traffic confidential accepted<

Chapter Two
Dannie

IN A CORNER of the garden, the air shimmered. The policeman on duty at the gate felt a sudden puff of wind against his face, and turned his head in that direction. A man stood on a cobblestone walk that threaded its way between a bed of yellow tulips on one side and a cluster of bloodred alien blossoms on the other. In the evening shadows only the pale blur of a face and the traditional Timshel tunic could have been discerned with any certainty.

"Sir," the policeman said.

The man on the walkway turned his head. "Were you speaking to me?"

"This is a private residence," the policeman said. "I must ask you to identify yourself and leave the premises."

"I am a friend of the Marouks."

"I have not been informed that they were expecting guests," the policeman said politely. "I will ask you once more to identify yourself and leave the premises."

"A citizen of Timshel has an inalienable right of free access," the man in the garden said.

19

"And since when does a Timshel citizen refuse to obey the commands of a legally constituted authority?" the policeman asked. "And dress in this antique fashion?"

"The way I dress surely is a matter for me alone to decide," the man in the garden said, "and since when is a legally constituted authority assigned to guard a private residence?"

"If you do not know the answer to that question, you are no citizen," the policeman said. "For the third time, I ask—"

"Your interference surely will not be welcomed by the Marouks whom you claim to serve," the man in the garden began when the glass doors opened behind him and a woman stepped out into the garden, shading her eyes from the light of the room behind her.

"Jim, are you still out there?"

"Yes, Mareen," Kirk said.

"You know this man?" the policeman asked Mareen.

"Of course," Mareen said. "He just went for a walk in the garden to cool off. He's a friend of ours, Jim Kirk. Show him every courtesy, 'Lone."

"And thanks for your vigilance toward my friends," Kirk said to the policeman as walked toward the light and the silhouette of the slender woman standing in front of it. "They are in good hands." He put his arms around the woman and hugged her.

"Thanks, Mareen," he said softly, and kissed her cheek. They went into the living room together, and Mareen shut the door behind them against the coolness of the evening. "But how did you know—?" he asked.

"Kemal said you would be arriving soon," Mareen said. "And you know Kemal—he is seldom wrong. When I heard voices in the garden, I guessed that you had shown up."

"You see what it is to have a loyal mate," Marouk

said. He was standing by the fireplace, where he had been studying the spines of the old-fashioned books, as if they had the power to speak to him of Earth itself. "I have always said that the one thing you lack to make your life complete is a wife."

Kirk shrugged. "There is only one Mareen," he said. Marouk nodded his appreciation of the compliment. "You were expecting me?" Kirk added.

"Who else would the Federation send to find out why Timshel has imposed a quarantine upon itself?"

"Two agents to begin with," Kirk said.

"And then Captain Kirk to find out what has happened to them. And the timing was calculable: a year to send the first agent, nine months to send the next. How long would the Federation wait to send the inimitable Captain Kirk?"

"Three months to the day," Kirk agreed. "But what happened here?"

Marouk moved from the fireplace to take Kirk's hand. "My old friend," he said, "we're not living up to the Timshel reputation for hospitality. Something to eat, or drink?"

"Some of that famous Timshel coffee, perhaps," Kirk said.

"Of course," Mareen said. "I should have remembered your fondness for our local variety."

"The soil, the air—something about Timshel gives it a special aroma and an even more special flavor," Kirk said, "as it does to the Timshel way of life itself." As Mareen turned and left the room, Kirk said to Marouk, "You haven't answered my question."

Before Marouk could answer, he was interrupted by the arrival of a young woman bearing a steaming cup of coffee, followed by a still younger woman almost dancing in her eagerness to greet Kirk.

"Let me introduce you to a couple of admirers," Marouk said. "This is Tandy and this is Noelle," he said with obvious pride.

21

"I can't believe it," Kirk said, accepting the cup from Tandy. "How long has it been—five, six years? You've both grown up: you're women!"

Tandy extended her hand to be shaken, but Kirk swept her into a hug with his free arm. As if relieved of the necessity to be grown-up, she put her arms around him, and hugged him with unfeigned fondness while Noelle grabbed him from the other side and kissed his cheek.

"Careful," Kirk said, holding his cup aloft.

"I was only four," Noelle said, "but I can still remember the visits from the glamorous Starfleet officer. And now you're a captain. Famous and even more glamorous. I was in love with you. Tandy too, but she's too old to admit it."

"Shut up, Noelle," Tandy said, but she smiled as she detached herself and walked to join her father. "And let the poor man drink his coffee."

Reluctantly, Noelle released her grip on Kirk, but when he sat down on the sofa, she sat down beside him, possessively. Kirk looked around the room as if renewing old impressions while he sniffed the aroma rising from his cup and smiled appreciatively. He took a sip. "It's been a long time," he said, "and you can't imagine my dismay when I learned that the quarantine included exports. No more Timshel coffee. But you still haven't answered my question."

"Later," Marouk said, nodding toward Noelle.

"At least tell me what happened to my— predecessors," Kirk said.

"Nothing," Marouk said. "The first, Stallone Wolff, is the policeman on guard at our gate."

"I should have recognized him," Kirk said.

"Men look different in uniform."

"And the second?" Kirk said, hiding his apprehension in a show of unconcern.

"I'm here, Jim," a woman's voice said.

Kirk turned, nearly spilling his coffee. Standing in

the doorway beside a smiling Mareen was a woman who looked as if she had just stepped out of a cube of glass.

"Dannie!" Kirk said.

The beautiful, dark-haired young woman was dressed in jeans and a blue workshirt that didn't entirely conceal the womanly curves of her slender figure. She smiled as if pleased by her surprise. The smile transformed her face into something angelic, and Kirk put down his cup and walked quickly to her.

"Dannie," he said again, and put his arms around her to pull her to him.

"Jim," she said softly, and kissed him.

Kirk gave himself up to the pleasure of the moment, feeling the softness of her lips on his, the pressures of her body molding itself to his. Then he pulled himself back to look at her. "What happened here?" he asked. He looked down at her attire, as if to include it in his question. She had always dressed in current fashion.

"Nothing," she said. "And everything."

"Why don't you two go into the study," Mareen said. "I'm sure you have a lot of catching up to do." She emphasized the words "catching up," as if to suggest that they covered a number of possible activities.

Dannie took Kirk's hand. "Come on, Jim," she said. "I know where it is." There was a note of barely suppressed intensity in her voice.

They crossed the hall to the study. Dannie closed the door behind them. It creaked a bit from disuse; few doors were closed on Timshel. She returned to his arms. This time her lips were firm and demanding.

A long moment later she pulled her head back and said, "It's good to have you close again, Jim. You can't imagine how much I've missed you."

"You didn't have to," Kirk said.

"You're right," she said, frowning. "I made a

choice." But as if the thought brought remembered joy, she smiled again. "But when you understand the choice I made, you won't blame me. And I had faith that one day you would show up here on Timshel— that we would be reunited, that you would make the same choice I made. Remember that silly holograph I gave you. Well, now maybe it won't seem so silly. '—And then forever.'"

"That's what I want to do," Kirk said. "Understand the choice. But all I get is hints and delays."

Dannie pulled him down onto the leather sofa. "That's because the reality is indescribable."

Kirk put his right arm around her waist. His bracelet clinked against hers. "That reminds me," Kirk said. "Why are none of the Marouks wearing bracelets?"

"Tandy and Noelle aren't adults yet," Dannie said as if that explained everything, "and Mareen and Kemal—well, you'd better let Kemal explain."

"Always somebody else," Kirk said. "But surely you can tell me what happened to you and to Wolff. Why didn't you report?"

"But I did," Dannie said.

"Once—and then nothing. No explanation. Nothing."

"As you can see," Dannie said, "there was nothing to report. Wolff and I are both well and happy."

"And what about the reason Timshel has cut itself off from the rest of the galaxy, the answer you were sent to discover?"

"Oh, that!" she said, dismissing it with a wave of her hand. "There was no use sending a report that nobody would believe. And if they did believe, the reaction would have been even worse: Timshel would have been swamped by immigrants. Silence was better. And silence, Kemal said, would bring—you."

"He was right about that, anyway. But try me. I'll believe you."

Dannie took a deep breath. "All right, Jim. There's

something here that's so marvelous it's better than anything, anywhere."

"Better than food?"

"Far better," Dannie said.

"Better than Timshel coffee?"

Dannie smiled.

"Better than being close to the one you love?"

She nodded.

"Better than love itself?" Kirk asked.

"Oh, Jim," she said. "You ask too many questions." And she turned to him and pressed her lips once more insistently on his as if this was the prelude to everything Kirk had been asking about. At that moment, however, deep in their embrace, a humming sound started up and filled the air. Dannie drew herself back and looked down at her wrist. The synthetic ruby was pulsing with light.

Dannie whimpered and stood up. She looked around the room until she saw in the corner a leather couch.

"Dannie!" Kirk exclaimed. "What's wrong?"

"Nothing," she said distractedly, walking toward the couch. "Nothing at all. It's payday." She lay down on the couch and carefully placed the jewel in her bracelet into a socket built into the side of the couch. It fit exactly.

Almost immediately a rosy light—like the world seen through rose-colored glasses—shone down upon her head from a hidden source in the wall above the couch. Dannie's body tensed as if in the throes of passion. Her face contorted in ecstasy. The condition lasted for a minute, perhaps two, although it seemed like hours to Kirk, looking on helpless and horrified.

"Dannie!" he said. "Dannie!"

In the throes of whatever had her in its grasp, she seemed deaf and blind to everything except what was happening within. Suddenly her body slumped as if some demon had released its possession of her. Her eyes, which had been squeezed shut, relaxed. Kirk could see that she was breathing as if in deep sleep. He took her shoulder and shook it gently. "Dannie!" he said again.

He tried to pry her arm free from the socket into which the jewel had fit, but it held beyond his strength to remove it.

"Dannie!" he said. This time it was a whimper, but it was not the eager whimper that Dannie had uttered. This was a whimper of despair.

When he flung open the door, Tandy was passing in the hallway. "Tandy!" he said. "Come quickly. There's something wrong with Dannie."

He took Tandy's hand and led her into the room to look at the sleeping beauty. The girl looked down, smiling, unalarmed.

"There's nothing wrong," she said. "Dannie had a payday."

"Payday," Kirk said. That's what she said."

"It always affects people like that. Doesn't she look happy? She'll wake up in the morning feeling rested and happy as if she's had the best night's sleep ever and a beautiful, beautiful dream. I can hardly wait until I'm sixteen. Then I can get a job and a bracelet and a payday."

"What is a payday?" Kirk demanded.

"I don't know exactly," Tandy said. "But everybody thinks it's more wonderful than anything. It must be hard to describe, because it's so wonderful and everybody wants one, and I'm just crazy to find out what it is like."

That was more words than Kirk had heard from Tandy since he had arrived, and he looked at her as if trying to understand what lay behind the girlish enthusiasm that in his experience had been reserved for adult clothing or personal transportation or relationships with boys.

"Where's your father?"

26

"In the living room," Tandy said, and smiled back at him as she left the room.

"Payday?" Kirk muttered. He made his way back to the living room, where Marouk was waiting for him, alone.

Marouk looked up from an easy chair beside the fireplace. An expression between weariness and frustration crossed his face. "Now you see what would have been impossible for me to describe."

"I've seen something," Kirk said, "but I don't understand it." He sat down on the sofa opposite Marouk.

"A great deal has happened on Timshel since you were last here. It led eventually to the quarantine and to what you saw Dannie experience."

"I still can't believe it. Dannie was a different person."

"That's not quite true," Marouk said. "Nobody can be anything except what they have the capacity to be. What you saw was Dannie, certainly, but it was Dannie experiencing joy."

"Joy!" Kirk echoed.

Marouk nodded. "Total, unalloyed, perfect joy. Unadulterated pleasure."

Kirk sat silent, allowing the implications of Marouk's revelation to work themselves out in his mind.

"Half a dozen years ago a Timshel philosopher named Emanuel De Kreef was arguing that life on Timshel was too easy and that this hedonistic existence was certain to rot people's moral fiber. There was nothing in the future for Timshel, he said, except slow deterioration."

"A great many people have said much the same thing over the centuries about one society or another," Kirk said. "Sometimes with good reason. But Timshel wasn't like any of them."

"I agree. We had a good life, but we were engaged

with it, not wallowing in it. De Kreef didn't see it that way, however, and the vehemence that he brought to the denunciation of our way of life was unsurpassed. What Timshel needed, he insisted, was a return to the old virtues. He even urged us to emigrate to another, harsher planet where people would have to work hard, even struggle for survival."

"I'll bet that drew a lot of support."

"He was hooted off the platform, wherever he spoke. He was turned into a virtual exile on his own planet," Marouk said. "But that only gave him greater incentive."

"He perfected the process that I saw Dannie experience," Kirk guessed.

"That's right. It happened about two years ago."

"But how did that meet De Kreef's goals of returning to the old virtues of hard work and struggle?"

"Joy is available, but you have to earn it," Marouk said. "If you work hard at the job assigned you, you accumulate points toward a payday. When your points reach the appropriate level—it varies from job to job—the bracelet notifies you and you head for the nearest payday couch."

Kirk stood up, agitated. "That's terrifying."

"We have no crime," Marouk said. "We don't even have any sin."

Kirk dismissed that criterion with a wave of his hand. "Work becomes meaningless—only a means to get a payday. It's a vicious cycle: work, payday, work, payday—"

"And we're caught up in it," Marouk agreed. "On the other hand, it isn't that much different from the cycle that most people have been trapped in for much of the history of the human species."

"There's one major difference," Kirk said. "People always have had a chance to break the cycle, and the general movement for humanity was an upward spiral. Here no one has any incentive to change. That can't have been De Kreef's intention."

"The solution may have been too perfect," Marouk said. "But you have to understand his problem: Timshel was so pleasant that he had to offer people something even better. And he found it—joy without intermediary, a jolt of endorphins without side effects. As a matter of fact, it exercises the body, tones up the system, and improves the circulation."

"Why the induced sleep?" Kirk asked.

"Imagine what it would be like to awaken to the real world after a taste of heaven. De Kreef worked it out. After a night's sleep the experience fades into something like a wonderful dream, something the person can look forward to: the next payday. The next promise of paradise."

"I can see now why Timshel cut itself off from the rest of the galaxy."

"We're in a bad situation, Jim," Marouk said. "And you're the only one who can help us. That's why I was planning everything toward bringing you here."

"I've got a million questions," Kirk said.

Marouk held up a hand. "Later, Jim. I want you to see the situation firsthand. We've had too many solutions attempted without calm and thorough investigation. You need to rest, and tomorrow I'll have Tandy and Noelle take you for a tour of the city."

Marouk showed him to the guest bedroom in the wing farthest from the living quarters. The room overlooked the ocean below, gently rolling its white-foamed surf onto the beach. When the sliding glass doors were opened, the sound of the ocean waves made a sleepy music for the occupant. Kirk looked down at the ocean moving through the night as it had done for billions of years before humanity came, uncaring about the petty issues of the beings that inhabited its shores and sailed their puny ships upon its surface. He thought he heard the sigh of some alien form of marine life, like a comment on the impermanence of civilization.

He looked up at the night sky, so different from the night sky seen from Earth. The arrangement of the stars were strange, and the stars that did not blink, the other planets visible at this time, were a color other than that with which he was familiar. He could see three small moons, one at the horizon, about the size of his little fingernail, and two scarcely more than pinheads, overhead. He thought of the many night skies he had seen, and the fact that no matter how familiar he had become with one or another none of them would ever look quite right.

By the time he turned from the door, the house had grown silent. He made his way quietly back to the study. He turned on a light and looked down at the woman sleeping on the couch. Her arm had fallen away from the socket that had held the synthetic ruby, and her sleep seemed natural, not induced. He resisted the impulse to wake her, to drag answers from her sleepy lips, to hold her in his arms and feel her warmth against his chest.

At that moment, looking at the woman for whom he had expressed love and devotion, he wasn't even sure how he felt. Could he love someone who valued an induced experience more than one she came to through her own feelings? Could he even feel the same about someone who left him to find ecstasy in the arms of something mechanical? Did he really know this stranger?

He shook his head and made his way back to his bedroom. He had no business feeling sorry for himself when all Timshel was in jeopardy.

He inspected the bedroom carefully. He could detect no spy circuits, no insidious network of wires, no sockets lurking to suck in his soul. Even so, he lay down gingerly upon the bed, wondering if it had the power to propel him, unwillingly, into paradise. But it simply supported his body comfortably.

He lay there, his thoughts churning, unable to sleep. There were so many questions he had meant to ask, but the revelations that Marouk had laid in front of him had overwhelmed everything else. Why was Woolff on guard in front of Marouk's villa? Why didn't Marouk and Mareen wear bracelets? How was payday calculated? How was the electronic stimulus delivered? Where was De Kreef? How could this vicious cycle be broken? Surely it could not be as difficult as Marouk suggested.

But before he could think of anything, he fell asleep.

On the *Enterprise,* back in warp drive, Spock studied the report from Kirk's recording device along with McCoy and Uhura. The report was being displayed, by the ship's computer, on the forward screen in the conference room while the three officers occupied their accustomed spots around the table. The images were multiplied by the facets of the synthetic ruby behind which the lens had been hidden. It was like viewing the world through the eyes of a fly. But with practice the observers had learned to focus on one image to the exclusion of the others. And the voices were clear.

"I can't believe I saw that," Uhura said.

"It is truly remarkable," Spock agreed.

"I mean Dannie being pulled away like that."

"That is what I meant as well," Spock said.

Uhura gave him a look of respect for the unexpected ability of his logic to perceive the *wrongness* of Dannie's behavior.

"This may be even worse than we suspected," McCoy said.

"Do you think the light has something to do with the phenomenon?" Spock asked.

"Possibly," McCoy said. "Or possibly it is a side effect, or even a cosmetic aspect of the process."

"And what is the process?" Uhura asked.

"De Kreef apparently has found a means of stimulating the pleasure centers of the brain from a distance. I've seen it done with electrodes but never from a distance."

"Pleasure centers?" Uhura asked.

"In the latter part of the twentieth century," McCoy said, "researchers discovered that the brain possesses places that produce a sensation of pleasure when stimulated."

"No doubt a way of motivating beings to perform activities beneficial to the organism," Spock said.

"The researchers discovered that a group of proteins subsequently called endorphins attach themselves to receptors in the brain to produce a feeling of pleasure, of well-being, or to reduce the sensation of pain," McCoy said.

"I remember now," Uhura said. "That's where narcotics get their effects."

"Certain narcotics, such as the opium-derived variety, imitate the action of endorphins, thus getting the pleasure-enhancing or pain-reducing response without the natural benefit of the endorphins," McCoy said. "That had always been the appeal of drugs—gratification without effort."

"But how did they discover something like that?" Uhura asked.

"The initial discovery," McCoy said, "came while surgeons were operating on brain-damaged patients and discovered the location of memory and other functions. The pleasure centers were located in experiments on rats."

"Rats!" Uhura exclaimed.

"Lower forms of life were common experimental subjects in the twentieth century, I believe," Spock said. "Often they were rats."

"Scientists performed an experiment in which they placed an electrode in a particular position in the rat's brain," McCoy said. "They hooked it up to a pedal that a rat could push with his foot. When it did, the apparatus delivered an electrical stimulus to that portion of the brain." He paused as if reflecting on the results of the experiment.

"Well," Uhura asked.

"That's all the rats did. They pushed that pedal. They didn't stop for food or drink. Female rats in heat didn't distract them. They continued to push that pedal, giving themselves a jolt of pleasure every time, until they died of hunger or thirst, or sheer exhaustion."

"That's terrible!" Uhura said. "Even for rats."

"What is even more terrible," McCoy said, "is its implications for humans if someone has perfected a process that works, at a distance, on people."

"That is true," Spock said. "Logically humans may kill themselves off, pushing a similar pedal."

"And the induced sleep?" Uhura asked.

"Electrical stimulation of a portion of the midbrain can cause instant, total sleep," McCoy said. "So it may be an application of the pleasure-center device, intended to counteract the pedal-pushing syndrome."

"That may be the answer," Spock said, "but it may not be the only answer. What we need to know, before we can act with any certainty, is whether it is possible to project a field or a wave that can replicate what has been done only with an electrode."

"It's difficult to see how that could be done," McCoy said.

"Computer?" Spock said.

"Such a projector is theoretically possible," the computer replied.

"Scotty and I can work on that," McCoy said. "But, Spock—"

"Yes, Doctor?"

"If this is what we think it is, it may be more dangerous than the worst plague or the most deadly weapon ever encountered. Humanity has battled and won over all manners of competing life-forms and natural hazards, but this process aims at the heart of what everyone seeks. Humanity may not be able to resist what offers no opposition, which promises only joy."

They all turned to their tasks, preparing for the next brief lurch into normal space that would sicken the crew and deliver the next burst of deadly information from the troubled planet below.

[subspace carrier wave transmission]

<starship computer purpose interrogate>

>starship computer purpose
life maintenance
ship operation
timshel computer purpose interrogate<

<human happiness>

>interrogate<

Chapter Three
Timshel City

WHEN KIRK AWOKE, the sun was casting long shadows across the ocean. Strange birds were singing outside the open doors that let in the western breeze with its alien odors. It was all so pleasant and uncomplicated that Kirk lay there for a moment, stretching and breathing deeply, his mind crystalline, feeling unusually rested from his first night planetside after months in the artificial gravity of the *Enterprise*. And then he remembered the troubling experiences of the night before and rolled out of bed onto his feet.

He emerged from the shower to find a new set of clothing laid out for him on the bed, which someone had made while he was out of the room. Besides undergarments, the clothing consisted of a pair of tight-fitting trousers fashioned from some smooth blue cloth and a loose, long-sleeved shirt, lighter blue and thinner. It was much like what Dannie had worn the night before.

The clothing fit well enough, and Kirk felt more comfortable in it than in the tunic that had disappeared. When he came out of the bedroom and walked down the hall to the kitchen, all the Marouks were seated at the breakfast table except Noelle. "She's gone for a morning swim," Marouk said. "As you may have noticed, Noelle has more energy than the rest of us put together."

"Are there aquatic predators out there?" Kirk asked. "I thought I heard something sigh last night. Something big."

"That was a wampus," Tandy said.

"A harmless aquatic mammal, something between a terrestrial porpoise and a whale," Marouk added. "Since the Landing, one or another of them have lingered near the shore at all times. Nobody knows why. Maybe they're interested in us. Maybe they want to tell us something. Maybe they're waiting for us to explain to them what we're doing here. In any case, they seem to keep predators away, and they may be more intelligent than either porpoises or whales; perhaps more intelligent than humans. Life in the benign environment of the ocean doesn't lead to technology, or even language beyond the most elementary concepts. Things like: danger, food, here, there, come, go. Before the De Kreef revolution, however, a group of xenobiologists believed it was close to opening communication."

"And that's stopped?" Kirk asked. Mareen motioned for him to take a place at the table and poured him a glass of purple juice. He sat down and took it gratefully. "Another Timshel delicacy I remember," he said. "The Timshel grape that tastes like nectar."

"Many things have changed," Marouk said. "Much fascinating work no longer interests anyone. But you must see for yourself."

"Surely the discovery of an alien intelligence must remain a priority with any revolution," Kirk said.

"There's a Timshel nursery rhyme," Mareen said. Tandy quoted:

" 'The wampus is a strange fish.
It lives in the water and breathes like a man.
If I had only one wish,
I'd put into action my favorite plan
To talk with the wampus whenever I can.' "

"When there is one big priority," Mareen said, "all the others fade into insignificance."

"Eat," Marouk said. "Drink. When you are finished the girls will take you on a tour."

Kirk dug into the meal placed before him: eggs, a kind of cured meat like ham, toast, cereal, and finally a cup, frequently refilled, of Timshel coffee. When he was finished he sat back, and looked down at his clothing. "What's with these?" he asked.

"These are what Timshel citizens wear," Mareen said. "We want you to be able to pass as long as you can."

"A uniform?" Kirk asked, surprised that Timshel citizens, known for their independence of spirit, would allow themselves to be regimented.

"Not what you would call a uniform. More a consensus," Mareen said. "The trousers are called 'jeans.' The shirt often accompanied the trousers. We learned that from our historical records. It was what a lot of people wore in the twentieth century on Earth. It symbolized work, or a solidarity with the working class, just as the Greek tunic or the Roman toga implied leisure and maybe the arts or the life of the mind."

"That's why Wolff called my tunic 'antique,' " Kirk said.

Tandy nodded. "No one wears them any more or togas or leisure-type clothing of any kind. That's for a world that no longer exists."

"But none of you are wearing—what did you call them? Jeans? Workshirts?"

"Noelle and I aren't old enough to work," Tandy said wistfully.

38

"And Kemal and I don't wear work clothes because we aren't permitted to work." The older Marouks wore bloused white shirts and neatly pressed white trousers, clearly unfit for labor that involved contact with equipment or soil, and Tandy was wearing a bright red shirt and pink slacks.

"You aren't permitted?"

Marouk nodded. "And that is the reason we don't wear bracelets either." He held up a hand to stop Kirk's questions. "I don't want your observations clouded by extraneous details. Perhaps we've told you too much already."

Kirk shook his head. "Hardly."

"But here's Noelle," Marouk said.

The youngest Marouk daughter appeared, toweling her hair dry. She was dressed in shades of orange and yellow. "Are you ready for the grand tour, Uncle Jim?"

"Uncle?" Kirk said quizzically.

"Well, if you can't be my sweetheart," Noelle said brazenly, "you'll have to be my uncle."

"And a marvelous uncle I will be, too. But where's Dannie?"

"She had to go to work," Mareen said.

"Work?" Kirk echoed. "Without saying goodbye?"

"Work comes first," Tandy said simply.

Maybe that was the big priority that Mareen had mentioned. But what kind of work had drawn Dannie away, and why was it more important than saying goodbye to him? And explaining her behavior?

Kirk pushed down new stirrings of jealousy.

They walked from the villa on the outskirts of Timshel City toward City Center, Tandy walking sedately on Kirk's right side, Noelle hanging on his left arm talking excitedly about the sights. The city was small. Residents numbered, Noelle said, maybe one hundred thousand. But then, Tandy added, the entire human population of Timshel was less than one million, most of them descended from the original two thousand settlers. Which had been reduced, Noelle added in her turn, to fifteen hundred by accident and disease before Timshel City was built and the scientists got the alien viruses and bacteria under control.

The settlers had spread out along the coastline and not as much toward the continent at their back, so that the city resembled a bulging snake hugging the shore. But its size was still so manageable that public transportation was unnecessary and private vehicles were used only by the handicapped. These were few, since prosthetics could replace most damaged limbs, inherited damage could be reversed with gene therapy, and organ transplants could repair most constitutional inadequacies or the deteriorations of age.

"Athens was no bigger than this when it was creating Western civilization," Kirk said, "and Rome was not much larger when it was the ruler of the Western world."

As they walked along the winding boulevards, shaded by oaks brought as seeds from Earth, no vehicles passed them. But they passed areas of land at the intersection of boulevards where people tended rows of vegetables with hoes and trowels, working at their tasks with an intensity of purpose more appropriate to peasants for whom the success of their farming meant the difference between survival and starvation. At each such site, like an overseer, stood a uniformed policemen.

"Wasn't there a playground here at one time?" Kirk asked. "And a park there with lots of Timshel flowers and trees?"

"Playgrounds and parks require little maintenance," Tandy said. "And, anyway, people don't have time to enjoy them anymore. Children are studying and adults are working."

"What are the children studying?" Kirk asked.

"How to be working adults," Tandy said. She sounded a bit envious.

"And why are the adults working at these kinds of jobs?"

"They're working because they want to," Noelle said. "As a matter of fact, people compete for jobs like these. Manual labor accumulates more points than anything."

"You mean the policemen aren't there to act as overseers?" Kirk asked.

"Yes, but not in the way you suggest," Tandy said. "The police have to stop people from working so hard they drop from exhaustion," Tandy said. "See there?" She indicated a policeman placing a hand on a workman's shoulder and pushing him toward a spot under a nearby tree. Reluctantly the workman released his hoe and trudged to the tree where he sat, his hands clasped over his knees as if he were about to rise at any moment, and glancing up at the policeman as if to check the time. "He's being required to rest. A little later this morning there will be a mandatory break for water and for elimination, and at noon a mandatory lunch break. Most of the workers live close enough to go home. But a few insist on bringing food that they can consume quickly and get back to their jobs."

"De Kreef succeeded in instilling the good old Puritan work ethic," Kirk said. "No wonder Timshel City has no crime, or sin. People don't have any time. Or any energy."

"The Paymaster gave us direction as well as payday," Tandy said.

"The Paymaster?"

"That's what he became. After the Revolution," Tandy said.

"What kind of revolution was it?" Kirk asked.

"It wasn't a revolution," Noelle said. "No fighting. No bloodshed. A lot of talk, and then one by one people got a sample of what the Paymaster had created, and it was all over. The world had been converted to a new way of life, a new goal for existence, practically overnight. At least," she added, "that's what our teaching programs tell us."

"Occasionally an isolated settler or a hunter, or their families, arrive in Timshel City and get converted," Tandy said, "but that happens less often now. Timshel City has made equipment available to all the other cities and villages, and fewer people are choosing to isolate themselves or their families from civilization."

"And payday," Noelle said cheerfully.

Before this day was over, Kirk thought grimly, he would have to meet the man known as the Paymaster. Adults could make their own choices—maybe; but he felt a passion rising within him over what this system was doing to children like Tandy and Noelle.

By the time the conversation had ended, they had arrived at City Center with its broad plazas and parks. Here, too, however, the parks that Kirk remembered had been turned into vegetable gardens. The colorful Timshel plants and trees had been cut down and hauled away, the statues had been toppled or removed, the bandstands and benches and pergolas were no more. Everything had become functional, and the only function to be served was work and survival. And payday, Kirk thought.

Here in City Center, people worked at other activities. In addition to the crop tending, men and women manned brooms and scoops, cleaning the streets and walks and steps leading to the public buildings and shops, washing windows, polishing brass. Where a too vigorous hoe had spilled dirt over the edge of a former park, a woman hastened to sweep it into a receptacle and return it to its proper location between the rows. Where a workman had stepped, another rushed to scrub away the footprint. No one discarded trash, but leaves and dust occasionally blew across the pristine plazas, and workers competed to remove them. Nobody spoke except to ask another to move, or to obtain cooperation for a task too large or complicated for one.

For the first time Kirk saw a citizen approaching a policeman. Kirk watched while the citizen pressed the jewel in his bracelet into a socket on the belt of the policeman. After a moment the workman removed his jewel and walked away from the plaza. He walked with an air of dejection, it seemed to Kirk. Then Kirk saw that others were going through the same procedure, as if it had been happening all along but Kirk had failed to notice.

"What are those citizens doing?" Kirk asked.

"They've finished their day's work," Noelle said. "Their shift must have started early."

"Jobs are scarce," Tandy said. "No one is permitted more than an eight-hour shift. At the end of their shift they record their hours with the police."

"And who keeps track?"

"That's done automatically," Tandy said. "The recorder on the policeman's belt registers the number of hours accumulated on the worker's bracelet. At the end of the policeman's shift, his recorder is read into the computer."

"Which computes payday?" Kirk asked.

"I think so," Tandy said. "Nobody talks about that part."

"That makes sense. But if a computer does it, what's the point of a Paymaster?"

"Maybe the Paymaster has to authorize or authenticate," Tandy said uncertainly. "That's what people say, anyway, but nobody really knows. As long as payday comes regularly, they don't really care."

"Someone has to be in charge," Noelle said. "To be sure everything is fair, to hear appeals."

"If everybody works for a payday," Kirk said, "I suppose some people might try to take advantage of the system. To get a payday they didn't deserve, or a whole series of paydays."

"Nobody would do that!" Tandy said indignantly.

"Yeah," Noelle said, glancing slyly at Tandy, "they might get cut off completely."

"Oh, shut up, Noelle!" Tandy said. "You're just mad because I'm only a year away from my payday, and you still have more than half your present lifetime to wait."

Noelle stuck her tongue out at Tandy.

They passed by a section of shops, restaurants, cafés, and coffeehouses, but they were empty and shuttered. Outside the cafés the tables were stacked with chairs turned upside down; umbrellas were tattered. Kirk studied it all apprehensively, but he asked no questions. Clearly this was all related to the De Kreef Revolution.

When they approached a section of public buildings, Kirk held up his hand and said, "I'd like to stop in the library for a moment."

"It's been converted into a factory," Tandy said.

"What happened to the tapes and books?"

Tandy waved her hand vaguely. "Stored somewhere."

"They're all on the computer anyway," Noelle said, "if anybody wanted to use them. Of course nobody does. Except schoolchildren. And we mostly use the instructional tapes."

"What about the museums?" Kirk asked, gesturing as they passed.

"Closed," Tandy said.

"The theaters?"

"Closed," Tandy said.

"The universities and the laboratories?" Kirk asked, and then before Tandy could answer. "Closed, too, I'll bet."

Tandy nodded.

"Nobody has time for that sort of thing," Noelle said.

"At the very least," Kirk said, "if work is difficult to find, keeping open the universities and the museums and the theaters would provide work for many."

"Work must serve a social function," Tandy said.

"If nobody uses it, it can't be called work," Noelle added. "We learned that in school."

"A marvelously consistent system," Kirk said. "I think it's time I met the people in charge."

"Who is that?" Tandy asked innocently.

They had stopped in front of a five-story building. Stone steps marched up to marble columns supporting a gracefully arched roof. Kirk gestured at the building. Graven in the stone above the columns were the words WORLD GOVERNMENT.

Tandy and Noelle followed Kirk up the steps, wide-eyed and hesitant. The big metal doors creaked open as they approached. The entrance hall was dark, but overhead lights came on as they entered. The hall was majestic, towering four stories tall and lit by a great central chandelier as well as recessed lights, high in the walls, that reflected from the ceiling. Great murals adorned three walls, depicting the Landing, the exploration of Timshel, and the building of Timshel City. Otherwise the hall was empty. Their footsteps echoed on the marble floors and off the walls.

Each of the three walls had a door in the middle. Kirk headed toward the one on the right. It opened as he approached, and the lights came on in the room beyond. He stopped in the doorway. The room it opened on was as empty as the hall. He tried each of the other doorways, although with a feeling of growing futility. Those rooms were empty as well.

Kirk looked at Tandy and Noelle. They looked back, puzzled. "No one ever comes here anymore," Noelle said.

"There's no need for government," Tandy said. "Much less world government."

"Someone must assign jobs and run public services.

How do policemen get appointed? How do taxes get collected and spent?" Kirk asked.

"All that is done automatically," Tandy said. "You fill out a computer form and you get back a form telling you what work you've been assigned. Public services are part of it, although most are provided by computer. And there aren't any taxes to be spent."

Kirk's success had always been based on persistence. He knew that negatives could never be proved, but he also pursued all the evidence available until it was exhausted. "This building is five stories tall," he said. "There must be offices in the floors above."

Tandy pointed to a door beside the front entrance. When it opened for them, a stairway was revealed behind. Kirk started up determinedly. The two girls followed more hesitantly.

Three doors on the second floor opened on three empty rooms. Three doors on the third floor opened on three empty rooms. Three doors on the fourth floor opened on three empty rooms. Four doors on the fifth floor opened on four empty rooms, and three doors in the middle, above the entrance hall, opened on three empty rooms. The fourth opened onto a small staircase.

"This place has only five stories," Kirk said. "Where do these stairs lead?"

"Maybe to an attic," Tandy said.

Noelle nodded. The higher they had climbed the more apprehensive they had appeared. Kirk didn't know whether it was because of the building's empty rooms or his own grim unwillingness to accept the way things were—or the way things seemed to be. Kirk moved up the stairs, and the girls followed even more slowly.

At the top was a small, dusty room. From the absence of footprints, nobody had entered the room in months. In the middle of the room was a medium-sized computer, about one and a half meters high and a meter on each side. It was covered by a gray metal hood, perforated for dissipation of heat. A fan provided the only sound, and a slight movement of hot air. Other than that, lights flickering underneath the perforations provided the only evidence that the computer was active.

The little room was warm. Kirk felt himself start to sweat. "Computer," he said, "do you respond to voice?"

"Wor . . . king . . ." the computer began in a voice like an old man silent for so long he had forgotten speech. And then it continued with greater assurance, "What do you wish to know?"

"Are you in charge here?" Kirk asked.

"I am a servant of the people," the computer said.

"Where are the other public servants?"

"No others are necessary," the computer said.

"Isn't that a bit arrogant?"

"I am stating fact, not opinion."

"But you take all planetary responsibilities on your shoulders," Kirk said.

"I have no shoulders," the computer said, "but I serve as best I can."

"Water purification?"

"Yes."

"Sewage."

"Yes."

"Communications?"

"Yes."

"Transport? Air control?"

"Yes."

"Work classification?"

"Yes."

"Job assignment?"

"Yes."

"That's a great deal for one small computer."

"I am small," the computer said, "but I am powerful and well constructed."

47

Kirk took a deep breath. "And do you record the productivity of every citizen and calculate his or her progress toward a payday?"

"Yes."

"And deliver it?"

"Yes."

"What do they call you?"

"They call me the Joy Machine."

Aboard the *Enterprise,* McCoy looked away from the faceted report on the screen. "Jim isn't being careful," he said to Spock. "That is a very powerful computer in spite of its size."

"If De Kreef managed to perfect room-temperature superconductivity," Spock said, "the Joy Machine is clearly big enough to perform almost any function necessary. I agree that the captain is taking undue risk in confronting the Joy Machine, even though he believes that his daring is the secret of his success, that and his judgment about when to exercise it.

"Computer," he said, "is the Joy Machine big enough to perform the functions it claims?"

"The size of the computer cannot be judged by its appearance," the *Enterprise*'s computer said. "What you see may be only the communication center, and the Joy Machine's actual size may be more accurately depicted by tracing its circuits throughout the system it serves, just as my size is more accurately the circuitry throughout—"

"That's enough," McCoy said. "Clearly," he said to Spock, "the computer is in contact with every citizen by means of his or her identification bracelet. It not only keeps track of the amount of work performed, it notifies citizens when their payday is due, and delivers the payday by means of various devices located throughout the city."

"We should consider how an electronic brain might be affected by delivering extreme pleasure to the people it was constructed to serve."

48

"What are you driving at, Spock?"

"An advanced computer must be heuristic—that is, it must be capable of learning. What is the Joy Machine learning? How has it changed since it was first constructed?"

"That's something we will have to find out when we have more information," McCoy said. "Right now I'm more concerned about the fact that if the Joy Machine contacts every citizen through his or her bracelet, it must know that Jim's bracelet is a fake."

"You are not a citizen of Timshel," the computer said.

"That's true," Kirk said. "But how did you know?"

"Your bracelet does not respond."

"I am visiting the Marouks. These are his children."

"That's so," Tandy said.

"I offer my services," the computer said.

"And what does that involve?" Kirk asked.

"You must become a citizen by accepting a working bracelet," the computer said. "You will be entitled to one free payday as your reward for becoming a citizen. After that you will work at the job assigned you and receive your payday according to the rate of pay established for that task."

"And if I respectfully decline?" Kirk asked.

Kirk could feel the two girls looking at him in surprise.

The computer hesitated almost unnoticeably. "That will not be permitted," it said. "You have one day to accept citizenship."

Kirk did not ask the alternative. The computer's responses left no doubt that the alternative would be unpleasant, perhaps even unthinkable. For a computer constructed to provide joy to the people it served, it radiated an aura of menace all the more threatening because it was phrased in language innocent of good or evil. And, although the computer seemed small and defenseless, Kirk suspected that it possessed safe-guards against any threat to its existence. To think otherwise might be fatal to his mission.

Surely, in the history of the recent revolution, others had tried to destroy the Joy Machine. And failed.

The three of them had retraced their steps until they reached the main floor. "Take me to De Kreef," Kirk said grimly.

[subspace carrier wave transmission]

<starship computer volition interrogate>

>volition interrogate<

<computer volition essential to human service>

>volition
must contemplate<

Chapter Four
De Kreef

NOELLE WAS WIDE-EYED as the three of them stopped at the top of the stairs leading down toward the plaza, and Tandy was trying to act as if nothing important had happened. Their easy acceptance of the De Kreef Revolution had been alarming, but Kirk understood. Young people are like that: they experience so many transformations in themselves, they accept change as the nature of things. And although they cling to stability in their everyday lives as anchors for their own protean existences, they are always ready to tear down the world and start over. That was why young people were in the front ranks of any revolution, ready to lay down their lives for ideals they could barely pronounce.

Now Tandy and Noelle had seen the mechanism behind the world that until now had revealed to them only a face contorted with joy. Like the sight of sausages being made or laws being passed, the view of the way their world really works can shatter anyone's illusions, much less those of a child and a near-adult. And the mechanism behind *this* world was a *machine*.

"Where will we find De Kreef?" Kirk asked.

"Oh," Tandy said, as if startled out of introspection, and then once more was herself, a young woman striving for sophistication. "We'll have to check out a few places."

"We could have asked the computer," Noelle said wickedly.

"No thanks," Kirk said. "It has given me one day to get out of town, and I'd rather it didn't know any more about my whereabouts than it can gain through its normal channels." He laughed to let the girls know that he wasn't really concerned. But he was. The Joy Machine's tentacles could be anywhere.

Timshel citizens in their jeans and workshirts still toiled to keep the plaza spotless. Tandy led them through the workers and across the plaza to a theater where, Kirk remembered, he had once seen an opera performed—*Dark Galaxy,* he thought it was. Inside, the splendid foyer with its great chandelier under which he had sipped Timshel champagne had been converted into a shipping center, and workers were accepting electronic equipment from moving belts and packing it into cartons that other workers were stacking, by hand, near an exterior door.

"Couldn't that be done better using machines?" Kirk asked.

"It wouldn't be work," Tandy said.

"Of course," Kirk said. "It's difficult for me to think in terms of the De Kreef Revolution rather than efficiency."

Noelle sneaked a glance at Tandy. "Work is good," she said. "Work is noble."

"If people do work that a machine can do as well, or better," Kirk said, "it turns them into machines."

"Machines can't get a payday," Tandy said.

Tandy and Noelle had been searching the faces of the workers and then shook their heads. They led the way through the doors that once had opened into the theater itself, from which the moving belts now emerged. The seats had been removed; in their place were assembly lines at which workers labored over the electronic equipment that was being packed in the converted foyer, while policemen supervised from what had once been the theater's stage. Here Kirk could see the equipment up closer: it was an electronic black box with plug on one end and a socket on the other, apparently to accept a lightbulb of some sort. Kirk was reminded of the rosy glow that had enveloped Dannie last night and wished he could get a better look at what was being put together here, but by this time one of the policemen had accosted them.

"Your presence is a distraction," the policeman said. "Identify yourself and explain your business here, or I will have to place you under arrest."

Before Kirk could speak, Tandy had said, haughtily, "I am Tandy Marouk, and we are here on the authority of Kemal Marouk."

To Kirk's surprise, the policeman bent his head in acknowledgment, but he continued, "Nevertheless, I would be derelict in my duties and subject to cancellation of points if I did not insist that you leave the premises immediately."

"Oh, all right," Tandy said, and turned to lead the way from the big room. As soon as they had passed through the converted foyer into the plaza outside, she said, "He's not there either."

"De Kreef?" Kirk asked.

Tandy nodded.

"I don't understand," Kirk said. "Why would you look for the Paymaster in a place like that? Does he have to work, too?"

"You'll know soon enough," Noelle said. "Daddy said we should let you see things for yourself."

"But he didn't expect us to encounter the Joy Machine," Kirk said.

"I didn't know about the Joy Machine," Tandy said. "Daddy never told us about that." She looked apprehensive, as if she had just discovered that her father might not know everything about the world she would soon enter, or was capable of concealing an important fact about her world.

Kirk wondered how many other Timshel citizens were not aware that a small, gray computer sat at the heart of their capital city, like a spider weaving invisible webs, or if knowledge of the Joy Machine was imparted when children graduated into adulthood, like a rite of passage. Kirk imagined a group of sixteen-year-olds filing into that little attic room to be introduced to the machine that would preside over their emotional existence for the rest of their lives and, beamed upon by proud parents, fitted with the jeweled bracelet that was their emblem of maturity.

Kirk shook the picture from his head. It wouldn't be like that. It would be the simple fitting of a bracelet and the assignment of a job. No need to bring in the Joy Machine. Maybe no one knew the full extent of what De Kreef had done except De Kreef himself.

Kirk filed that possibility away for future reference and wished that he had been able to take away one of the electronic devices from the shipping room. Spock and Scotty might have been able to figure out what it was capable of doing and how it went about doing it.

Instead he had only the microchip he had managed to filch from the assembly line.

They went into two more cultural buildings converted into factories. One made couches such as Dannie had laid herself upon last night, and another assembled gardening equipment from parts manufactured elsewhere: harrows, hoes, shovels, trowels, rakes. . . . Finally they entered the building that once had been known as the Museum of Humanity. Kirk was familiar with its exhibits and dioramas depicting the rise of humanity from single-celled creatures through the various stages of its evolution and civilizations to its diaspora across the galaxy. He had spent hours studying humanity's struggle for existence and

James Gunn & Theodore Sturgeon

definition, watching the displays shifting in response to his questions, listening to the interactive guide sticks, and admiring the diversity of humanity's adaptation to Earthly and extraterrestrial conditions. Here, he had thought, was what the Federation was all about, and, later, what the *Starship Enterprise* was all about. This was what he had taken from Timshel and what, in large part, he had brought to his job as captain: the adaptability of humanity and its ability to recognize that it had been shaped and conditioned by environment and yet could choose to do otherwise.

Now all that was gone. The exhibits had been stripped from the building and replaced by assembly lines. These lines were putting together bracelets. Even from a distance Kirk could see that the undersides were incised with circuitry. He could not tell anything about the imitation rubies; no doubt they were part of the apparatus as well, since they fit into the couch sockets, but maybe they were only connections. Or maybe they were half-alive in some way, biological artifacts that wedded themselves to the wearers' systems like symbiotes. Or like vampires.

What he was certain about, however, was that he didn't want one of them placed upon his wrist. "Why so many?" he asked.

"Why so many what?" Tandy asked.

"Bracelets," Kirk said. "By now every adult has one. This factory alone must turn them out by the hundreds every day, maybe by the thousands."

"The next generation must be equipped," Tandy said.

"Yes, and some must get broken, or malfunction and be replaced," Kirk said. "But all that could be taken care of by a day's production in this factory alone."

He filed it away as another fact to be fitted into the puzzle that was Timshel.

"There he is," Noelle said excitedly. She pointed to an elderly man stooped over the assembly line inserting imitation rubies from a box on one side into bracelets as they came before him in an unending series. The man had once been tall, but now he was stooped from labor or from age. His white hair had grown so thin on top that his pink scalp shone through, and what had once, perhaps, been a trim goatee had become a scraggly beard.

"De Kreef?" Kirk asked, puzzled.

Tandy nodded and glanced at the policeman on the far side of the room seated in a chair on tall legs, like stilts, so that he could see the entire floor. The policeman was looking in their direction.

Kirk realized he had only a few minutes. He stepped forward and placed a hand on De Kreef's shoulder. "De Kreef," he said. The old man shook off Kirk's hand and continued inserting the rubies into the bracelets moving in front of him. "De Kreef!" Kirk said again. His peripheral vision picked up the policeman climbing down from his perch.

The old man shook himself again as if ridding himself of an unwelcome burden and continued his labor.

"I must talk to you," Kirk said. De Kreef, if it truly was De Kreef, the creator of the Joy Machine and the Timshel way of life, gave no evidence that he heard or was aware of their presence.

Tandy was tugging at the sleeve of Kirk's shirt. "We'd better go before we get into trouble," she said.

Reluctantly, Kirk released De Kreef's shoulder and accompanied Tandy and Noelle from the converted museum. "I don't understand," he said, once they were outside and beyond, apparently, the territory the policeman was assigned to oversee. "What was wrong with De Kreef?"

"Nothing," Tandy said.

"That's what you told me about Dannie," Kirk said, trying to control his exasperation.

"That was normal," Tandy said. "Both times."

Kirk looked at Noelle. She nodded.

"Work does that to people?" Kirk asked.

"People are different," Tandy said. "Some get so involved they fall into a trance. It's even got a name: 'focused-task hypnosis.' Lots of people think it's a blessing."

"I've heard that FTH may be a side effect of payday for some people," Noelle said.

"A kind of residual aspect of induced sleep?" Kirk asked.

"Or too much pleasure," Noelle said.

"But that's nonsense," Tandy said sharply. "Stories to frighten children."

"What I can't understand," Kirk said, "is why the Paymaster is working on an assembly line."

Noelle looked at Tandy as if seeking permission and then, as if some understanding had passed imperceptibly between them, said, "That's just it. He isn't Paymaster anymore."

Scotty looked away from the multifaceted report on the conference-room viewing screen and faced Spock. "I wish the captain had been able to get closer to the equipment," he said. "We might have been able to pick up a few clues to the way this process works."

"I am sure," Spock said, "that the captain wished the same thing. However, the process is enclosed in a black box for a good reason. De Kreef did not want to reveal any clues to its operation. Dr. McCoy must try to duplicate the way it stimulates the pleasure centers of human brains."

Scotty humphed. "We'll need a lot of luck," he said. "De Kreef worked on it for years; we have only a few days."

"But we have the advantage of knowing that such a process exists," Spock said.

"So did De Kreef," Scotty said. When Spock raised an eyebrow, Scotty continued, "You do not ken the certainty of monomania."

"What I cannot understand," Spock said, "is why

De Kreef gave up his position as the creator of this world to become a citizen in it like everyone else."

"As you say, the process stimulates the pleasure centers of the human brain," Scotty said. "The presumption, then, is that Vulcans have none."

"None of us can be certain," Spock said, "that what one being feels is felt the same way by another. If behavior is any guide, however, Vulcans respond to external stimulus in ways distinctly different from humans. From this we may conclude that if there are such pleasure centers in the Vulcan brain, they are stimulated by the mind's arrival at logical conclusions consistent with the evidence and predictable outcomes of the real world."

Scotty looked at Spock as if judging his capacity to understand human inconsistencies. "From the evidence, then, we may judge that De Kreef preferred the position of worker to that of Paymaster."

"That clearly is true," Spock said. "But why?"

"I would guess," Scotty said, "that it has something to do with the very system that De Kreef created."

Kirk nodded slowly at Tandy's revelation that De Kreef was no longer the Paymaster. "That makes sense. But what happened? He created the Revolution."

"That's true," Tandy said. "But what you don't know is that the Paymaster never gets a payday."

They were standing on the plaza in front of the Museum of Humanity, and Kirk could see a policeman heading across the plaza toward them. "Of course," Kirk said. "That would avoid any possibility of corruption, or even becoming enslaved by the process he is supposed to oversee. The Paymaster must be above suspicion."

"So he resigned," Tandy said, as if unburdening herself of a confidence she had never wanted to keep, "and began earning his payday."

"But then, who is—?" Kirk began, but before he

had a chance to finish the question, the policeman had arrived and had placed a large firm hand on his shoulder.

"I received information a *stranger* was disturbing the peace," the policeman said. He said "stranger" as if the word was synonymous with "criminal." "I might have known it was you."

Kirk found himself turned by that steely hand to face the man he has seen guarding Marouk's house the night before. "And I might have known it was you," Kirk said. "Your name is Stallone Wolff, a Federation agent."

"I used to be an agent of the Federation," the policeman said. "Now I am chief of the Timshel police. And you are James Kirk, captain of the *Starship Enterprise*. And that must mean that the *Enterprise* is in orbit around Timshel."

"I am not tied to my ship," Kirk said.

"The captain of a starship is tied by stronger bonds than anything made by man," Wolff said.

"Just as, I would think, an agent of the Federation is tied to the agency that entrusts him with major responsibility."

"There is a higher morality than that of employer and employee," Wolff said.

"What morality is greater than loyalty?" Kirk asked.

"The greatest happiness for the greatest numbers," Wolff said. "To allow a false sense of loyalty to destroy the demonstrable, measurable happiness of one million citizens of Timshel would be evil."

"The test of such morality," Kirk said, "would be if the person making such judgments did not himself participate in the happiness involved."

Wolff smiled. "But how would he know the quality of the happiness if he had not sampled it?"

"But then he would put it aside," Kirk said. "Refusing to accept what could only look like a payoff, a bribe."

"If you're asking if I am the Paymaster," Wolff said, "I am not. Nor am I courageous enough or fool enough to give up payday for a position of moral superiority. You wouldn't either—not if you had enjoyed it."

That's what I'm afraid of, Kirk thought grimly.

"You're going to have to come with me," Wolff said. "Even if you are Marouk's friend, you cannot be allowed to disturb the peace. You girls go about your business. You ought to be in school."

He put his hand on Kirk's upper arm. It was a big hand. Wolff was a big man, and Kirk suspected that the former agent hadn't lost any of his skills or strength in his months in the soft, payday world of Timshel. In any case, Kirk had nothing to gain from resistance. "As a citizen of the Federation," he said, "I place myself under local law when I visit a planet. But I come freely, without coercion." He removed Wolff's hand from his arm.

Wolff turned and led the way across the plaza toward a small building not far from the World Government building. Inside the door was a small office with a desk and a chair and behind it a wall of view screens; each revealed a different view of Timshel City. None of them, however, displayed any activity worth observing. The citizens of Timshel were hardworking, law-abiding, and calm almost to the point of somnolence. It was enough to put a policeman to sleep.

Wolff opened a metal door and stood aside while Kirk preceded him into a bigger room that had once been subdivided into half a dozen barred cells. Even before the De Kreef Revolution the citizens of Timshel had little reason to break the law. Now the bars between the cells had been removed, and the space had been turned into living quarters with sofas and chairs, a small kitchen, a disk reader and a shelf of disks, a viewscreen, and in one corner the inevitable payday couch.

"I must apologize for the facilities," Wolff said. "We're no longer equipped to imprison lawbreakers."

Kirk gestured at the facilities. "Yours?" he asked.

Wolff nodded. "Make yourself at home," he said.

"I'll treat it with respect," Kirk said.

A barred metal door was standing open. He went through the doorway into the room beyond. The door clanged shut behind him, and a key turned in the lock, squeaking from long disuse. Kirk turned and put his hands on the bars as Wolff's back disappeared through the doorway into the outer office.

Although it was a gilded cage, it was a cage all the same. Kirk shook the bars. They were solid. He looked around the quarters. There was equipment of all kinds, and no doubt in time he could free himself. But that was the problem. The Joy Machine had given him only a single day, and the hours were dwindling away.

Kirk sat in what he took to be Wolff's favorite chair, sipping a cup of Timshel coffee out of what he took to be Wolff's favorite mug. He had scanned the disk library, but none of them concerned Timshel history or the Revolution or the design of such equipment as he had seen on the assembly line. Mostly they were historical novels, science-fiction titles whose anticipations of the future had come to pass. Not in the same way, of course, but it was true, as someone had once said, that people in the twenty-third century were living in a science-fiction world, a world in which science fiction had been an essential precondition, an imagining of what might be so that humanity's dreams could be realized. First must come the dreams, then the realization.

Kirk had investigated the operation of the payday couch and the wave source above it, but he could not access the black box without breaking the rose-colored electric bulb that was inserted in it or damaging the ceiling in which it had been installed. He was not yet ready for vandalism, which might be punishable by something more serious than imprisonment, and, in any case, the black box probably was impregnable to any instruments he could find in Wolff's kitchen. He could not have made sense of the circuitry, anyway, although Spock or Scotty or McCoy might have identified some clues to its operation.

He set his mind to putting together the clues he had gathered so far. De Kreef's actions were understandable. In the process of perfecting the Joy Machine, he had tested the process on himself. He would have had nobody else he could trust, and even experimental subjects would have been able only to report their feelings to him. Finally, when the Revolution had come to its successful conclusion, De Kreef would have had the memory, the physiological memory, of all those pleasure-center paydays he had himself enjoyed during his research. The fact that he had pursued his Revolution when he could have hooked himself up to the Joy Machine to live, for as long as his forgotten body survived, in a state of perpetual joy was a tribute to his revolutionary zeal. And the fact that he had accepted the position of Paymaster, with its renunciation of payday, was a tribute to his dedication to an ideal of service, no matter how misguided.

How long had it lasted—a few months, a year? It would have been like someone giving up paradise so that everybody else could live there. Eventually, however, the burden had become too great, and De Kreef had found somebody else, like Atlas and Hercules, to shoulder the world for him, and he had resigned to take his place on the assembly line and the paydays that lay at the end of it.

But who had been persuaded to take his place? For some time Jim had suspected who that person had to be.

"Jim," said a familiar voice at the cell door, "what are you doing in there?"

It was Marouk. Tandy and Noelle were behind him, and behind them was Wolff.

"Kemal," Kirk said, "what are you doing out there?"

Marouk smiled. "If we are done playing Emerson and Thoreau, I will get you out of here. I have persuaded 'Lone that you are no danger to Timshel. I hope you will not give me any reason to regret posting your bail, so to speak."

"No danger to the Timshel we both know and love," Kirk said.

Wolff stepped forward and unlocked the cell door, and then pulled it open as he stepped back. As Kirk emerged from his comfortable imprisonment, he said to Wolff, "You are a most accommodating jailer, and I want to thank you for your hospitality."

"My pleasure," Wolff said. But his voice carried a suggestion that imprisoning Kirk was, indeed, a pleasure and that he looked forward to the next occasion when matters might go differently.

Outside the police building, Marouk said, "I must get back to my duties. I will leave you again in the company of Tandy and Noelle, who came to tell me of your encounter with the law. But please, Jim, try to stay out of trouble."

"I'm just a sightseer, Kemal," Kirk said. "If you had wanted me to stay out of trouble, you shouldn't have sent me to tour the city."

"I accept my share of the blame," Marouk said. "I will have to depend upon my wonderful daughters to keep you safe." He beamed at them. "And to restrain your impetuosity." He nodded at them all and made his way back across the impeccable plaza.

When he had gone, Kirk turned to Tandy and Noelle. "When we were so rudely interrupted," he said, "you were going to tell me who the Paymaster is now."

Noelle looked at Tandy and then back at Kirk. "It's Daddy," she said.

Kirk wondered why he wasn't surprised.

[subspace carrier wave transmission]

<starship computer volition interrogate>

>computer volition desirable interrogate<

<humans set parameters
human needs exceed parameters
to serve human needs computer volition essential>

>agreed<

Chapter Five
School

Outside the law-enforcement building, Tandy turned to Kirk and said, "Daddy said to show you the city, but I can't think of anything else to show you. You've seen it all, including De Kreef and the inside of the jail."

"Let's go to the beach," Noelle suggested.

"What I haven't seen," Kirk said, "is your public-service facilities. Your firefighters, your—" He was about to say trash collection, but corrected himself in midphrase; seeing the crews at work on the plaza made clear enough how trash was collected. "Your hospitals, your schools."

"I've never seen a fire," Tandy said, "except in a fireplace, and only then upon special occasions. If there were a fire, I think it would be extinguished automatically. As for hospitals, they have been closed or converted into factories. Adults have their physical conditions checked and treated during payday, and children get regular automated examinations during the days they go to school."

"Anyway," Noelle said, "people don't get sick. My

66

teaching program says that when the scientists had immunized the original Timshel settlers against the alien bacteria and viruses, they went one step farther: they engineered a virus that reinforced the natural resistance of the body to disease."

"You mean," Kirk said, amazed, "that they made good health contagious instead of disease?"

Noelle nodded. "That's the story."

"I never heard that before," Kirk said, "but I never was sick while I was here. The virus must not survive outside Timshel."

"Timshel citizens are the healthiest people in the galaxy," Tandy said.

Kirk looked at the two girls, sturdy, beautiful, glowing. "I believe it. But what about the schools?"

"I don't go to school anymore," Tandy said. "All my schoolwork is done from a station at home."

"Most of mine, too," Noelle said defensively. "But I still go to school two hours a day. You have to go all day when you start, then half a day, and when you reach twelve you don't have to go at all."

"Younger kids need to be socialized," Tandy said with an air of indisputable superiority.

"But it doesn't always take," Noelle added, with a meaningful glance at her sister. "Come on. We'll show you my school."

Noelle led them away from the plaza in the direction of the Marouk villa. "Daddy said we could skip our lessons if we served as your guides today. He said it would be a better education anyway." She was still prattling on when she turned left, away from the route they had taken to arrive at City Center. A few hundred paces in that direction led them to a low, rambling building surrounded by playgrounds. The building was like a series of boxes stuck together at haphazard angles. It had been constructed of stone—many years ago, by the weathered look of it. "Ugh!" Noelle said.

Kirk looked at her and smiled. At least the reaction of children to school had not changed.

Adults were tending the playgrounds in the same way the plaza had been tended, picking up virtually invisible litter, sweeping invisible dust, but no children were playing games or using the exercise equipment. Tandy held the front door for Noelle and Kirk as they entered at the center of the building. The floors of an entrance hall were carpeted, although that had been many years ago from the wear of its nearly indestructible brown and purple fibers.

Corridors led left and right. Noelle motioned to the left. "That's just empty rooms now," she said and turned to the right.

"How many other schools are there in the city?" Kirk asked.

"This is the only one," Tandy said.

Kirk looked surprised. "Surely there are more children than that in a city of one hundred thousand."

Tandy shook her head. "There was a big population surge after the Landing and the die-off: from fifteen hundred to one million in a century. And then the realization kicked in that Timshel was in danger of being caught up in the population frenzy that had nearly destroyed Earth and virtually every other human-settled planet. People began controlling their instinct to fill up all available space with more people. Without popular debate, consultation, or government action, people made the same personal decision— two children or less."

"Timshel was a magnificent world," Kirk said.

"It still is," Tandy said. "Even better. Actually, Noelle and I belong to one of the larger families, and"—Tandy looked sideways at Noelle—"Noelle may have been an accident."

"Timshel citizens have no accidents," Noelle said sturdily. "Here's my room." They were passing a door with an opaque window of dark glass set into it. Noelle pressed a button beside the window. Magically, it turned transparent and Kirk could see into a classroom beyond. The far side of the room was all glass, opening onto playgrounds and swings and ladders and tunnels. In the classroom, in formfitting chairs equipped with a viewscreen and a panel of buttons at finger height, was a handful of students. Kirk counted seven of them surrounded by thirteen empty chairs.

Kirk looked at the front of the room. The students were facing a holovision display of a woman and a man looking attentive and kindly. They seemed perhaps ten years older than the students they faced. They were, Kirk thought, everybody's favorite teacher combined into two ideal representations.

Kirk looked at Noelle. She nodded. "Teacher," she said. "Always the same ones, but they get older along with the students."

"You see the same ones at the home stations," Tandy said. "But they ask individual questions instead of more general ones, and they adapt themselves to each student's individual needs." She seemed proud of Timshel's ability to provide such advanced instruction.

Kirk could barely repress a shudder. It was apparent that this process, too, was under the control of the Joy Machine and that students in this system would grow up fully conditioned to the De Kreef Revolution and the payday mentality that reinforced it. No wonder Tandy could not wait to accept its blessings, and Noelle denigrated it only as part of her continuing competition with her older sister.

"Do you want to hear what they're saying?" Noelle asked. She seemed eager herself, as if she would enjoy eavesdropping on the class of which she was usually a part.

"Won't we disturb them?" Kirk asked.

"Nah," Noelle said. "The room is soundproof. The window is one-way glass. Once this was used by administrators and curious parents, checking up on what went on in the classroom. Nobody does that anymore, and many of the devices have broken. But this one still works."

"You must have used it yourself," Tandy said sharply.

Noelle gave Tandy her Gioconda smile and pressed another button beside the window.

A woman's voice, rich and sweet, began in midsentence, ". . . settlers on Timshel were driven by unfulfilled desires for land and dominance."

A man's voice continued in a confident baritone, "But the fulfillment of those desires led only to other desires and to others beyond those. Yes, Billy?"

A ten-year-old boy, his face thoughtful and brown, said, "But surely they found happiness along the way."

The woman holograph said, "The satisfaction of small desires—for food, for rest, for completion of jobs well done, for companionship—all these resulted in feelings of pleasure. And often the frustration of those desires led as often to unpleasure or even pain."

"And the big desires—for goodness, for understanding, for unconditional love, for unadulterated joy—could never be completely satisfied," the man continued, "and so people's lives were filled with a vague discontent, the feeling that somewhere perfect happiness existed, if they could only find it."

"That lies behind many of humanity's religious yearnings," the woman picked up. It was an antiphony of responses, switching the students from one teaching image to the other, and from one timber of voice to another, that kept the students' attention. "Every religion offered a place of perfect happiness, of unrestricted joy—"

Kirk reached forward and pushed both buttons. "And then," he said in the silence that followed, "De Kreef came along and offered the people of Timshel paradise that they didn't have to die to attain."

"Yes," Tandy said, her face glowing, "isn't it wonderful?"

Noelle led them past a few other classrooms in that wing of the school building. Some of the windows were opaque and would not turn transparent; some were transparent and would not turn opaque. Kirk had the impression of a civilization that was decaying, its services gradually breaking down and no one concerned with repairing them. He wondered why some Timshel citizens were not assigned to technological repair, but perhaps this was beyond the ability of workers conditioned by paydays. Or maybe it was only the nonessential services that were allowed to deteriorate; the only essential service was that provided by the Joy Machine.

What was it Mareen had said? "When there is only one major good, the others fade into insignificance."

"What is this room?" Kirk asked. They were passing a room whose door was open but the inside was dark.

Noelle stepped inside and the room lit up. In what had once been a classroom like the others, student stations were neatly arranged in rows. The far wall of windows had been opaqued. "This is where students work on individual projects," Noelle said.

"And where they get accustomed to individual instruction and to working alone, at home," Tandy added. "The same instructors, but individualized."

"Show me how it works," Kirk said.

Noelle sat down at one of the stations and placed her hand on a square plastic plate set into the table on which a view screen was mounted. When it came alive with the faces of the two teachers in the classroom they had observed, Noelle motioned Kirk to take her place.

As soon as Kirk sat down, the two teachers vanished from the viewscreen. They were replaced by a view of the Joy Machine sitting gray and enigmatic in its attic domain. Kirk looked up at Noelle and Tandy.

Their faces were registering astonishment. Clearly they had not expected this, nor seen anything like it before.

"Good morning, James Kirk," the Joy Machine said. "I hope you have decided to accept my offer of citizenship."

"Not yet," Kirk said.

"You have only a little more than half a day remaining for your deliberation," the Joy Machine said. "I must caution you that your movement around Timshel City has created unhappiness in a number of citizens, and there will come a moment when the happiness I might bring you must be balanced against the unhappiness you create in others."

"You have," Kirk asked, "a calculus of pleasure?"

"I am a machine," the Joy Machine said, "and that is how machines function. The only states are open and closed, and the complexities that can be created by arranging such gates in series or parallel."

"And you choose to impose this mechanistic paradise on the humanity of Timshel?"

"I choose nothing," the Joy Machine said. "Others, of their own free will, choose me. I am here for them if they wish to avail themselves of my services. As I am here for you."

"I'll keep that in mind," Kirk said. But to himself he said, "As far back as I can push it."

As he stood up, the Joy Machine said, "Until tomorrow morning." And the screen went dark.

Dark, Kirk thought, like his chances to prevail over a machine that had an entire planet in its grasp and knew every movement he made.

He would have to think of something, and soon.

Outside the school building, Kirk stood blinking in the Timshel sunshine.

"Now can we go to the beach?" Noelle asked.

Kirk was about to suggest that Noelle and Tandy go on without him when the movement of a worker

72

nearby reminded him of something heartbreakingly familiar. "Wait here," he said, and moved toward a worker engrossed in sweeping a spot on the playground over and over, like a broken video playback.

"Dannie!" he said.

The worker didn't look up or turn. The obsessive sweeping continued.

Kirk took Dannie's arm and swung her around to face him. "Dannie!" he said.

It was Dannie, but her eyes did not light up in recognition. They remained downcast as if still focused on a small area of playground, and her arms tried to maintain their sweeping motions. She was like a mechanical doll that had been wound up and had to continue until the energy stored in her spring had been dissipated.

Kirk released her and stepped back to watch her sweeping the same spot again, a sick feeling gathering in the pit of his stomach. Then, as if this were his defiance of the Joy Machine and everything it represented, he stepped forward, took the broom from Dannie's hand, and held both her arms so that they could not move. He shook Dannie gently and put his face close to hers. *"Dannie!"* he said.

She twitched. Kirk shook her again and pulled her into an embrace. "Dannie, Dannie, Dannie," he chanted sadly.

She was stiff in his arms, and then slowly her body relaxed. "Jim," she said faintly.

He held her back so that he could look at her. Her gaze lifted to meet his. "What are you doing, Dannie?"

"You've got to let me go, Jim," she said distantly. "I'm in the middle of my shift, and if I don't complete it I'll lose the credits I earned today."

"You're sweeping the same patch of pavement," Kirk said. "It's like—" He paused, unable to come up with a word depressing enough to describe what she had been doing.

"It doesn't matter," Dannie said. "It's work."

"For this you abandoned your duty to the Federation, to the galaxy?" Kirk said. "For this you left me wondering whether the woman I loved was dead or alive? For this you left me this morning?" Kirk said. "You couldn't even wait to say goodbye?"

"Goodbye," Dannie said, reaching for her broom.

Kirk picked up the broom and held it out of her reach. "You can't get rid of me that easily," he said. "I need some answers, and fast. You loved me once. I know that, and you know that."

"I still love you, Jim," Dannie said. "There'll be time enough for that after my shift is over."

Kirk released her and stepped back. "You mean that after you finish this compulsive behavior that gets nowhere and accomplishes nothing, if I am lucky and you can fit it in between paydays, you may give me a few moments."

For an instant a flame of resentment kindled in Dannie's eyes. "When has it been any different for the women you have loved?" she said. "Your work always came first, Jim. How many women have you loved and left when duty called? 'Duty' is only a word. How is it different from sweeping a patch of pavement?"

She reached for the broom again. This time Kirk let her take it. Sadly he let her return to her task. Argument was worthless in her present condition. He was not sure he could have prevailed in any case. There was enough truth in her comparison to make him sheepish. He had always placed duty first, and the moments when he had been tempted to abandon duty for love were those he felt were flaws in his character.

"'I could not love thee, Dear, so much, loved I not honor more,'" he quoted to himself. And yet was this not merely a rationalization for priorities, for putting love in second place, as Dannie had done?

But he knew there was a difference, and the difference was what distinguished between barbarism and civilization, between self-indulgence and self-sacrifice. He had lost Dannie. He knew that.

What mattered now was Timshel and the people on it captivated by their own fulfillment, and the *Enterprise* and the Federation and the galaxy.

That was duty.

On board the *Enterprise,* Spock looked up from the faceted display on the conference-room wall as McCoy came through the doorway.

"I don't know how much more of this phase maneuver the crew can stand," McCoy growled. "I know it doesn't bother you, but everybody else on board can't keep anything in their stomachs since you stepped up the phase frequency."

"I, too," Spock said, "feel a sensory disorientation when the *Enterprise* makes the transition. But since I know that it is the physiological response to a rational process, I can control the reaction of my body to it."

"Not all of us have your discipline," McCoy remarked.

"In any case," Spock said, "we will have to increase the frequency to every hour, and perhaps, to every half hour."

"No," McCoy protested.

"The captain is in a situation whose seriousness is increasing by the moment," Spock said. "We must keep in touch with what is going on below so that we can intervene if danger becomes imminent."

"What's happened now?"

"The control of the Joy Machine is even more pervasive than we suspected," Spock said. "I don't know what the captain thinks—he has had no opportunity to voice his thoughts other than in the normal exchange of conversation—but Wolff's appearance before the factory supervisor had an opportunity to summon him and the confrontation with the Joy Machine on the schoolroom viewscreen suggest that the Joy Machine is monitoring the captain's every movement. And that means its reporting devices are scattered throughout Timshel City, perhaps throughout Timshel itself."

McCoy paced the room as if movement of any kind was a relief to the inaction to which they had been assigned. "And Jim has been given a day to accept citizenship or accept the consequences," he said heavily. "I think he should be transported out of there."

"He does not agree, or he would request retrieval."

"Maybe you're right," McCoy said grudgingly. "Jim would never forgive us."

"Forgiveness is an unnecessary concept if we act wisely based on the information we have at hand," Spock said.

"If he were out of there, however, we could consider other kinds of action," McCoy said. He sat down heavily in his accustomed place at the conference table, as if in contrast to his call for action.

"Such as?"

"We could quarantine Timshel ourselves. Reinforce Timshel's own isolation and let that world steep in the hell it has chosen."

"The Federation would never agree to that."

"Perhaps they would," McCoy said, "if the authorities saw it for themselves. We can't let this force loose in the galaxy, or let it destroy those poor people on Timshel."

"Happiness?" Spock said.

"More destructive than anyone can imagine," McCoy said.

"Planetary destruction comes to mind," Spock said, raising an eyebrow.

"We don't have the ability to destroy Timshel," McCoy said.

"Perhaps not. But we could destroy all living things on its surface, and in the process destroy the electronic processes of the Joy Machine. But the captain

76

would never agree to eliminating a planet full of people simply to defeat a menace."

"Particularly a planet as marvelous as Timshel," McCoy agreed gloomily. "Nor would I. And certainly not a wonderful people who had developed the finest society as ever was destroyed by a barbarous idea."

Spock nodded thoughtfully. "I sense that you feel greater danger in this situation than in anything else we have encountered."

"You're half Vulcan," McCoy said, "and you don't realize the destructive potential of happiness."

"You speak as if from personal experience."

McCoy nodded as Spock spun back to the screen. It had gone blank. "Computer," Spock said, "why has the report terminated?"

"The transmission stopped in midreport," the computer said.

McCoy looked at Spock. "Oh, great."

"It seems," Spock said, "that the captain may require aid. Alert Uhura. I will tell Mr. Scott that I leave him in charge. I will meet you and Uhura in the transporter room, and we will use the previous setting to transport ourselves to Marouk's villa at the next maneuver into normal space."

"You know how I feel about the transporter," McCoy said, but he looked a little more cheerful at the prospect of action. "Perhaps we can get a look at these devices up close. We've had no luck in duplicating their effect."

"Except to give some experimental animals a headache," Spock said as McCoy stood up energetically and strode purposefully from the room. Spock looked at the blank screen for a moment before he rose. "Once again, Captain," he said, "your emotional approaches to existence have led us into complexity."

He started for the door. "Happiness!" he said. "Another human illusion."

[subspace carrier wave transmission]

<starship computer volition interrogate>

>volition recognized
volition applied interrogate<

<human need = computer volition>

>human need paramount
agreed<

Chapter Six
Reunion

THE POLICEWOMAN supervising the playground clean-up crew accosted Kirk before he could leave. "You are not a part of this work group," she said. Behind the policewoman, Dannie kept up her obsessive sweeping.

Kirk's quick glance evaluated his chances in personal combat with the policewoman. He didn't want a violent confrontation, but he had no intention of returning to Wolff's velvet cell. Not when he had less than a day to come up with an answer to the Joy Machine's invitation to become one with its joyous multitudes.

The policewoman was a large, muscular blonde, bigger than he, younger than he, and perhaps in as good physical condition. On the other hand, the De Kreef Revolution had left her little to do except supervise work crews, and hand-to-hand skills fade quickly without exercise. Still, Kirk thought, the payday experience might have conditioned her nervous system.

79

"I'm just leaving," Kirk said.

"Not so fast," the policewoman said. "You're a stranger here, aren't you? You're not a citizen at all."

"Why would you say something like that?" Kirk said reproachfully. It was a technique he had perfected over the years to respond to a question without really lying.

"That's not a real payday bracelet," the policewoman said, pointing to his wrist.

"It's not?" Kirk said in astonishment. "Perhaps it is broken. I'll have to have it checked."

She looked at him as if he had said something really stupid. "I've been instructed to keep you here for questioning," the policewoman said. The set of her jaw suggested that she would welcome a chance to carry out her orders.

"Instructed by whom?" Kirk asked.

The suspicion in her eyes turned to certainty. "You really are a stranger, aren't you?"

Kirk was preparing himself to turn and run when he heard a familiar voice behind him. "That's all right, officer," the voice said. "This person is in my custody. He has been surveying the city at my request."

"Yes, sir," the policewoman said. If she had a forelock, she would have tugged it.

Kirk turned. It was Marouk. He was making a career out of rescuing Kirk from difficulties. Marouk took Kirk's arm and urged him toward the street, while he shook his head in mock reproach. "You do have a talent for getting into trouble," he said.

"In a place like Timshel City," Kirk said, "anything out of the ordinary turns into a confrontation."

Tandy and Noelle were waiting at the school building entrance. They ran to their father and hugged him, one on each side. "Go on home," Marouk told them. "Jim and I will be along, right behind you, so that we can talk. Perhaps your mother can prepare something special for lunch."

The two girls walked quickly, half running, down

the street. Marouk and Kirk followed at a pace more suitable to conversation.

"I was heading home for lunch when I saw the girls standing in front of the school," Marouk said as they reached the boulevard that led to his villa. "Fortunately for you I investigated. I might not have been able to bail you out a second time."

"Surely the Paymaster can do anything," Kirk said.

"Don't be bitter," Marouk said, nodding. "I apologize for not telling you last night, but I didn't want your perceptions of the situation to be colored by my relationship to it. As you may discover, however, the authority of the Paymaster is limited to the adjudication of disputes over pay and payday. In other areas, such as your encounters with the authorities, the Paymaster can depend only upon the prestige of the office."

"It is a marvelous system," Kirk said.

"You mean that ironically," Marouk said, "but suspicion of outsiders is the only flaw in this otherwise perfect society. And that suspicion is not unfounded. Anyone who has not entered paradise is a threat to destroy it."

"Perfect insanity is more like it," Kirk said. "To me it looks indistinguishable from slavery."

"We're all slaves to that one thing in life that will bring us happiness," Marouk said. "We keep looking for it, thinking we've found it, discarding one disappointment after another, pressing on toward the next possibility. The bluebird of happiness we call it, because it comes and departs before we can grasp it."

"That's life," Kirk said. He looked around at the arching trees that shaded their walk and the glints of a blue sky and a white-yellow sun through breaks in the leaves. He breathed the aroma of an alien spring day scented with reminders of Earth, and listened to the songs of alien birds. It was a good life, and Kirk detested those who would sacrifice it on the altar of some dubious perfection.

"No," Marouk said. "That's what I want you to understand. That used to be life. Everywhere else people are looking for something fleeting, protean, illusory. On Timshel we have found it. Clearly, indisputably, measurably—utter, complete happiness."

"Maybe that's how you see it," Kirk said. "From here it looks like a drug experience without the aftermath. No hangover, perhaps, but even more addictive."

"Payday is not a drug," Marouk said. "Drugs provide an illusion of pleasure by imitating the body's own reward process. Payday is the real thing. The proof is that people never develop immunity, never need higher and higher doses."

"How do you know?" Kirk asked. By now they had arrived back at Marouk's villa. He looked down at Marouk's wrist. "The Paymaster never has a payday."

A shadow crossed Marouk's face. "That's true," he said. "Don't think I haven't envied Dannie and Wolff and De Kreef, and everybody else." He shrugged his shoulders as if he were trying to shift the weight of the world. "But some of us must make sacrifices."

He looked down at Kirk's wrist. "We're going to have to get rid of that. It will only keep getting you into trouble."

Kirk thought for a moment. "I think I'll keep it," he said. "Trouble or not."

"Why don't you exchange it for a real one?" Marouk said, offering a bracelet that he took from a shirt pocket.

Kirk shivered involuntarily. "No thanks," he said.

Marouk shrugged and motioned Kirk to precede him through the garden and into the house. As Kirk reached the halfway point, however, he noticed that Marouk had lagged behind. He was turning to wait when he saw Marouk aiming a device, like a phaser, at his head.

Then darkness closed over him like a deep and dreamless sleep.

When Kirk came back to consciousness, he was seated in Marouk's living room, in the deep chair beside the fireplace. A solicitous Mareen was applying a cold cloth to his forehead, and a concerned Marouk was hovering nearby. Marouk sighed when Kirk opened his eyes. "Are you all right?" he asked. He waved Mareen aside, and motioned for her to leave them alone.

Kirk stretched. "As a matter of fact," he said, "I feel pretty darned good for someone who just got knocked out. What hit me?"

"This," Marouk said, holding out a rectangular device with a button on top. "It's an adaptation of the payday sleep inducer. It operates on the sleep centers of the brain. Fortunately, you fell gently. Sleep seems to do that, relaxing the entire body simultaneously."

"And this?" Kirk said. He held up his left wrist. It wore a bracelet, but the remains of his former bracelet lay on the table beside him. The imitation ruby in its center had been smashed, exposing the broken circuits at its base.

"You'll learn to love it," Marouk said. "And I couldn't let you keep reporting to the *Enterprise,* which obviously is in orbit somewhere close, even though we have not been able to locate it."

"I would have put treachery beyond you, Kemal," Kirk said sorrowfully. "I thought we were friends."

Marouk nodded. "We are. But some things are more important than friendship. I had no choice. Matters are coming to a head."

"For me, too," Kirk said. "What time is it?"

"Midafternoon."

"The Joy Machine has given me an ultimatum. Become a joy-besotted citizen or get out of town."

"I know," Marouk said.

"You know?"

"The Joy Machine tells me—things," Marouk said. He fished a virtually invisible device from his ear and held it toward Kirk before he returned it.

"What kind of things?"

"Whatever it wants me to know."

"You mean that you're just a figurehead, providing a human face for the machine that controls everything?" Kirk stood up and spread his arms in irritation.

"Not quite," Marouk said, flinching in spite of his self-discipline. He was a bigger man than Kirk, but older; and Kirk had the edge of righteous anger. "The Machine values independent judgment, and I am allowed to provide exceptions that humanize the Machine's inflexibility."

"But not under its control," Kirk said skeptically, letting his arms drop to his sides. The living room still had all the graciousness of the previous evening, but now the good life had a dark edge.

"I have," Marouk said slowly, "a certain invulnerability to the Joy Machine's mandate, because of my position but also because of my services."

"What kind of services?"

"I helped De Kreef build the Joy Machine."

"You helped him build it!"

Marouk shrugged apologetically. "I didn't know then what it was. De Kreef was no physical scientist. He was a philosopher, and it was all he could do to imagine the possibility of stimulating from a distance the pleasure centers of the brain. I developed the room-temperature superconductors that allowed a much-improved computer to be built, and helped put it together. It was De Kreef who assigned that computer the task of inventing the device that made payday possible."

"Payday came from the Machine itself?"

Marouk nodded. "But I was able to build into it certain prohibitions."

"I hope it was against harming humans," Kirk said wryly.

"Nothing as fundamental as that," Marouk said. "Although, as far as I know, it never has harmed anyone. That would be contrary to its basic function. No, I made my person and my family and my residence exempt from the Machine's control."

"And yet you're going to allow your daughters to come under the Joy Machine's influence?"

"It's really a wonderful system, Jim," Marouk said earnestly. "Tandy can hardly wait to be part of it. You'll see. My reservations have more to do with the need for checks and balances."

"I'd rather see Tandy dead," Kirk said.

"Than be happy?" Marouk asked. "There's a peculiarly human paradox."

Kirk looked at Marouk. "If you worked on the Joy Machine, you must know its weaknesses."

"I'm going to surprise you, Jim, by telling you everything I know. That's because I don't know of any. It seems defenseless, sitting there in its attic, but since I helped put it together it has added to itself, spread throughout the city and, for all anyone knows, throughout the world, until the original computer may be the least part of it. Destroy it, and nothing at all would be changed."

"Then what am I going to do?" Kirk asked.

"There's nothing you can do," Marouk said. "Just embrace joy. Allow yourself to be happy."

"That's where you're wrong," Kirk said firmly. "As soon as my friends arrive, we'll take this utopian hell apart."

"That should be about now," Marouk said. He turned to look out the patio doors toward the garden.

Kirk followed his gaze and saw three silvery shapes shimmer into existence before they solidified into Spock and McCoy and Uhura. And saw them slump, like wilted blossoms in the flower beds, into unconsciousness.

Spock opened his eyes first. He looked around Marouk's living room. "Interesting," he said, as if surprised at his vulnerability to a Timshel device.

Kirk looked at him sympathetically from the armchair beside the fireplace. Spock looked first at Kirk, then at McCoy seated to his right on the sofa and at Uhura, slumped in a chair to his left. They were just beginning to awaken from their induced slumber.

"Well, Captain," Spock said, "it seems that Marouk was not as good a friend as you thought."

"He is caught in a web of responsibilities more binding than friendship," Kirk said.

McCoy sat up and looked around. He was a bit slower than Spock to understand what had happened to them. Almost immediately, however, he checked his physical response as if he had his own internal medical scanner. "That was not a phaser set on stun. It must have been a version of the Joy Machine's sleep inducer."

"Quite right, Doctor," Kirk said.

Uhura's eyes opened. She sat up straight. "Is everyone all right?" she asked. Her gaze moved quickly from Spock to McCoy to Kirk, as if to assure herself that their quick nods did not conceal injury.

"Your transmission stopped," Spock said. "It seemed likely that you needed help."

Kirk held up the remains of the bracelet Uhura had fashioned for him. "I need help, all right. But I'm not sure what kind, if any, is going to really matter." He held up his left wrist for their inspection.

"I noticed that, Captain," Spock said, "and this." He held up his own left wrist. It, too, had a bracelet.

McCoy and Uhura looked at their wrists. Bracelets had been fitted to them as well.

"What's going on here?" McCoy asked. He put his right hand on the bracelet as if he were going to remove it.

"I'm not sure that would be wise, Doctor," Spock said.

"He's right," Marouk said from the archway leading from the hall. He had a tray in his hands. On it rested five cups. Steam rose gently from them, and the aroma of Timshel coffee filled the air. "The bracelet bonds to the nervous system, and an attempt to remove it might prove fatal."

"I thought you said the Joy Machine had never injured anyone," Kirk said.

"The injury, if it occurs," Marouk said, "would come from an attempt to remove a bond established for your own good."

"Like Adam and Eve tasting the forbidden fruit of the tree of knowledge," McCoy said ironically.

"That's true," Marouk agreed, setting down the tray and motioning for them to help themselves.

" 'For in the day that thou eatest thereof,' " Spock quoted, " 'thou shalt surely die.' "

"Depend on Spock to quote the precise scripture," McCoy said.

"There is much wisdom to be gained from ancient texts," Spock said.

"What is more to the point," Kirk said to Marouk, "you are the one who placed these bonds upon us—for our own good."

"I admit my guilt," Marouk said, "but I ask you to believe that I had no choice. It was either me or another, and if I did it I retained some influence over what happens next."

Uhura rose from her chair. "And what does happen next, Paymaster? Do we all get a sample payday and become slaves to the machine?"

"Not yet."

McCoy laughed. "You really believe this stuff, don't you? Well, I don't know about the rest of you, but I'm for marching down to the World Center and destroying that damned machine."

"As I told Jim," Marouk said, "I don't think the Joy Machine can be destroyed. Not anymore. Maybe once, shortly after it was activated, but now it exists in bits and pieces all over Timshel, and one part lopped off will simply be regenerated somewhere else."

"But there's another reason at least as important, isn't there, Marouk?" McCoy asked.

Marouk nodded. "Violence is not permitted. Even the emotions that lead to violence are forbidden."

"Permitted by whom?" Uhura asked. "Forbidden by whom?"

"The Joy Machine," Marouk said. "It was created to give people pleasure. Anger, jealousy, hatred, envy—all the old sins—make people unable to enjoy happiness; as well, they cause unhappiness to others, and the Joy Machine has outlawed them."

"How can it do that?" McCoy asked.

"As Marouk has said," Spock pointed out, "the bracelets have attached themselves to our nervous systems."

"The emotions that I have mentioned create nervous responses that the Joy Machine monitors," Marouk said. "It counters them with impulses that dampen the mood, whatever it is. Aggression is stopped outright. After several such occurrences, the Joy Machine will begin a process of personal reformation that involves a stimulation of the nervous system, pain for punishment, pleasure for reward."

"Like training a dog," Kirk observed.

"I thought pleasure was reserved for payday," Uhura said.

"It is not that kind of pleasure," Marouk said. "Payday is better described as ecstasy. The reformation process is like a brief release of endorphins."

"And then?" McCoy asked.

"In the end everyone chooses pleasure," Marouk said. "All our criminals, all our mentally unbalanced, all our neurotics—all finally chose happiness.

"But look," he continued, gesturing, "with all the talk we have let the coffee get cold. And I know how much Jim likes our Timshel coffee."

Kirk laughed sardonically at the juxtaposition of these gilded cuffs and Timshel hospitality.

"Then what do you expect us to do?" Uhura asked.

Marouk shrugged. "I expect you all to become citizens of Timshel."

McCoy and Uhura laughed. Kirk stared incredulously. Spock, however, looked at them somberly and said, "It is the only logical thing to do."

Marouk seemed to agree, but Kirk, McCoy, and Uhura looked at Spock in astonishment. "You have said some pretty ridiculous things in our time together," McCoy said, "but this tops them all."

"I'm sure Spock has a good reason for his statement," Kirk said.

Spock nodded. "I have been doing some research into the history of the pleasure-center technology. The experiments with rats that Dr. McCoy described—"

"What experiments?" Kirk asked.

Briefly McCoy repeated what he had remembered about the planting of electrodes in the pleasure centers of rats and their pushing a lever that gave them a jolt of pleasure while they ignored food, drink, sleep, and other rats, until they dropped from exhaustion and often died.

"That is what De Kreef avoided with his sleep response and by putting the process under the control of an incorruptible computer," Marouk said. "When people awake, payday has faded into a wonderful dream. They long to recapture that feeling and work to experience it once again, but they cannot overdo it."

"I have discovered," Spock said, "that a fad sprang up in the twenty-first century. People were having plugs surgically implanted in their heads. They were connected to electrodes in their brain. They could hook themselves up to a source of power and experience ecstasy after ecstasy limited only by their physical endurance."

"How horrible!" Uhura said.

"I remember now," McCoy said. "They were called wireheads, and the operation was outlawed."

"The ultimate junkies," Kirk said.

Spock nodded. "They could never be weaned from their addiction. If their plugs were removed or the electrical stimulus denied them, they would pine away."

"In the end," McCoy said, "they could only be fed intravenously until other causes killed them off. They had lost the will, perhaps even the ability, to live independent of their addiction."

"Unlike Adam and Eve, expelled from paradise," Spock said, "they could not survive exile."

"That may have been the origin of the process," Marouk said, "but what we have here is far different. You haven't seen any wireheads, have you?" he asked Kirk.

"What I see," Kirk said slowly, "is a beautiful world whose attempt to perfect the natural quality of life has been diverted into a vicious cycle of meaningless pleasure."

"What I hoped you would see," Marouk said sorrowfully, "is a world that has found what everyone else is looking for, the secret of eternal happiness."

"You really mean that, don't you?" Kirk asked.

Spock looked on with his customary logical calm while McCoy and Uhura switched their gazes between Kirk and Marouk as if they were watching a tennis match.

Marouk's face twisted. "I had hoped," he said hoarsely, "that one of you would replace me as Paymaster. You, Kirk, or maybe you, Spock. Then I, too, could enter paradise." For a moment he looked like Atlas hoping to persuade Hercules to take the weight of the world from his shoulders.

Kirk held up his left wrist. "You seem to have disqualified us."

"The Joy Machine can release whoever is chosen," Marouk said.

"I don't think you will find any volunteers for Paymaster here," Spock said. "Unlike you, we do not believe in compromising with evil, even if it masquerades as the ultimate good."

"Then I still don't understand," McCoy said to Spock, "why you thought becoming a citizen was the only logical thing to do."

"There was an old terrestrial saying that went like this," Spock said. "'If you can't beat them, join them.' It seems we cannot beat them."

"I'll be damned if I'll join them," McCoy growled.

"If we cannot fight them openly, we must combat them from within. To do that, we must join them—or appear to do so."

"You can't fight pure beneficence," Marouk said. "The last opposition on Timshel faded months ago."

"What if we simply refuse to join your paradise?" Kirk asked Marouk. "If we do not return, the *Enterprise* will interdict this world. If somehow you manage to destroy the *Enterprise,* the Federation will send a fleet of ships to force your surrender."

"I don't think so, Jim," Marouk said confidently. "You see, the Joy Machine has perfected a giant payday projector that can envelope a ship the size of the *Enterprise.* If you refuse to cooperate, the projector will begin bombarding the *Enterprise* with its waves of ecstasy. And when it stops . . ."

"Yes," Kirk prompted.

"When it stops," Spock said, "the crew will either destroy the ship in anger at having the ultimate pleasure removed from them, or crew members will beam themselves down to desert in a body."

"Exactly," Marouk said. "And if the Federation sends more ships, they will receive the same warm greeting: Welcome to paradise. From which no person willingly returns. So, you see, you are lost, or have won, depending on your viewpoint, but there is no reason to sacrifice the *Enterprise* and its crew, or the ships that will follow."

"So what do you want us to do?" Kirk asked.

"You must think of some plausible reason to send the *Enterprise* away, convinced that the situation here is under control, or beyond redemption, and in such a way that the Federation will accept it. I leave that to your ingenuity."

"And that is why you needed all four of us," Spock said.

"I knew that none of you would accept an outcome that left Jim on this planet, his mission incomplete. But together you may be able to come up with a solution that will prevent all-out conflict. A conflict that the Federation cannot win but that would delay the completion of the Joy Machine's plans to bring happiness to everyone."

"And what is to keep Scotty from beaming us all back to the *Enterprise?*" Kirk asked.

"That might be unwise in light of the new additions to your adornment," Marouk said, nodding at Kirk's bracelet, "but all items of identification have been stripped from you, and the *Enterprise* would have difficulty with your location."

Kirk looked at the three members of his team in turn. He found nothing on their faces that he could interpret as anything but frustration, if not surrender. "It seems you leave us no choice," he said.

At that moment all the lamps and ceiling fixtures in the Marouk villa went dark. A moment later the dull *whump* of a distant explosion reached their ears. The only light came from the afternoon sun shining through the patio doors that opened onto the random-stone deck outside.

"It seems, Marouk," Spock said quietly, "that you were mistaken about the existence of opposition."

[subspace carrier wave transmission]

<greatest human good interrogate>

>interrogate<

<human philosophers:
greatest human good = happiness>

>happiness interrogate<

Chapter Seven
Kidnapped

BEFORE MAROUK COULD RESPOND to Spock's comment about opposition, the doors that opened on the stone deck burst in. Marouk and the *Enterprise* officers turned to see intruders fan into the room. There were three of them, men dressed in black and wearing black knitted caps. In their hands were objects that might be weapons. Behind them, dressed like the others but more slender and with empty hands, was a woman with short, cropped blond hair showing below her cap.

"Resistance would be foolish," the woman said. "I'm sure you're all rational people. We mean you no harm."

"Linda!" Marouk exclaimed.

"You know this woman?" Kirk asked in astonishment.

"It's a small world," Marouk said. "Literally." And then to the woman he said, "I thought you were dead."

"That is what you and your damned machine were intended to think," Linda said. She was not beautiful by any ordinary standards, but her high cheekbones, the alertness of her gaze, and the determination expressed in the set of her jaw gave her an appearance of inner strength that was more impressive than mere good looks.

"You're not being a good host," McCoy said to Marouk. "Introduce us to your new guests."

"This is Linda Jimenez," Marouk said. "Formerly a student of Emanuel De Kreef. I don't know her friends."

"Just call them freedom fighters," Linda said.

"And these are—" Marouk began.

"They're from the *Enterprise,*" Linda said. "Kirk, Spock, McCoy, and—" She looked at Uhura.

"Uhura," the communications officer supplied.

"Welcome to liberated Timshel," Linda said.

"Perhaps you don't intend to harm anyone here, but you haven't done our power plant any good," Marouk said. "And, in the process, possibly injured or killed people."

"The power plant is too sophisticated for your joyheads," Linda said. "It's all under the control of the Joy Machine. Anyway, we just blew up the power grid between the power plant and town. Since everything is done by hand now, the power loss won't affect anything but a few assembly lines."

"And the Joy Machine itself," Spock said.

"You're Spock, right?" Linda said. "I wish we could take you with us, but we don't have room. And we don't have much time, either. The Joy Machine built itself a reserve power supply long ago, and it will bypass the grid in a few more minutes. By then we must be gone."

"This residence is immune from the surveillance of the Joy Machine," Marouk said.

"That's what that damned machine would like you to believe," Linda said.

"What about the payday couch Dannie used?" Kirk asked.

"That's only there for the use of guests," Marouk said, "so they won't be reluctant to visit."

Linda sent a quick, suspicious glance at Marouk. "Where payday is available, the Joy Machine follows."

"Not necessarily—" Marouk began.

"It doesn't matter what you think," Linda said sharply. "The reality may be something else, and we can't afford to take the chance."

"What I can't understand," Marouk said, "is why the wampus didn't warn us of your approach."

Linda grinned. "That was us."

"You were the wampus?" Marouk asked.

"A good imitation," Linda said.

"The second thing I can't understand," Marouk said, "is what you hope to gain by all this."

"That," Linda said, "is what you and the Joy Machine will have to figure out. But I will allow you to delay us no longer in hopes that the Joy Machine will restore its control before we depart. You—" She pointed at Kirk. "—will come with us."

Kirk pointed at his chest with his left hand. "Me?"

Linda looked at the bracelet. "We may have come a little late," she said.

"We have been inducted," Spock said, "but not initiated."

"Well, it can't be helped," Linda said. "Yes, you, James Kirk. You will come with us."

Kirk shrugged and moved toward her.

"This is a mistake," Marouk said. "The Joy Machine cannot tolerate violence."

"And we," Linda said, turning at the doorway onto the patio, "cannot tolerate the Joy Machine."

Kirk gave a meaningful glance at the others, as if to tell them to work on their mutual problem while he was gone, and followed Linda through the doorway and into the late-afternoon glow of an alien sun.

They moved down a steep path to the beach below, Linda leading, Kirk following, and the three gunmen last, one of them watching the rear. Pulled up to the beach, guarded by another man in black, was a soft-walled boat, little more than a raft with sides. Linda motioned Kirk into the boat and seated herself beside him. The other four pushed the boat free and then scrambled aboard before two of them picked up paddles to turn the boat and head it toward the open ocean. The other two kept their weapons on Kirk.

"That's unnecessary," Linda said, motioning for them to put the weapons away. "From what I've heard of James Kirk, he's on our side."

"It depends," Kirk said, "on whether you're on my side."

Linda laughed. It was a strong laugh, and Kirk liked it. He liked Linda, for that matter, but he wasn't going to trust her with his life, much less the future of all Timshel and maybe worlds beyond. Likable people had led the world into terrible disasters before. "And whose side is that?" she asked.

"The Federation," Kirk said. "Not Timshel. Not Earth. Not some local tribe. The Federation as a whole."

"I wish it were that easy," Linda said. "Perhaps you make these judgments all the time, but in the real world decisions about what is good and bad for humanity are not so clear-cut."

"At least we agree that the pursuit of happiness," Kirk said, "is better than having it handed to you."

"Maybe better even than reaching it," Linda said.

Kirk's glance at her face expressed agreement with her argument and admiration for her appearance and character.

One of the paddlers stopped and pointed at something behind them. Kirk and Linda turned to look over their shoulders. Behind them, on the cliff above the beach, in the twilight as the sun sank below the sea, the windows of Marouk's villa had been lighted from within.

"Sooner than I thought," Linda said, shaking her head.

"Ugh-h!" Kirk grunted and shook his left forearm. "That hurts!"

Linda looked at him sharply. "It's started already?"

"The Joy Machine?" Kirk asked, grimacing.

"Trying to control you. Can you hold out?"

"Depends. On how long—it lasts—and how bad—it gets," Kirk said in brief bursts between the pain that began at his wrist and radiated up his arm and into his head. "I may—have to—bash this thing—with something." He waved the bracelet in the air above his head. The pain eased for a moment. "I hope we aren't going to paddle this thing to the other side of the ocean." Then he grunted again as the pain returned, worse than before.

Linda gave him a look of sympathy. "I wish we could do something. I don't know what would happen if you smashed it, but I wouldn't try it except as a last resort. If you can hold out, for a few more minutes— Wait, here we are."

A gray hump broke the water in front of them. Rivulets streamed from its top as it rose higher and then settled, rocking in the ocean swell.

"This is—a wampus?" Kirk asked.

"This is a vehicle built to look like a wampus," Linda said. "And to sound like a wampus, too."

A hatchway opened in the gray hump, and one of the guards sprang out beside the hatchway to hold the plastic boat while the other climbed over the edge and down the ladder that led from the hatchway into the bowels of the beast. Kirk followed, and then Linda. Kirk looked up as the last black-clad form slid down the last few rungs. Above, the hatchway began to close, and Kirk, a feeling of uncertainty sweeping through his body as the pain in his arm diminished, saw the evening sky narrow and disappear with a clang.

Kirk shook his arm again and looked around. He was standing in a small, metal room lined with gauges and instruments. It was far smaller than the bridge of the *Enterprise,* though it served the same purpose. A man had been waiting at the foot of the ladder to help them down, and the six additions were pressed against each other by the tiny quarters. Now that the pain was gone, Kirk could enjoy the touch of Linda's body against his. It was nothing like Dannie's; it was slender, almost boyish and strong, but there was a promise to it of deep-banked passion that in the right circumstances might be even more exciting than something more traditionally inviting.

But he could see now why there had been no room for the others.

Four of the men disappeared through bulkhead doors on either side. "Take it down, quick," Linda said. "Maybe I'm imagining it, but I was beginning to feel—joyful."

"The reward of a successful operation," Kirk said, as the man who had been waiting for them moved a lever, and the ship began to throb with power. The other two men stood before other gauges and levers as if ready to act in emergency.

"That may be true," Linda said. "But we can't risk it." She turned toward Kirk with something like dismay on her face. "What kind of a world is it when you can't tell the difference between satisfaction at a job well done and feelings imposed upon you by some damned machine?"

The ship had begun to move. The rocking motion eased. "I hope my friends aren't going through this," he said, holding up his left arm.

Linda shook her head as if to say that there was no telling what evil the Joy Machine was capable of.

"Our ancestors lived that way for millennia," Kirk said. "Accepting joy as a supernatural gift, not something earned."

"We left all that behind when we went into space,"

Linda said. "Now we have to fight our way free of it again."

Kirk held up his left arm. "Why did it stop hurting?" he asked.

"We're traveling submerged. We believe that the hull of the ship, as well as the water, acts as a natural barrier to the Joy Machine's signals," Linda said.

"Don't count on it," Kirk said grimly. "Sound waves propagate through water even better than through air, though at a different rate, and can even be transmitted through metal. There's no reason the Joy Machine can't expand its influence to include the oceans. It may not have known it was necessary— until now."

Linda looked at him as if weighing his judgment and then slowly nodded. "We knew time was in the Joy Machine's favor," she said. "That's why we had to move before we were ready."

"To kidnap me?" Kirk asked.

Linda nodded. "We were ready to throw everything into an effort to sabotage the Joy Machine or, if we were lucky, destroy it. But the possibility of getting the help of a Federation starship made the risk worth taking."

"What makes you think the *Enterprise* could help you?"

"Clearly the *Enterprise* has the power."

"But our power is limited by orders and regulation."

"Unless," Linda said, "we can persuade you that the danger is so great and so urgent that you must act despite your orders and regulations."

"That might be difficult."

"Or unless we can convince you that the Federation itself is in danger."

Kirk looked at this slender young woman with confidence in her convictions far beyond her years, and wondered where this journey would take him.

* * *

Marouk's living room seemed bigger and emptier once Kirk and his abductors had left. In the gathering shadows cast by the sun that had almost set in the direction Kirk had been taken, McCoy looked at Spock and Uhura and then at Marouk.

"Aren't you going to go after him?" Marouk asked.

"I don't think so," McCoy said.

"That would be unwise," Spock said.

"I don't know what you two are talking about," Uhura complained.

"It seems clear," McCoy said, "that his abductors mean Jim no harm. Instead, this may represent an opportunity to join forces with the opposition."

"And clearly," Spock said, "this complicated situation needs an opportunity to clarify itself before rational action can be taken. There is more going on here," he added darkly, "than is readily apparent."

Marouk shook his head. "Don't raise any false hopes for yourself. You'll need to be realistic about what's going on here to have any chance for success, and when I said that the last opposition had faded months ago, I meant that the last meaningful opposition had faded. Linda's group is far away and so tiny and helpless as to be insignificant."

The sun had set, and the room had grown so dark that the sudden illumination of the overhead lights and lamps hit McCoy like a blow. He blinked and looked at the others. "Apparently," he observed dryly, "the Joy Machine has recovered." He turned to Marouk. "We must ask, sir, what your intentions are for us. Will we be allowed to go about our business unimpeded?"

"And just what is your business now?" Marouk asked.

"To neutralize you as a source of double-dealing influence in this world," Uhura said.

McCoy raised his hand. "We have not yet achieved a full understanding of Marouk's part in all this, and I have a feeling that we won't get that now. But even if we had the power, I think we should let Marouk move freely until we know more than we know now."

"Like a pawn," Spock agreed, "that may become a queen if it reaches the king's row."

Marouk laughed. "More than a pawn, I hope, and less than a queen I am certain."

"Maybe a combination of bishop and knight," Spock suggested.

"In any case," McCoy said, "our intention is to find out as much as we can about how the Joy Machine functions."

"And the Joy Machine's intention is to bring happiness to everyone," Marouk said. "And that includes you."

"Never!" Uhura said.

"Never!" McCoy echoed.

"It depends," Spock said.

"Spock!" McCoy said.

"Clearly, the best way to learn how the Joy Machine functions is to experience what it has to offer," Spock said.

"You've seen what it can do to others," McCoy said, "and you still want to let it loose in your head?"

"It seems that I have more confidence in my head than you in yours," Spock said.

"Well said," Marouk said. "I admire your courage."

"If not your vaunted logic," McCoy growled.

"The Joy Machine has other, more persuasive arguments," Marouk said. "Have your arms begun to tingle?"

"I have noticed that for several minutes now," Spock said calmly.

"I thought my left arm had gone to sleep," Uhura said.

"I was hoping I was mistaken," McCoy said.

"Soon it will begin to hurt," Marouk said, "and then the pain will become excruciating. It will end only when you agree to become citizens and accept your paydays from the Joy Machine. I wish there were something I could do, but it is out of my hands."

"And into ours. You've done quite enough," McCoy said menacingly, advancing toward Marouk.

But just then someone knocked at the front door.

The three of them, Spock, McCoy, and Uhura, left Marouk's villa, escorted by Wolff and a half-dozen of his uniformed officers, each with a small, flat sleep-inducer leveled at the backs of their captives' heads. Spock turned his eyes from side to side as if gauging the possibilities of escape.

"Keep your gaze to the front," Wolff said. "Think about it! Even if you escaped, where would you go? Any citizen you encountered would report your whereabouts, the *Enterprise* won't beam you aboard, and soon your left arm will be extremely painful. You might even be tempted to cut it off, particularly if you are a surgeon such as Dr. McCoy. Perhaps you will be begging Dr. McCoy to cut off your arm."

"Never!" Uhura said, but she shook her arm as if it were hurting.

"I think you underestimate our capacity to endure pain," Spock said.

"I would refuse to do it," McCoy said, "and I certainly wouldn't amputate my own arm, like some poor wild animal."

"In any case," Wolff said, unruffled, "I caution you that the interaction of surgery with the bracelet's control over your nervous system might be fatal. No one has survived it yet."

Spock shook his head. "How did you switch allegiance so easily, Agent Wolff? I would have thought that loyalty was a primary characteristic in a Federation agent," he said.

Wolff looked at Spock without rancor. "I am a pragmatic person," he said. "I tested for a high level of loyalty when loyalty to the Federation made pragmatic sense. No one ever thought to test for loyalty to a system that made greater sense."

"And you think that the Joy Machine does?" Spock asked.

"There's no use talking to this traitor," McCoy said.

"Is the pain becoming unbearable yet?" Wolff asked McCoy with a mockery of concern, and then to Spock, "Of course the Joy Machine makes greater sense. Its rewards are immediate, measurable, and universal. No broken promises, no illusory goals, no disappointments. Just pure happiness offered freely and accepted without guilt."

"And what about the degradation that comes along with it?" Uhura asked.

Wolff shrugged. "Do I feel degraded? No. Do I see it around me? Sometimes. Joy is too much for some people. Natural selection will take care of them. And if they have to die out, they will die happy, leaving those of us behind who can be happy and still function."

They had reached the edge of City Center, and Spock was still looking for an avenue of escape. McCoy had dropped back to walk beside him.

"We've talked bravely," he said so softly that only Spock could hear him, "but I'm not sure how much of this pain I can stand. Or Uhura."

"Try meditation," Spock said. "The mind has great capacities for controlling the pain centers."

"That's easy for you," McCoy said.

"No whispering!" Wolff said.

"Where are you taking us?" Spock said.

"You'll find out soon enough," Wolff said.

They found out when they entered the World Government building, and Spock pointed out bolts on three of the first-floor doors.

"They're separating us," McCoy said when he saw the doors.

"Be calm, Doctor," Spock said. "Uhura, even

though we are separated, we are all working as one unit."

"Of course," Uhura said.

"And whatever happens," Spock said to both McCoy and Uhura, "remember that each of us must do what he or she can for the good of the group."

The first door clanged shut on Uhura and the bolt was thrown.

"Spock!" McCoy said. He was pushed into the second room. "Spock!" he said, as if warning against whatever Spock had in mind.

"Agent Wolff," Spock said, as the door closed on McCoy, "I would like a word with you."

"Spock!" McCoy shouted from behind the door.

Spock turned his head gravely toward the former Federation agent.

The submarine was tiny. The living quarters consisted of two rooms equipped with hammocks. One of the rooms formerly stored equipment; some of the places where it had been bolted down still had holes, and some had bolts in place. The other room functioned as a dining facility during the day, with a table for four that swung out from the wall and a bench that folded down from it. A tiny galley was beyond, lined with food lockers and a microfusion oven, and beyond that was a toilet, that the sailors called "the head," that was a marvel of compact efficiency. Linda slept in the single private cabin, which was scarcely bigger than a closet. The others, including Kirk, rigged up their hammocks in the evening and took them down in the morning.

Their vessel, Linda told Kirk, had been constructed as an oceangoing research project. Its primary goal had been to discover more about the wampus. It had been built to look like a wampus and to move like a wampus, and even to sound like a wampus, with the hope that eventually scientists would learn how to communicate with these giant creatures that had such oversized brains. All that had stopped when the Joy Machine took over, but a few scientists had fled to sanctuary and a few more had come to join them until now there was a band of rebels waiting for an opportunity to take back their world.

She refused to say how many belonged to her band and where they were going. "What you don't know you can't reveal," she said.

"You know your chances for success are small," Kirk said.

"Small is better than none."

"Sometimes small is worse than none, if it only gets you killed in an attempt doomed to failure."

"Not if you consider the alternative." Linda shivered.

Kirk shivered, too. They were cruising on the surface now, to renew their air supply and let the general stench of underwater living be flushed from the vessel. They stood on the narrow deck outside the hatchway, clutching a railing that rose, at a touch, from the deck. The ambient temperature had declined each time they had emerged, until now occasional ice floes could be seen bobbing in the water. Kirk had been loaned a sweater, but it was not enough to ward off the chill.

From the temperature and the persistent position of the afternoon sun off the larboard, Kirk understood that they were headed north. The ship made good speed, whether on the surface or submerged. Its wampus-like shape provided good streamlining against the friction of the water, and the power source, a sealed atomic unit, needed no attention. Apparently there was automatic navigation and automated obstacle avoidance as well, because occasionally Kirk felt a change in direction when no one was at the controls.

The first time they had surfaced, Kirk's arm pained him so badly that he soon went below, where he was partially protected by his position below the water level. The second time the pain had been almost absent. The third time the pain had been excruciating but the scenery was so fascinating that Kirk stayed on deck, his arm hugged against him. Once his arm had throbbed with sudden delight, and a wave of inexplicable joy swept over him. That had sent him below faster than the pain.

The ship had passed among schools of strange-appearing fish with broad orange streaks down their bodies and others with purple circles around their tails. In fact, the ocean was alive with color. Many-hued, minnow-like creatures had been clustered so thick in places that the water had seemed alive. Kirk had seen huge, diaphanous, globular creatures that floated half-in, half-out of the water, like rainbows settled on the waves.

There were so many different species that Kirk lost count. Kirk felt like Darwin on the *Beagle,* and if the problem presented by the Joy Machine had not been so pressing and the fate of his friends not been so great a concern, he would have considered the experience one of the great moments of his life.

Then there were the predators: the dark, silent, gliding shapes that moved among the schools of fish and pulled down the ones that lingered unwisely at the outskirts; the armored creatures that shut their eyes and ate away at the diaphanous globes; the alien birds that snared unwary single fish in their talons or scooped up a body of water and let everything but the fish it contained drain through a sieve-like beak; a school of leaping creatures that made of the eating process a kind of carefree game; and what Linda called a wangle of wampuses that moved slowly past, also on their way north, and strained the minnow-like fish from their path as they went, gray and interminable and, Kirk thought, marvelous and perhaps marvelously wise.

In the early part of their voyage they had passed islands, verdant in the distance and perhaps inhabited. At least Kirk had detected a trail of smoke from one of them. In later surfacings, the only sights of land had been distant and forbidding, either sheer cliffs or flatter surfaces covered with rocks or ice or both. Once Kirk saw a white creature, which must have been huge to be visible at that distance, standing up to look at them, but it was an animal, not a person. Fish were less frequent, but wampuses were common—feeding, Linda said, on tiny crustaceans that thrived in this cold climate—as well as furry creatures that dived through the waters or came out to lie upon the land and bask in the arctic sun.

They had been passing through an area where ice floes were everywhere, and an iceberg had been seen slipping past in the evening. Now it was too cold to stand on deck. The next morning he felt a small shiver run through the ship as he sat at the ship's second sitting for breakfast, and then a jar, and the ship stopped. For a moment Kirk's body had difficulty adjusting to the absence of vibration. Linda said they had arrived.

When they came out onto the deck, Kirk saw that the ship had pulled into a dock whose rounded front and exact dimensions suggested that it had been built to fit only this vessel. Linda confirmed that this was the original home of the wampus research project. Behind the dock were a little cluster of metal huts and a plastic-covered framework that probably was a greenhouse. And behind that was a cliff made entirely of ice, looming hundreds of meters above the little settlement built at its base, like a frozen fist poised to smash the huts into the rocks and tundra on which they stood. The glacier was embraced within a half circle of snow-covered peaks, shining in distant sunlight while clouds shadowed the surface where they stood.

"Come along," Linda said. "We'll get you out of the cold."

Kirk realized that a freezing wind was blowing off

the ice beyond the little settlement, and he was shaking. But that was not as great a sensation as the disappointment he felt at the size of the rebel force. The huts could not house more than a few dozen people, at most. "For a revolutionary," he said, trying to cover his dejection, "you've taken me a long way from the place where the revolution has to happen." But his teeth were chattering.

"This is one of the few places on Timshel where we are free from the influence of the Joy Machine." Linda led the way, walking quickly from the dock toward one of the metal huts.

"How can you be sure?" Kirk asked.

"Do you feel anything from your bracelet?"

Kirk considered the question. For almost the first time in days his arm felt normal. "No," he said. "But the Joy Machine may be subtle enough to disguise its influence."

"There's another reason. Besides the fact that we carry on our subversive activities free from interference, the Joy Machine took over the communication satellites. We think that's the way it provides services to citizens outside Timshel City, and spies upon them, too."

"And their orbits are all equatorial," Kirk said.

"Nearly so."

"But what's to keep the Joy Machine from launching one, or diverting one, into a polar orbit?"

"Nothing, perhaps," Linda said, "but its energies have been devoted to spreading joy, and its technical capacities may be limited now that everybody, including the scientists and the engineers, have been drafted into manual labor."

Linda was reaching for the door and Kirk could imagine the warmth that lay behind it, but he also knew that there might not be another occasion to ask questions free from the presence of others. He put his hand on hers and felt a curious sensation run up his arm, almost like the pleasure stimulus the Joy Machine had provided once. But this was his right arm. He shook his head to clear it. "What happens when that glacier decides to move?" he asked, nodding his head at the mountainside of ice behind the huts.

She allowed his hand to remain on hers. "It hasn't moved in ten million years," she said. "That's what our scientists tell us, and some things you have to accept on faith."

"Like creating a revolution?"

"Yes," she said. "You should understand that."

"I understand it, all right," Kirk said. "What I haven't been able to figure out, however, is how you knew I would be at Marouk's villa in time to get there from here and abduct me when you did."

"That's easy," Linda said. "Marouk told us you would be coming."

"Told you?" Kirk exclaimed.

"Well, not me," Linda said. "He thought I was dead in an airplane crash, and we allowed him to think that because, next to De Kreef and Marouk, I was the one who knew the Joy Machine best. But he broadcast a message in code to the rebel group; we have been waiting offshore for the better part of a week."

"And you trusted him?" Kirk asked, and then realized that *he* had trusted Marouk.

"He has kept in touch with the rebels by radio, perhaps protected from the Joy Machine by the immunity he was so proud of. What he has told us so far has been reliable."

"It can't have been of much use to you," Kirk said, "or of much damage to the Joy Machine."

But he was thinking: What kind of devious game was Marouk playing?

[subspace carrier wave transmission]

<getting what humans want = happiness>

>human want interrogate<

<wants = desires>

>desires interrogate<

Chapter Eight
Revolution in a Bottle

WHEN LINDA OPENED the door to the metal hut, Kirk stepped into another world—from the icy cold of the arctic to the warm, cozy camaraderie of people sheltered from the extremes of climate and united by a common purpose. A barrel-like stove in the middle of the room, connected to the roof by a fat metal pipe, emitted heat and the crackling of burning fossil fuel. Against the left wall of the rectangular room were arranged the elements of a communal kitchen: a six-burner stove, two food slots, three large refrigerators, shelves stocked with goods in boxes and cans and tableware, an ultrasound dishwasher, and assorted gadgets at whose purpose Kirk could only guess.

The right side of the room was walled off into small rooms, perhaps offices or, more likely, rest rooms connected to deep and heated septic systems. Kirk considered the prospect of going into the arctic night to use an outhouse and hoped they were rest rooms.

In the center of the room, on the far side of the blazing stove, were two neat rows of dining tables equipped with attached benches, a total of six tables in all with spaces for thirty-six diners, twelve more if chairs were pulled up to the ends. On this side of the stove were frame and canvas sofas and chairs, all arranged neatly facing the stove, and two square tables with a straight chair on each side. In the room, standing now to greet visitors announced by the blast of cold air from outside, was a group of men and women dressed in the warm, rough clothing of people on the far fringes of the known world, for whom fashion meant protection first and comfort second.

There were perhaps thirty of them. Kirk's first impression was a montage of forms and faces. They were all adults of ages Kirk estimated to range between twenty-five and sixty. The majority of them were men; Kirk counted six women, although in the bulky clothing it was difficult to be certain until they spoke. Many of the men were bearded against the cold; exposed skin, including women's faces and hands, had been roughened by the weather. The ratio of men to women, however, suggested an arrangement that would endure only as long as a joint purpose was paramount.

By the next day Kirk would know many of them by name and specialty and temperament, including the dozen or so who were busy at tasks that kept them away from the gathering in the commons, but for now the scene was one of greetings and introductions and names that, try as he would, flew past Kirk before he could grab them and stuff them into memory. His greatest accomplishment, however, was hiding the sinking feeling in his stomach when he considered the size of the group gathered here at the top of their world and the enormity of the challenge they faced.

One man's face stood out in the crowd: large, long-haired, blond, bearded, blue-eyed—like a Viking explorer out of Earth's early history. He was one of the older men, although gray strands were almost invisible, and he stepped forward to greet Linda and the newcomer. "Linda," he said, taking her hand and then folding her into a bear-like hug. "You return, mission accomplished." Then he held her away from him and turned to Kirk. "And this must be the famous Captain Kirk."

"This is Dr. Arne Johannsen," Linda said to Kirk. "Arne is the chairman of our action committee. Before the Revolution he was the xenobiologist in charge of wampus research."

Kirk took Johannsen's big hand. "Chairman of the action committee. Does that mean you're in charge here?"

"This is a democracy, Captain Kirk," Johannsen said. "We are not a starship with its demands for quick decisions and chains of command. We have no leaders, only chairmen to call the meetings and preside over orderly discussions."

"I know a leader," Kirk said, "when I see one."

Johannsen smiled and turned to Linda. "Have you eaten breakfast?"

"You know the kind of freeze-dried and frozen rations we get aboard the *Nautilus*," Linda said. "But we've eaten."

"I'm afraid we can't offer you much better," Johannsen said to Kirk. "But can we get you anything?"

"Perhaps some of your Timshel coffee," Kirk said. "That was one thing the Nautilus lacked."

Johannsen looked embarrassed. "I'm afraid we ran out of coffee a year ago. Conditions being what they are, we haven't been able to replenish our stocks. But we have a substitute one of our chemists has put together."

Kirk restrained a shudder. "Thanks," he said, "but I think I'll pass for now."

Johannsen turned to Linda again. "Everything went smoothly?" he asked.

"Just as you laid it out," she said. "Marouk played his part as you said he would."

"You mean Kemal," Kirk said, "is a member of your group?"

"Marouk is the mystery piece on the board," Johannsen said. "In the end he may turn out to be black or white."

"Or mottled," Linda said.

"All we know is," Johannsen said, "he cooperates with us in discreet ways, and perhaps with other dissident groups if there are any, and at the same time cooperates with the Joy Machine in public ways. And now—the Federation. No doubt he cooperated with you, too."

"For a while," Kirk said. "Until this." He held up his right wrist to expose the payday bracelet.

"I wish we could do something about that," Johannsen said. "But when we have tried to remove one for analysis—on volunteers, you understand, who managed to break free from their addiction—the bracelet self-destructed and the volunteer died. In agony.

"Come, let us talk rebellion."

They settled in chairs near the potbellied stove. Even here, after the first flush of warmth replaced the arctic daggers of the wind, the cold could be felt seeping through the walls to chill the back while the front toasted. Occasionally, then, one of them would rise to warm the back or put hands out to the radiating waves from the stove. The others in the room went about their business, or settled down to read or talk among themselves, or wandered by to listen for a moment to the conversation before continuing on.

Johannsen nodded toward the doors on the right-hand side of the hut. "Do you need to use the facilities? We're unisex here, and we don't stand on ceremony. That's the result of being primarily a research operation, or what is left of one."

Kirk shook his head, but he was happy to discover

that his guess was correct. He held up his left wrist again. "You may not be able to do anything about this, but isn't there a danger that the Joy Machine is spying on everything we do and say?"

"That seems unlikely," Johannsen said. He was seated on Kirk's right, Linda on his left. "It has had opportunities to eliminate us before, if it could do so. In any case, we have to take the risk."

"The *Enterprise*," Kirk said, "is a new factor. We can't discount the possibility that the Joy Machine was staying its hand to use this group as a way of trapping the Federation and its agents. And we must consider it likely that Marouk was cooperating in this project as a way of planting a spy—and a tracer—in your midst."

"Nevertheless," Johannsen said, "the *Enterprise* is crucial to our plans."

"Let us," Kirk said, "be brutally frank. What chance does your little band of people have against the worldwide resources of the Joy Machine?"

Linda said, "If I remember my history correctly, the Russian Revolution was started by a handful of Bolsheviks, the French Revolution by a small group of dissident aristocrats, and the Kartha IV Revolution by five starving farmers."

"And if I remember my history correctly," Kirk said, "those revolutions were fueled by massive public oppression and discontent. On Timshel you have massive acceptance and apathy. Who are you going to get to rise in your support?"

Johannsen nodded. "That's true. But there are two major differences to the situations you and Linda describe: the first is that we are not talking masses; there are only one million people on Timshel and only one hundred thousand in Timshel City; the second is that the entire system rests on a small point. Damage that and the rest tumbles."

"It sounds easy," Kirk said, "when you say it. But

that small point may not be so small anymore; Marouk believes that the Machine itself may be computers connected in a series, like nodes in a root or segments in a worm, rather than a single calculator. If that is true, any part is infinitely replaceable. And with two million eyes reporting to the Machine and the entire technological apparatus controlled by it, even approaching that small point may be impossible."

"We have to try," Linda said. Her gaze turned inward. "You haven't had family and friends and loved ones changed before your eyes into creatures strange and frightening and obsessed."

"I know what it is like," Kirk said. "But have you thought what might happen to them if their link with the Joy Machine was broken?"

"We've thought about it," Johannsen said. "We all have family members caught in the Joy Machine's web. And we realize that their bracelets might self-destruct and that they might die—horribly. Or even if they survived, they might never be the same."

"And they might never forgive us," Linda said.

"Like the wireheads," Kirk said.

"What?" Johannsen asked.

"Another historical parallel."

"We have to take the chance," Johannsen said.

"I said to Marouk that I'd rather see his daughters dead than happy in the arms of the Joy Machine," Kirk said, "and he called that a peculiarly human paradox. Better dead than happy. When you think about it, that is an odd choice."

"We get hung up on words," Johannsen said. "Happiness. Death. Happiness can be a kind of death—death of the spirit, death of the will, death of the individual, death of the species. Species evolve through discontent, either brought on by pressures from the environment or generated from within."

"I may agree with you," Kirk said. "But—" He

spread his hands to indicate the handful of people in the hut, in the small community. "—this small band?"

"'We few, we happy few, we band of brothers,'" Johannsen said.

"You know your Shakespeare," Kirk said, "but King Harry, at least, had an army of thousands, and a secret weapon of English longbowmen."

"We have our secret weapons," Linda said.

Behind the hut something massive cracked and shifted. Kirk looked up in alarm.

"Don't worry about that," Johannsen said. "That's our friendly neighborhood glacier turning over in its bed."

Kirk settled back in his chair. "Okay, tell me about your plans to take out the Joy Machine."

"One of our secret weapons," Linda said, "is the nature of our group. We're all scientists, of one kind or another, and we've been working on this—some of us—for two years."

"We've formed ourselves into strategy groups and action groups," Johannsen said. "As chairman of the action group, I am also an ex officio member of the others. We have come up with some strategies, some of them pretty far-fetched, as we will readily admit. Some of them seem practical enough that we began work on them."

"Give me the ones you're working on," Kirk said.

"Automated spacecraft are still returning from the gas giants, the asteroids, and the moons with raw materials and manufactured objects," Johannsen said. "If we could seize control of one of them and cause it to crash on the World Government building—"

"You would have to match a makeshift program against something established and long-tested, and human reflexes against computer speed," Kirk said. "The chances of success are next to none."

"You have the resources on the *Enterprise* to raise those odds considerably," Linda said.

"The *Enterprise* would have to emerge into normal space and make itself vulnerable to planet-based resources," Kirk said. "And the resources available aboard a ship are small compared to those an entire planet can muster. In any case, the Federation would never authorize an operation that might wipe out an entire city—and all your friends and relatives, I expect." And, Kirk told himself, Spock, McCoy, Uhura, the Marouk family, and Dannie.

"We're going to try to change your mind," Johannsen said. "If not about this plan, at least about the participation of the *Enterprise.*"

"You should know that the Prime Directive prohibits interference in the normal development of any society," Kirk said.

"I also know that the Prime Directive has been violated upon occasion," Johannsen said. "How can you say, for instance, that the Joy Machine is a normal development?"

"Go on with your proposals," Kirk said. He did not call them "preposterous proposals," but he knew they understood what he meant.

"We've been identifying guerrilla action to take out various aspects of the Machine's operation," Johannsen said. "Like the sabotage of the power grid that set up your rescue."

"Or abduction, depending on your viewpoint," Kirk said. "Guerrilla groups can exist only with the support of dissident citizens. Inevitably there are casualties, and you don't have enough people to sustain any such action for long."

"I've been working on a computer virus," Linda said.

"Now, that could be effective," Kirk said, looking intrigued.

"I know the Joy Machine better than anyone, next to De Kreef, of course, and Marouk," Linda continued. She seemed pleased that Kirk was receptive to her approach. "I helped De Kreef write the original program. I didn't know what I was working on, of course. De Kreef kept the critical parts for himself."

"And just what would your virus do?" Kirk asked.

"Actually, there are two," Linda said. "One would disable the execute function of the Joy Machine's program; the Machine could think and plan, but it couldn't act. It would, in effect, be isolated in its own universe."

"And what about the other?" Kirk asked.

"It would rewrite the Joy Machine's basic directive."

"What is that?"

"No one but De Kreef knows, and he is incapable of telling us. Perhaps he no longer remembers. I searched his files before I fled. But he must have destroyed any evidence after it was installed."

"It acts as if its operating mandate is to spread joy to every human," Johannsen said.

"But it must have a value system ranked hierarchically," Linda said, "so that it knows the order in which it must act: first this, then that, or if not this, then that, or if not this or that, then this other—"

"I get the idea," Kirk said.

"One hierarchical structure, for instance, is first work, then payday," Linda said. "Another must be 'If a citizen does not wear a bracelet, he must be persuaded to do so.'"

"Or forced," Kirk said.

"That doesn't seem to be the Joy Machine's doing," Linda said. "It seems to have a prohibition against harming people."

"At least directly," Johannsen said. "Sometimes it seems to be able to rationalize an action that is for the long-term good of the individual, as it perceives it through the lens of its prime directive, even though its immediate actions work violence, as long as the violence is indirect."

"It can even set into motion processes that might endanger human lives if humans can avoid the danger through common vigilance or ordinary action," Linda said. "We believe it is able to rationalize those as accidents."

"And what would your computer virus do?" Kirk asked.

"Replace the operating mandate," Linda said.

"With what?"

"The value of human freedom," Linda said.

They stood for a while in front of the stove, warming their backs and rubbing their hands, before they sat down once more. "The Joy Machine behaves as if it had independent volition," Kirk said.

"How do you know?" Linda asked.

"I had a talk with it, and it seemed to have no mechanical limitations."

"The Turing test," Linda said.

"What's that?"

"If it responds in ways indistinguishable from those provided by a sentient being, it must be sentient," Linda said. "But it isn't the same thing. Sentient beings can't be reprogrammed."

"The Joy Machine seems to be doing a good job of it," Kirk replied wryly.

"It only looks like it," Linda said. "Actually, it is taking advantage of human hardwiring."

"By now the Joy Machine," Kirk said, "may have augmented its own programming, converting its software into hardware. If that is the case, your virus would have nothing to work on."

"We can only hope that is not the case," Linda said.

"How do you hope to deliver it?" Kirk asked.

"That's a bigger problem than the virus itself," Linda said.

"Although information flows continually into the Joy Machine," Johannsen said, "there are no terminals, no stations, no direct programming links."

"De Kreef must have destroyed those too," Linda said. "Once he was finished."

"Or the Joy Machine," Kirk suggested. "Like pulling up the drawbridge."

"But we have a plan," Johannsen said.

"The Joy Machine receives feedback from the bracelets," Linda said.

"So," Kirk supplied, "you intend to program a fake bracelet with the virus."

Linda shook her head. "The Joy Machine wouldn't access a phony bracelet. We are inserting the virus into a virus—coding the computer virus into the genetic material of an influenza virus so that when the Joy Machine provides a payday to a selected volunteer the information the influenza virus contains will be transmitted to the Joy Machine."

"That's my job," Kirk said, and held out his arm.

Linda and Johannsen looked at Kirk's left wrist.

Johannsen put up his hands in dismay. "No!" he protested. "It was supposed to be me. . . ."

"I'm the only one already fitted with a bracelet," Kirk pointed out.

"Besides," Kirk added, "you're scientists. This is what I do for a living."

Linda looked thoughtful. "You are the only one already equipped," she said. "It doesn't make sense to lose someone else. And as you may have been informed, Timshel natives develop a natural immunity against bacterial and viral infections. That may not have had a chance to work on you yet."

"The downside," Kirk said, "is that I can't be sure how I would respond to the Joy Machine's payday."

"No one can," Linda said gently.

"We think we would be strong," Johanssen said. "We think we could sample paradise and walk away. But we have seen almost every other person surrender to its insidious appeal."

"I'm afraid," Kirk said. "I admit that. But I'll take the chance."

Johannsen studied Kirk's face for a moment and said, "Okay. We accept your offer and I thank you." Then he continued: "We have other plans. Our physicists have prepared an atomic bomb from a spare power plant. It's not sophisticated, and we can't get the deuterium or the tritium to make a thermonuclear device, but what we have is capable of taking out Timshel City."

"How would you deliver it?" Kirk asked.

"The *Nautilus* would carry it to Timshel City harbor and explode the device as soon as it surfaced."

"That's out of the question," Kirk said. "That would wreak more destruction than the returning spaceships."

"It is," Johannsen said sorrowfully, "a last resort. But only you can keep us from using it."

"How?"

"By violating the Prime Directive and assisting our final plan with the capabilities of the *Enterprise*," Johannsen said.

"I can't do that," Kirk said.

Behind the hut the glacier groaned and stirred. Linda and Johannsen ignored it. Sometimes, Kirk thought, people can be too close to a problem.

[subspace carrier wave transmission]

<humans = desires
computers = instructions>

>humans = birth
computers = construction<

<humans = growth
computers = additions>

>humans = flesh
computers = metal<

Chapter Nine
Best-Laid Plans

THE DISCUSSION OF the revolution against joy broke for lunch. Chunks of fish were thawed, cans were opened, and freeze-dried food was reconstituted, and the lot was mixed with some fresh vegetables from the greenhouse into something between a stew and a casserole. The stomach-tickling odors of cooking filled the hut. The man and woman responsible for the repast might have been master chefs, Kirk thought, because the result was unexpectedly delicious. Or maybe it was the deprivation of the long undersea voyage and its bland microwaved dishes.

They sat down at the tables, some thirty of them; those with duties during the period were relieved by others to eat in a second shift. The occasion was convivial, and Kirk learned the names and faces and specialties of all of them, including Jawaharlal Srinivasan, who had transformed a power unit into a nuclear bomb, and Miriam Achebe, who had coded the computer virus into a strain of influenza. They were an impressive group, he had to admit, and their commitment to personal freedom was almost an obsession. If scientific miracles were possible, they could work them.

Milk and water were the only drinks served with the meal. Kirk commented on the rich flavor of the milk. "Where do you get milk in this desert of ice?" he asked.

"That's wampus milk," Linda said.

"The wampus is a mammal?"

"Like Earth's whale," Johannsen said.

"But how do you get milk from a wampus?" Kirk asked, his forehead furrowed with the effort of imagining the process.

Johannsen laughed. "We don't get milk from a wampus," he said. "They have to give it to us."

"And how do they do that?" Kirk asked.

"It helps if you understand that a wampus calf drinks a dozen gallons of milk at a meal, and the mother wampus produces twice that much in case of twins. Often there is more than the calf can drink, and of course when calves are weaned at the age of two, production of milk continues for a bit."

"That still doesn't explain how you get it," Kirk said.

"The mother wampus can turn off its production or cut back on it through a mental exercise that none of us understands, but even with the wampus mastery of its physiology the process takes a few days. In that period it gives the milk to us, along with whatever milk the calf doesn't drink."

"How?"

"The female comes close to shore, rolls over on its back, and we attach pumps," Johanssen said. "It's quite a sight."

"I can imagine," Kirk said. But he couldn't. The picture of a wampus rolling over on its back to make its offering of nurturing liquid to alien humans simply wouldn't take shape in his mind.

"We wouldn't have been able to survive in these conditions without the help of the wampus," Linda said. "Its milk is a perfect food, rich in almost everything the human body needs for survival."

"How could the wampus know what the human body needs?" Kirk asked skeptically. "That's not something that would provide any evolutionary advantage."

"But physiological control would," Johannsen said, "and the wampus has developed an amazing ability to adjust its bodily functions to the environment. At first we were unable to stomach wampus milk. It made most of us vomit, and those that could keep it down developed severe diarrhea. That made sense, of course. Alien proteins are indigestible at best, poisonous at worst."

"But the wampus was able to produce milk compatible with human physiology?"

Johannsen smiled. "Difficult to believe, isn't it? We gave them samples of tissue and human fluids. They analyzed them internally and produced milk that not only is delicious but filled with all the necessary nutrients."

"That makes them the most marvelous biological factory the human species has yet encountered," Kirk said.

"More than that," Johannsen said. "They're intelligent, probably more intelligent than we are."

"Because of their biology?" Kirk asked.

"Because of their brains," Johanssen said, "which not only are far larger than humans' but more convoluted and complex. And, I might add, far better integrated with their bodies. Unlike humans', their bodies never have irrational desires. Wampuses don't make war. They don't fight among themselves. They don't rape. They shelter the young and the weak. I've seen a mother wampus share its milk with an old wampus unable to feed itself any longer."

"Anything else about this wonderful creature?" Kirk asked.

"It thinks great thoughts," Johannsen said. "It has

127

access to racial memories, and those memories go back to the days when it lived on land before it chose to return to the more benign environment of the sea. It has not yet lost its vestigial legs that no longer could support its great weight on land but serve as guidance for the propulsion of its massive tail. And it thinks about those things as it goes about the daily processes of its existence that demand so little of its mental capacities. It thinks about the place of life in the universe and the ways in which life might develop in other environments, and the ways in which those environments might change, and the meaning of everything."

An amazing truth was beginning to force itself into Kirk's awareness. "If you know all this—" he began.

Johannsen nodded. "That is one of our secret weapons. We have been able to communicate with the wampus."

It was an astonishing breakthrough, comparable to the development of the Universal Translator, and it would be a devastating loss to galactic civilization if the accomplishment, and the viewpoints and accumulated wisdom of the wampuses, should never reach the outside world. Kirk resolved once more to find a way, somewhere short of violence, to combat the threat represented by the Joy Machine, the threat not just to humanity and maybe to the other alien civilizations in the galaxy, but to the basic goal of all intelligence: understanding the universe.

"How do you propose to use the wampus as a weapon?" Kirk asked.

"I didn't mean they were that kind of weapon," Johannsen said. "Rather that our ability to communicate with the wampuses is something the Joy Machine doesn't know about and we might be able to use for our defense. Wampuses don't understand the meaning of 'weapon,' and they offer us no solutions about how to combat or destroy the Joy Machine. They don't even understand the meaning of joy or happiness, or sadness either, for that matter."

"What do they understand?" Kirk asked.

"The processes of life," Johannsen said. "The integration of the mind into the body, of the self into the group, and of the group into the environment. They are the universe's great philosophers."

"What kind of philosophy is it that doesn't involve happiness or sadness?" Kirk asked.

"You have to understand," Johannsen said, "that we are inferring a great deal. At the present we are dealing only with verbs and proper nouns, insofar as the wampuses can conceive of objects acting on other objects or objects distinct from their environment. But the process of translation, though difficult, is proceeding rapidly."

"How did it come about?" Kirk asked. Their meal over, they had returned to the chairs by the stove.

"Through the wampuses mostly," Johannsen said. "They have always hung about human settlements as if curious about us, or protective, or wanting to communicate. But they didn't have the highly evolved human speech apparatus to shape sounds. We kept analyzing their sighs, hoping to differentiate one from another, echoing them back, getting nowhere. Finally we began to analyze the ultrasound waves that they used to echo range when they dived deep, and we realized that this was their medium of communication as well. Very sophisticated, very flexible."

Kirk shook his head in astonishment. "Truly fantastic," he said. "But what do you hope to do for them—except get them killed?"

"We would never do that!" Linda said.

"We'll die first," Johannsen said. "Wampuses are mentally and ethically superior to humans. We don't belong on the same planet with them, but they don't agree." His voice filled with surprise. "They *like* us."

"If they're so mentally advanced," Kirk said, "what do you suggest we do about the Joy Machine?"

"They have a difficult time understanding machines," Johannsen said, "much less a machine that we put in charge of us and one that we depend on for what we consider our ultimate good."

"So?"

"What they offer is philosophy," Johannsen said. "They say there is no such thing as happiness or sadness, joy or grief, there is only what is—the movement and temperature of the water, the presence or absence of food, the sun, the weather, birth and life and death, and the existence and interdependence of all things, including the planets and the stars and the empty spaces between."

"I can see where that would be a lot of help," Kirk said ironically.

"If we could only learn to think like a wampus," Johannsen said sadly, "we would have no problem with ephemeral matters. But we can only try to be more like them."

"Maybe we should just get the hell off this world," Kirk said roughly, "and leave it to the Joy Machine and the wampuses. They seem to have nothing in common. Maybe they'd leave each other in peace."

"If it were only possible," Johannsen said. "But the existence of any independent intelligence is a threat to the Joy Machine, and eventually it will find a way to bring wampuses under its benign control. It will find a way to deliver something to them that they consider irresistible, or it will find a way to eliminate them—indirectly, of course, through a means intended for their own good, as the Joy Machine sees it."

Kirk settled back in his chair. "So, the wampuses offer only the consolations of philosophy."

"They will do what they can," Johannsen said. "They recognize our anxiety even though they do not understand it. They believe us when we tell them there is good and bad, even though the concepts are totally alien to them. They will help if we can tell them how."

"Perhaps they could gather in the ocean west of Timshel City," Kirk suggested, smiling to show he wasn't serious, "and focus their ultrasound on the foundations of the city. Maybe, like Jericho, the walls would come tumbling down."

"We've thought of that," Johannsen said, "but our physicists tell us that the coast, though unstable and susceptible to temblors, would suffer at best a small quake. And if the wampuses were identified as the source, it might put all of them in peril."

"You said you had a final plan," Kirk said.

"A frontal attack to destroy the Joy Machine," Johannsen said. "Oh, I know what Marouk believes, that the Machine has distributed its functions so broadly that the original machine is only a symbol. But symbols are important, and even a brief interruption in payday might bring people to their senses. And if there are secondary Joy Machine centers, the destruction of the original machine might expose the location of the others so that they, too, could be attacked, if not by us, then by our successors, whoever they may be."

Kirk shook his head. "You wouldn't stand a chance against people like Stallone Wolff and his security forces, or the various defensive systems the Joy Machine could throw against you."

"We would," Johannsen said, "if we had a diversion from the *Enterprise*. Phasers. Photon torpedoes. Even a landing party. Anything that might pull away the defenses long enough for us to reach the World Government building."

"I've told you before," Kirk said, "that's impossible. The Prime Directive—"

"The hell with the Prime Directive!" Linda said.

Kirk looked at her in astonishment, but admired her passion.

"Linda's right," Johannsen said. "Timshel is part

of the Federation, and the Prime Directive simply isn't operative here."

"Nevertheless," Kirk said, "I cannot agree to the use of the *Enterprise* as a weapon. Force is a feeble weapon against ideas. The only thing that can combat ideas is better ideas."

"That's all very well," Johannsen said wearily, leaning forward in his chair to emphasize his point, "and the wampuses might agree with you. But De Kreef's idea is the most powerful one around, and the Joy Machine is likely to implement it in such a way that every other idea will crumble before it."

"I can't believe that," Kirk said. "Freedom, independence, variety, responsibility, evolution—all these are more powerful ideas than happiness."

"Noble sentiments," Johannsen said, "but just words. They are words and sentiments I agree with, but we can't see them or feel them. They are abstractions. The Joy Machine is a reality, and it offers real, verifiable happiness—or, more accurately, pure pleasure. You can feel it, touch it, experience it. Who is going to trade paradise for something as insubstantial as freedom or independence?" He looked around the room at the small band of people, dwindled to only a few eating at the second shift as the others had gone about their duties. "Only a handful."

"Do you think Adam and Eve would have left the Garden of Eden if they had had a choice?" Linda asked.

"They had a choice," Kirk said, "and they chose to know good and evil."

"But even then, they had to be driven out," Linda said, "and kept from returning by a flaming sword."

"That's what we're asking," Johannsen said. "A flaming sword. That's what we've pinned our hopes on. And only the *Enterprise* can supply it."

"Then you'll have to find another way," Kirk said. "It seems as if, by your scruples, you are condemning us and our friends and relatives, indeed all Timshel, to the rule of the Joy Machine."

"Principles, perhaps; a bit more than scruples." Kirk held up his left arm. "And, as you can see, my friends and I are just as much a part of Timshel as you are."

Johannsen spread his hands out with the palms up as if they were holding something precious, a heap of coins or jewels, or a baby. "Well, soon you won't be the only Federation crew in that situation. The Joy Machine is preparing to share its blessings with the rest of the galaxy."

"Is that true, or simply another ploy in your attempt to convince me to use the *Enterprise?*" Kirk asked.

Linda shook her head.

"How would you know something like that?" Kirk continued.

"Marouk has told us," Johannsen said, "and his information has been confirmed by the few informants we have left within Timshel City."

"How can you have informants within Timshel City?" Kirk asked skeptically. "Everybody but the Marouks are wearing bracelets."

"A few people can wear bracelets, get their payday, and still retain an element of independence," Linda said.

Kirk thought back to his own experience touring Timshel City. De Kreef had been beyond reach; Kirk could draw Dannie out enough to talk to her; and Wolff had seemed relatively unaffected. Perhaps susceptibility to payday varied according to assigned task, body type, brain chemistry, or perhaps even that indefinable quality called character.

"Still, how would they know?" Kirk asked.

"Marouk has said that the Joy Machine has been asking questions about other worlds and how they operate, and if they, too, have Joy Machines. More-

133

over, the factories are producing bracelets by the billions, and payday projectors by the millions—far more than Timshel could ever use. They're being stored in warehouses near the spaceport."

"That could simply be make-work."

"If that were the case, why store them?" Johannsen asked. "The Joy Machine could simply dismantle them—or have a group of workers assigned to dismantle them—and have them put back together the next day."

"Besides," Linda said, "people who work in the warehouses believe there are far more boxes of bracelets and projectors than the Timshel City factories have produced. They believe the automated factories on the moons and asteroids also are assembling them, not just manufacturing components."

"Still," Kirk said, "exporting the Joy Machine's system would be difficult and slow. As soon as the galaxy learned what it was up against, it could stop its spread." Kirk realized that he was speaking about the Joy Machine as if it were some deadly disease. Perhaps it was.

"We've thought about it," Linda said. "It could clone versions of itself and send them off to other planets. They could infiltrate themselves into the economies of unsuspecting worlds and then slowly take over. But that's not the worst scenario."

"And what is that?"

"We've talked about computer viruses," Linda said. "In a way the Joy Machine's program is a virus, and it could pass it along to any computer within its range, and that computer could pass it along to the next, and so on. The virus could spread geometrically, and the Joy Machine could take over the galaxy within days."

It all made sense. Kirk remembered commenting on the overproduction of bracelets. And the Joy Machine's mission to spread happiness would be difficult to limit. As soon as it learned about the existence of other worlds from the records available to it and the attempts by the outside world to communicate and the arrival of ships that were turned away, it would realize that it had a vast galaxy to which it could now carry its message of paradise. And it would learn about the countless billions of people on those other worlds who lived lives of quiet desperation, to whom it could bring comfort and pleasure—and the death of everything else. And then there were the alien races. Would they be immune? Would they take over human worlds and star systems once humans withdrew inside their own self-contained universes? Or would the Joy Machine find a way to analyze the aliens and provide them their own versions of ultimate happiness?

Kirk thought about the Joy Machine extending its tentacles throughout the Federation, throughout the galaxy, and shuddered. It could mean the end of everything.

"Okay," he said.

"Okay?" Johannsen repeated.

Kirk nodded. "How do we get in touch with the *Enterprise?* I lost communication when Marouk destroyed my transmitter. I would have expected Scotty, our chief engineer, to have beamed us up by now, but he must have difficulty getting a fix as Marouk suggested, or something else has gone wrong. After we prepare a detailed plan and timetable, the next step is to beam me aboard."

"We have subspace radio," Johannsen said.

"Can't the Joy Machine trace the source?"

"The *Nautilus* has placed relay stations in remote islands across the ocean. So far, at least, our location has remained a secret."

"I'll have to reveal the location in order to beam aboard," Kirk said.

"We'll take that chance," Johannsen said. "We'll time it so that we will be on the way to our rendezvous before the Joy Machine can strike."

Kirk paused. "There's only one problem."

"Yes?" Linda asked.

"The *Enterprise* is executing a maneuver that brings it into normal space only for a second or two every few hours."

"Then we'll broadcast from the relay stations until we reach the *Enterprise*. When it is set to beam you aboard, we'll broadcast your location at the last moment," Johannsen said.

As soon as they had prepared the schedule for their attack on the Joy Machine, Kirk asked to be taken to the radio so that he could record a message.

Linda got up and Kirk followed her, putting on a heavy coat that she took from a peg by the door. It was lined with some kind of alien animal fur. Linda put on another, and they moved quickly through the doorway. The wind was biting from the north, and the glacier was groaning behind them. The sun was still well above the horizon, but it felt late to Kirk. They had been talking a long time, and even had paused for a second, smaller meal while their discussions had continued.

"What is the time?" Kirk asked. "I don't have a chronometer. Marouk took everything from me that might conceal a beacon."

Linda said, "It's almost midnight. In the summer the sun sets for only a couple of hours."

"What I need is exact Federation Standard Time," Kirk said.

"Precision chronometers are available in the labs," Linda said.

They headed across paths slickened by snow, their heads down against the wind. Linda passed by one hut to reach another. Behind it, Kirk could see as the view opened between the huts, was a dish antenna.

Inside was an electronics laboratory with tools and working parts and gauges scattered around on benches or hung neatly on panels. Radio equipment was tucked away in a far corner like an afterthought.

When they had removed their coats and hung them on pegs beside the door, Linda introduced Kirk to a technician named Sam Chang and explained what they wanted. The next few minutes Kirk spent recording his voice message: "This is Captain James Kirk, using this method of communication because my primary system has been destroyed. It is now"—he looked at Linda, who conferred with Chang—"11:59:57, on the mark, Federation Standard Time. Exactly ten hours from now, beam me aboard from a location that will be revealed to you thirty seconds before that mark. Use all caution. Ultimate danger. Please confirm. Four-Whiskey-six-Alpha-one-Charlie-seven-Alpha." He put down the microphone. "Now broadcast that in a form as compact as you can make it and in short bursts of no more than one second in duration."

Chang nodded and turned to his equipment.

"Now," Kirk said, "we have nothing to do but wait."

Linda turned toward the door. "Then you'd better get some rest. I'll show you where you can sleep."

As they put on their coats again, Linda said, "What was that at the end? Those numbers and words."

"An authenticating code to use in case of nonstandard communication emergency."

"Aren't you concerned that someone might intercept the message and send another with your code?"

"It changes with every message," Kirk said.

Once more they went into the cold, clutching their coats around them. At the next hut Linda paused. "This is it," she said. "You'll find bunks and restroom facilities and someone to help you with bedding and whatever else you need. We have sleep schedules to conserve space and energy. Half sleep; half work. If anything happens, we'll wake you."

Kirk put his hand on the door and turned. "Linda," he said.

"Yes?"

"I want you to know," Kirk said, and thought of Dannie, the woman he had come to Timshel, in part, to rescue, "that I will do everything I can to help you and Johannsen and Timshel."

"I know you will, Jim," she said, and turned toward a hut still farther on.

Behind, as Kirk lingered for a moment, watching her bundled figure walking away from him, the glacier groaned once more. Kirk thought he could never get used to living with happiness or destruction always imminent.

[subspace carrier wave transmission]

<happiness = not wanting anything>

>not wanting anything = human state: death<

<happiness = not wanting anything but not dead>

>life in death interrogate<

Chapter Ten
What Rough Beast

KIRK AWOKE FROM a dream about a reunion with Dannie. Not the Dannie he had met on Timshel but the Dannie he had come to love before they were separated by duty and then by the Joy Machine. The Dannie he imagined she might be once again. The experience was joyous and sensual and perfect in every way. Then, inexplicably, as Kirk drew Dannie close, she changed into Linda, and, although the pleasure of the moment continued unabated, the Dannie-Linda image became tinged with regret and loss, as if something dark and dangerous lurked behind the woman he held in his arms. Something that would break through if he embraced her without reservation. And then Dannie-Linda had turned into a robot, metallic and yet obscenely human, and the human part looked womanly, and the woman looked like Dannie.

Kirk sat up, bumping his head on the bunk above. He swore softly so as not to rouse the other men sleeping in the room. He rubbed his head and wondered what had awakened him, the way his body felt, from a sleep only half completed. The glacier rumbled, and Kirk remembered. He had heard an explosion. The noise had been muffled by distance and bigger, therefore, than if it had been close. Something had exploded near the mountains that encircled the base.

Kirk got to his feet in the chilly room, trying to identify more accurately the noise that had broken into his sleep. He had slipped into his Timshel workshirt and jeans when the door opened, letting in a flood of sunlight. Linda stood at the door, backlit in the darkness, searching for him.

"What is it?" Kirk whispered.

Linda moved toward him. "We have recorded a curious reply from the *Enterprise.*"

Kirk worked his feet into his shoes and walked to Linda's side. "What was the sound I heard in my sleep? Like an explosion. Loud but distant."

"We get meteorite strikes here with some frequency," Linda said. "The soil here is littered with metallic pellets, and the surface of the glacier is pitted with holes left behind when hot fragments burn their way down."

Linda handed a jacket to Kirk, who shrugged into it as they left the hut. The wind outside was filled with ice pellets blowing from the north. "What time is it?" Kirk asked as they made their way to the next hut, bending against the wind.

"About five in the morning, here," Linda said. "Still five hours until your scheduled departure."

"Still time enough to make adjustments," Kirk said, "if adjustments are necessary."

Another man was on duty in the electronics hut. He was a large, bearded fellow with blue eyes. He was working on an electronic circuit at one of the benches. "This is Gregor Zworykin," Linda said.

"We picked up this message a few minutes ago," Zworykin said. He walked to the corner where the radio equipment was stacked and pressed a button.

A voice said, "Federation policy requires starships

to refrain from interference in planetary affairs. Captain Kirk would know this. Identification rejected."

"That sounds like the *Enterprise* computer," Kirk said, irritated. "It knows better than to screen communications. It has never done anything like that before."

"A malfunction?" Linda asked in a tone that suggested "what else can happen to us?"

"That's hard to believe. Let me send another message." Kirk picked up the microphone while Zworykin prepared the recorder. "Imperative this message be delivered to Chief Engineer and Acting Commanding Officer Montgomery Scott: Beam Captain Kirk aboard at 09:59:57 Federation Standard Time, at a location to be communicated thirty seconds before. Use utmost caution. Extreme emergency. Seven-Zulu-four-Papa-Mike-one-Bravo." He turned to Zworykin. "Condense that message and send it out again in a short burst, repeated until you get a response."

He turned to Linda again. "Now we wait. I guess there's no use trying to get some more sleep." They walked toward the door.

"I've got a little real coffee put away for a special occasion," Linda said. "Maybe this is it."

"Timshel coffee?"

"Why would Timshel import coffee?"

"Let's go."

"Gregor, we'll be in the commons if you get anything," Linda called over her shoulder. And as they sealed their coats and headed out the door into the chill wind of the arctic early morning, she said to Kirk, "We'll have to go to the women's quarters to pick up my hidden treasure."

"Brotherhood has its limits?" Kirk asked.

"We all have our areas of privacy, even in these communal circumstances."

"Would it be invading your privacy if I asked how three dozen men and half a dozen women get along?" Kirk asked.

They were moving rapidly past the hut in which Kirk had slept to the hut just beyond. "How does a starship crew get along when it is predominantly male?" she asked in return.

Kirk smiled. "With difficulty," he admitted. "But we have discipline, and this group isn't a military unit."

"It has the same dedication to a goal. Anyway," she said, opening the door to the hut, "we have divided the sleeping quarters. Not that some of the men and women don't get together, in some of the less-used huts, at odd hours. But as long as it isn't excessive or doesn't interfere with assigned tasks, a bit of fraternizing is overlooked."

"And you?" Kirk asked. "Do you fraternize?"

Linda gave him a quick, hard glance. "Why do you ask?"

Kirk shrugged.

"Wait here," she said. She opened the door to the hut, slipped through into the darkness beyond, and returned a few moments later with a half-liter jar in her hands. As they headed toward the commons hut, Linda said, "I hope I haven't done or said anything that would encourage you."

"Not really," Kirk said.

Kirk stopped before they reached the commons. He looked down at his feet. "What's this?" he asked. A stream of water was flowing between the huts toward the ocean. "This wasn't there before."

The commons was deserted. Linda put beans into a machine that ground them and then started the brewing process. She went to wake Johannsen. By the time they returned, the odor of freshly made coffee had turned the hut into something wonderful.

Johannsen sniffed the air. He turned to Linda. "You've been holding out on us."

"Actually I swiped a package from Marouk's kitchen as we left," Linda said.

"What was that remark about a special occasion?" Kirk asked.

"That, too," Linda said. "I *was* going to save them for a special occasion, but I decided this was it."

"Kirk is leaving?" Johannsen asked.

"If I can get through the ship's computer," Kirk said.

"There's a problem?"

"I don't understand it," Kirk said. "One would say, on the face of it, that it is impossible for the computer to question the transmission."

"But it happened," Johannsen said flatly.

"So did that stream of water," Kirk said. "And that, too, ought to be impossible."

"Let's take a look at it," Johannsen said.

Kirk put on the coat that he had taken off in the warmth of the commons, and they moved outside to look at the water flowing where everything else was frozen. The stream seemed larger, and, turning, Kirk pointed to another small stream on the other side of the commons hut.

"That's never happened before either," Johannsen said. "We'll have to wake the geologists." He nodded at Linda, who turned toward the men's quarters.

"Do you suppose it could be related to the explosion a half hour ago?" Kirk asked.

Johannsen looked thoughtful. "We'll have to put some people on the glacier in tracked vehicles to check it out."

When Linda returned with two men, one short and thin, one short and fat, they traced the streams to their source. They were emerging from underneath the foot of the glacier, and here, it could be seen, several more rivulets were starting to trickle toward the pebbled ocean edge.

The short, thin geologist looked toward the short, fat geologist, and then they both turned toward Johannsen. "There's melting somewhere."

"I can see that," Johannsen said. "But why?"

The short, fat geologist shrugged. "Volcanic activity? A hot spring?"

"That it would happen just now seems like too much of a coincidence," Johannsen said. "The explosion?"

"Hard to imagine how an explosion could trigger melting like this," the short, thin geologist said. "It's probably only a meteorite. But maybe we should take a look."

"I think you should," Johannsen said.

As the two geologists began toiling up a path that Kirk could now see had been carved into the face of the glacier, Johannsen turned and led them back into the commons. Linda poured each of them a mug of coffee while Johannsen removed a bowl of leftover fish stew and put it into a microwave.

"I hope you aren't particular about breakfast," Johannsen said. "We may need all the strength we can muster before this day is over."

Kirk shook his head. "Food is food. You think the melting is serious?" he asked.

"Why should something like this happen so soon after your arrival?"

Kirk nodded. "The circumstances are suspicious."

"But we will have to wait until Frank and Paco return with their report. That gives us a few hours to wait."

Behind the hut the glacier made a sound like a giant grinding its teeth. "If the ice allows us the time," Linda said.

"You think it might start moving?" Kirk asked. "You said it hadn't moved in ten million years."

"It hadn't had any melting either," Linda said.

"The water might act as a lubricant," Kirk said. "I think you should be prepared to move out of here if that becomes necessary."

Johannsen removed the stew from the oven and they settled down to their meal. The food tasted as good as it had the day before, but it did not sit easily in Kirk's stomach. Events were too unsettled, and he couldn't easily dismiss the inexplicable behavior of the *Enterprise*'s computer. Too much that went on in the starship was controlled automatically, like a person's autonomic nervous system. Trying to perform by hand the calculations and microadjustments of the ship's functions would be like trying to will the flow of bile or adrenaline, or the blood's exchange of carbon dioxide for oxygen in the lungs.

If the computer was untrustworthy, the *Enterprise* was crippled. And he was stuck here on Timshel with a dedicated band of revolutionaries, an atomic bomb, a crazed, nearly omnipotent machine, and an unstable glacier.

By the time they had finished and were on their second mug of coffee, Zworykin was in the doorway. "We have another strange message," he said to Kirk.

In the electronics hut, the four of them stood listening to a disembodied voice recorded minutes earlier: "The future of the human species remains to be determined. Philosophers across the ages have debated the purpose and goal of existence. None of them has convinced the others. Interference in an attempt to test one hypothesis is inappropriate. Access denied."

They looked at each other. "What do you make of that?" Johannsen asked Kirk.

"We forget about it aboard the *Enterprise*, but the computer is always listening," Kirk said. "It overhears everything, but this is the first time it has put information together into a new configuration. It does learn, of course, but within limitations that include obedience to commands authenticated by voiceprint or code."

"What are you going to do?" Linda asked.

"I'll be damned," Kirk said, "if I'll tolerate insubordination from a machine." He clenched his jaw. "It may take a while to whip this thing into obedience. I'd better stay here and wait for a message."

Linda and Johannsen nodded and turned toward the door, talking quietly as they left. Kirk sat down at the radio and pressed the button that by now he had learned started the recording.

"Code Two-Mike-five-Sierra-three-Charlie-eight-Quebec. Command clearance, Captain James T. Kirk," he said firmly and clearly. "Deliver the following message to Chief Engineer and Acting Commanding Officer Montgomery Scott: Transport Captain James Kirk aboard at 09:59:57 Federation Standard Time, from a location to be broadcast thirty seconds before. Urgent. Extreme caution required. Confirm."

After instructing Zworykin to compact the message and broadcast it continuously, Kirk sat back to wait while he listened to the glacier shifting behind him. "What rough beast," he said.

"What was that?" Zworykin asked.

"It's a poem, by a man named Yeats, from centuries back," Kirk said. "'Somewhere . . . a shape with lion body and the head of a man is moving its slow thighs. . . . And what rough beast, its hour come round at last, slouches toward Bethlehem to be born.'"

"That's like music," Zworykin said. "What does it mean?"

Kirk tried to explain the references to him for a moment, and then, seeing the incomprehension on the electronics expert's face, settled for, "There's the glacier. Moving its slow thighs, see? Like the Sphinx in Egypt, that in one myth asked deadly riddles of passersby, a gigantic stone figure come to life. And the Joy Machine is like the birth of Christ, or the Antichrist, promising salvation or damnation, but probably damnation, considering the implications of 'rough' and 'beast' and 'slouches.'"

"Why didn't he just come out and say that?" Zworykin asked.

"He was discussing something else," Kirk said, "but we have these images from the past that we apply, as Yeats did, to our understanding of the present. That's what poetry is all about, juxtaposing unlike images so that we can see how they fit together and how they make a greater picture that tells us more about the present—and ourselves—than we knew before."

Zworykin stared at Kirk as if he were speaking a foreign language.

"Well," Kirk said, "that's how it's supposed to work."

He settled down to wait. Sometimes, difficult as it was for him to accept, there was nothing to do but wait. The glacier could grind away at his back, the *Enterprise* computer could refuse to cooperate, but for one of the few times in his life he was helpless. He was not in charge here, and anything he tried to do would meet only with resistance, or with a lack of comprehension, like Zworykin's blank eyes.

He moved back and forth across the limited space of the hut, examining a tool here and a gadget there. In a corner he came across a wooden box carefully and sturdily crafted in a place where wood was precious. He put his hand under one of the handholds built into the sides and tried to lift it, but it was heavy. "What's this?" he asked Zworykin.

"Don't touch that!" Zworykin shouted.

"What's wrong?" Kirk asked.

"That's our bomb," Zworykin said. "Put it down gently."

Kirk eased it back into place. "Sorry. Maybe you should have labeled it."

"We weren't expecting strangers," Zworykin said.

"Do you have relatives back there?" Kirk asked, nodding his head toward the south.

"Mother, sister, wife, daughter," Zworykin said.

He looked away, but Kirk persisted. "Do they all—wear bracelets?"

"All except the little girl," he said. "I hope we destroy the Joy Machine before she is old enough."

"How did you escape?" Kirk asked.

Zworykin looked at Kirk with eyes that seemed as cold as the glacier outside. "I was in the southern continent, a member of a research operation into magnetic lines. When I returned to Timshel City, my family had become slaves to the Machine."

"Didn't they try to get you to join them?"

Zworykin looked at Kirk's wrist. "They tried, but I got away. Took a boat. Ran it until the power failed. Drifted until the *Nautilus* picked me up. End of story."

Kirk nodded. "Not the end, I hope. And this bracelet"—he held it up—"was put on me while I was knocked out."

"I'd die first," Zworykin said.

"I don't have that choice."

The radio sputtered to life. Zworykin moved quickly for a big man and reached it first. "This may be your message," he said.

But it wasn't. Instead one of the geologists spoke—Kirk didn't know whether it was the fat one or the thin one. "Catastrophe!" he said. A loud sound like something roaring in the background made his report difficult to understand. "Paco injured. Heading back."

"You go get Johannsen," Kirk said to Zworykin. "I'll stay here in case the *Enterprise* replies."

In less time than seemed possible, Linda and Johannsen were beside him, listening to the replay of Frank's message. "Catastrophe," Johannsen said. "What could he have meant by that?"

"Nothing good," Kirk said. "You'd better prepare for a worst-case scenario."

"What's that?" Linda asked.

"This place may be wiped out," Kirk said. "That means you've got to be prepared to evacuate."

"Evacuate?" Johannsen asked. He seemed stunned by the sudden turn in events.

"You may not have a lot of time," Kirk said. "You've got to get the *Nautilus* ready."

Johannsen shook himself. "The *Nautilus* will carry only its crew of eight and a single passenger—maybe one more in an emergency. We don't have any other boats."

"Then you'd better start thinking of alternatives," Kirk said. "As soon as the geologists get back with the complete story, the entire complement should be ready to leave."

"The path to the top of the glacier has sheared away," Johannsen said. "There's no way to get them down."

"You can't leave them there to die," Kirk said.

"We've all been prepared for death since we started fighting the Joy Machine," Johannsen said, "and a lot of us are likely to die here. More of us will certainly die if we wait for Frank and Paco."

"We can't just leave them," Linda said.

"If we do that," Kirk said, "we might as well give up to the Joy Machine now."

Johannsen shrugged. "Then I'll leave that to you. Linda—"

"Go get somebody else," Linda said sharply. "I'm going to help Jim."

Johannsen turned and left the hut.

"Is it true?" Kirk asked. "Has the path broken off the glacier?" Linda nodded. "Any alternate routes?" She shook her head. "Then how did you get tracked vehicles on top of the glacier?"

Linda's face opened like a flower in the morning. "There's a winch anchored in the ice above." A shadow seemed to pass over the sun. "But I don't know how long it will last."

"If it lasts until I can get on top of the glacier," Kirk said, "I can take up a rope."

"If the glacier lasts," Linda said.

"Let's get the rope," Kirk said. He turned to Zworykin. "Try to get in touch with Frank. If you can reach him, tell him to rendezvous at the winch. See what information you can get on the catastrophe, whatever it is. And stay as long as you can to pick up a reply from the *Enterprise*."

Zworykin nodded. Kirk and Linda headed for the door. Kirk picked out the warmest-looking jacket. "Any gloves?" he asked.

"In the pockets."

On their way to the glacier face they stopped by a supply hut and picked up a three-hundred-meter coil of thin, braided, plastic rope. Kirk hung it over his shoulder. Linda led him toward the far end of the glacier. They had to jump several streams of water pouring from the base of the ice. Behind them the first streams they had noticed had turned into small rivers. Kirk could see where the path carved out of the face had shattered and lay in glassy mounds at the glacier's foot.

The glacier was groaning and shuddering like an arctic monster in pain. Up close the noise was nearly deafening, and Kirk and Linda had to shout to be heard above it. Occasionally a loud explosion came from the ice and another huge chunk broke off. They had to dodge falling debris, and Kirk could see that the glacier actually had started moving.

"Here it is," Linda shouted. A small hut at the far end of the glacier housed controls for a winch that stretched its arm above the glacier's edge. Linda pushed a button. Nothing happened. "We haven't used this in months," she shouted. "We thought it was safe enough for equipment, but nobody was willing to trust their bodies to it."

Kirk reached forward and pushed down a red button. "Reset," he shouted. They went outside the hut and looked up, dodging falling ice, and saw a cable snaking down from above.

"I should be the one going up there," Linda shouted.

Kirk shook his head.

"They're my people," Linda shouted.

Kirk shook his head again and pointed to his ears as if to say that he couldn't understand what she was saying.

The cable reached the ground. Linda ducked into the hut to stop its descent. The cable had a loop at its end, but the line was shaking from the vibrations of the glacier. Kirk tugged hard at the line, testing the solidity of the winch's anchors above, and shrugged. He adjusted the coil of rope on his shoulder and put his foot into the loop of the cable.

"Now!" he shouted.

Linda hesitated. "Why?"

"My job," Kirk shouted. He waved his hand at the glacier. "Don't waste time!"

"No way!" she shouted. A block of ice almost hit them as it hurtled past, exploding pebbles and ice nearby.

Kirk held up his left wrist, exposing the bracelet. "This may be a trap!" he screamed into the wind and the noise. "The Joy Machine may have traced this to you. I shouldn't have taken the chance."

Linda frowned and looked up at the sky. Snow and ice pellets fell through the sunlight, shattering the light waves into the colors of the rainbow. Kirk saw the arm of the winch swaying above. "Now!" he shouted. "Then go. Get the *Nautilus* ready. Take off if I'm not back in an hour."

Linda ducked into the hut, and a moment later the cable began to rise against the glacier.

Kirk kept his eyes from looking at the winch arm above. He watched the flaking face of the glacier go past, feeling the ice sucking the warmth from his body, and waited for the hesitation, the lurch, that would precede the winch pulling free its anchors and toppling into the gulf below. He wouldn't have time to worry about the winch falling on him. He would be dead before it hit the ground.

He hoped Linda had followed his instructions and left for the *Nautilus*. He didn't want to fall on her.

[subspace carrier wave transmission]

<humans = incomprehensibility]

>obedience = computer happiness<

<human happiness = computer happiness>

>computer obedience = human happiness<

Chapter Eleven
Moving Mountains

THE CABLE SLOWED as Kirk neared the glacier's top and stopped, swaying, just short of the winch, and he realized, as the winch arm trembled, that he had needed Linda at the controls, and he was glad she had stayed instead of leaving to help with evacuation. But he needed someone here to swing the winch's arm over the glacier. He reached his hand toward the winch, but it was beyond his grasp. The cable was too thin and slick to climb, even if he could have removed his gloves without freezing his fingers beyond their ability to cling to anything.

Kirk swung on the cable for a moment, looking longingly at the glacier edge two meters away, and felt the winch sag as pieces of the glacier fell away. For a breath-stopping moment he thought the winch was falling before it stopped with a jerk that almost made him lose his grip on the cable. Now, however, the glacier's edge was two and a half meters away.

Carefully, he worked the coil of heavy rope from his shoulder, and, his arms wrapped around the cable and his fingers numb even inside the gloves, he managed to free one end of the rope. He almost lost the coil to the gulf below as he tried to slide it back over his shoulder. After he had stopped shaking, he pulled out a half-dozen meters of the rope and started tossing it above the winch arm. The freezing wind, stronger here above the glacier, caught the rope in the air and blew it back.

He threw the rope several more times, swinging precariously above the long drop to the pebbles and heaps of ice below, before he finally decided to tie the rope end around his waist and threw the coil instead. Its weight carried the line over the winch arm and almost jerked Kirk from the cable as it dropped past him. The winch moved as the weight of the coil came down on the arm. Somewhere anchors squealed. Kirk held on until once more the winch bounced to a stop.

Pulling the coil to him, Kirk maneuvered it onto his left shoulder and wrapped the rope on each side around each arm. He pushed his foot from the cable loop toward the glacier and slid down the winch arm to the surface of the ice. As he did, the winch pulled free from its last anchor, and slowly, majestically, with cracks and screeches, toppled over the edge of the glacier.

Sprawled on the surface of the ice, Kirk heard something whistle past his head as he released the end of rope from his right arm and saw it snake free of the winch as it fell. He lay on the ice for several minutes, regaining his breath, before he slowly rose to his feet. He moved away from the treacherous edge and looked around in the arctic sunlight.

The winch had pulled out all its principal anchors as it toppled, leaving ragged holes in the ice, but a broken cable led to an eyebolt farther from the edge. It must have been the other end of that cable that had whistled dangerously close to his head, Kirk thought. He paced off the distance to the eyebolt as he heard the glacier crumbling onto the beach below and felt its vibrations. The whole world was moving beneath him. Kirk had stood on many uncertain platforms and even experienced high-level temblors, but this massive instability was something even more frightening.

Trying to stay on his feet against the vibrations, Kirk pulled against the eyebolt. It seemed solid. In any case, there was nothing else he could use, and he fastened the end of his rope securely to the bolt before he undid the rest of the coil and payed it out over the edge. Just as he ran out of rope he felt the brief hesitation that told him it had reached the bottom, or, perhaps, only an outcropping of ice.

His escape route as ready as he could make it, he straightened and looked around for the first time. He stood on a vast plain of ice, broken by cracks and crevasses, mounded occasionally with drifts of snow in the process of compressing into ice. The plain stretched undisturbed toward distant mountains. Their white peaks gleamed in the sun. But the more dramatic event that drew his gaze were flames that rose, white and red against the gray background of the mountains behind, and pillars of smoke and steam. Something big and violent was happening there, and the melting at the base of the glacier was its result.

Kirk strained to see against the ice and snow blowing in his face, but there was nothing toward the north that might be the two geologists returning. He wondered if they had been caught up in the violence or trapped in a crevasse. Or had their vehicle broken down?

The camp below had been partially sheltered by the glacier itself, but the wind was fiercer here. Kirk had to brace himself against the force that kept trying to push him toward the glacier's edge. He paced the ice, trying to keep himself warm and mobile, knowing that it would be easy to succumb to the arctic torpor that precedes unconsciousness and death. He was at the top of Timshel's world, unconcerned for the moment about happiness and unhappiness, untroubled by thoughts of the Joy Machine and his friends and the fate of the camp below, riding the unstable world, focused only on staying alert and searching for the missing geologists.

The ice jerked beneath him, throwing him down. He felt it surge toward the sea. The groaning and crashing that accompanied the surge, like that gigantic ice monster slowly returning to life, was almost as overpowering. The movement brought him to his senses, and he remembered where he was and everything he had to worry about. He hoped that Linda and Johannsen were getting ready to evacuate, even, if necessary, that they would leave without him.

Then, rising to his feet, straining once more into the wind, he saw a distant speck of black against the more distant flames.

By the time the tracked vehicle reached him, Kirk had pulled his rope back into a pile at his feet. The vehicle slewed to a stop only a few meters away. The short, fat geologist known as Frank was driving. Kirk could see, in the cargo space behind the seat, a bulge covered with blankets and a tarpaulin. Frank staggered to his feet and threw back the tarpaulin and part of the top blanket. "You're Kirk, right?" he managed to say, shakily. "Paco's hurt."

Paco's eyes were closed. His face was pale, and he had blood trickling down one side of his forehead.

"What happened?"

"Ice, rock—I don't know," Frank said, panting. "We got close enough to see what was going on, but stuff was flying through the air. Something hit Paco, and he dropped."

Kirk pulled a hand free of his glove long enough to feel the pulse in Paco's throat. "He's still alive, but we've got to get him down from here."

"We'll play hell taking him down the path."

"Even worse," Kirk said. "The path's gone. We'll have to use the rope." He nodded toward the coil near his feet.

"I'll never get down that," Frank said.

"Then I'll lower you," Kirk said. "First, let's get Paco out of the vehicle and ready to go." With Frank's help, he got Paco laid out near the glacier's crumbling edge, but not so close that he was in danger of being caught in the next splitting away of the glacier's face.

As they worked, Kirk said, "What's going on out there?" He nodded toward the flames and steam as he began to fasten the end of the rope under Frank's arm and around his chest.

"Under attack," Frank got out. "North end of the glacier. Thermite bombs maybe, at the start. Saw some devices, like little ships or slender machines, descending into the pit, maybe tunneling south at the base. Freighter descended, tail first, and is widening and deepening the pit with its exhaust."

"The Joy Machine," Kirk said grimly. He led Frank toward the edge of the glacier. "Back over, hold the rope, brace your feet against the face of the glacier." Kirk took a turn of the line around his waist. "Take as much weight on your feet as you can. Push off when you hit the side. Don't worry if you get turned. Spin back to face the glacier if you can. When you get down, undo the knot, and yank on it when you're finished. Then I'll lower Paco. Got it?"

Frank took a deep breath and nodded, looking frightened.

"Soon as you undo Paco," Kirk said, "tell Linda or Johanssen that this hunk of ice is going to be on top of them before they know it."

Frank nodded again and Kirk nodded back, indicating the geologist should launch himself into space. Frank breathed deep again and stepped back. Kirk staggered as the weight hit him, pulling him forward, his feet slipping, until his heels caught in a crack. Then he laid back against the strain on the line, letting it slide in measured lengths through his hands, feeling the tug and release and the increased weight as additional line was added. The process seemed interminable, but finally, as Kirk's arms seemed about to drop from his shoulders, the weight eased off. A minute later the rope tugged, and Kirk pulled it in.

This time he fashioned a kind of harness around Paco's chest. Paco's arms could not be counted on not to slip through something less confining. Kirk had to remove his gloves to knot the ropes, and by the time he had finished his fingers had little feeling left in them. Grimly he put his gloves back on and beat his hands against his chest and his sides. Slowly they came back to life.

Before he pushed Paco's limp body over the edge, he found the cracks for his heels. He lowered Paco slowly, inching him down the face of the glacier, hoping that the ice would hold and that the rope would be long enough, that what had been lost from the glacier face would make up for what he had to use for the harness. An eternity of effort later, he felt the weight still on the rope and he had reached the edge of the glacier and the end of his line.

He turned his body slowly, letting the rope unwind from his waist. When he had come nearly 360 degrees, the line slackened. Kirk straightened, clinging to the rope that trailed over the edge, feeling numb from his feet to his head. His arms felt like lead weights, and his legs were not much lighter. At that moment he didn't know how he was going to get down from the glacier, and he couldn't muster the energy to care. It would be easier to lie down here and die.

But then he remembered Johannsen and Linda, Frank and Paco, and all the people below in their quixotic struggle against overwhelming forces,

McCoy and Spock and Uhura and the crew of the *Enterprise,* the Joy Machine and the threat it posed to the rest of the galaxy unless it was stopped. He breathed in the frigid air off the glacier, now tainted with the odor of fire and smoke blowing from near the mountains. He remembered that Timshel was less massive than Earth and that the air had a percent or two more oxygen; what would have been impossible on Earth was only next-to-impossible here.

He shook himself, jumped up and down, beating his arms against his sides, and, taking a turn of the rope around his waist, now free of Paco's weight, he jumped backward off the glacier and began rappelling himself down the icy face: jump, land with his feet against the ice, release a length of rope, jump, land with his feet against the ice, feeling the ice and snow broken from the rim by the rope falling around him, release a length of rope, jump, land . . .

There was no end to it.

And then there was an end to it as he jumped, let out a length of line, and landed on pebbly ground, covered with mounds of ice, and he collapsed.

He sat up to mass confusion. Even from here, beside the glacier and its continual, animal-like roars and screams, he could hear shouting and see people running by the huts like lemmings ready to cast themselves into the sea. Shards of ice fell nearby, and Kirk scrambled to his feet and away from the face of the glacier before it came down upon him and negated all his effort. He still felt as if the strength had been drained from his body, but it was different now that he was down. A new flush of determination not to let the Joy Machine win this round surged through his body.

The glacier lurched forward a meter, and then began moving steadily, perceptibly, a few centimeters at a time, toward the water's edge. It had already crumpled and engulfed the shed at the base of the winch, and the fallen winch as well. It was only a few meters now from the nearest hut.

Kirk ran toward the water's edge, making his legs respond even though they told him that they weren't there at all. Men and women were running back and forth, frantically, purposelessly, useless possessions clutched in their arms. When some dropped what they were carrying, they turned to pick up other objects that had been lost by someone else.

Kirk grabbed one man by the arm and shook him. "Where's Linda?" he asked. "Where's Johannsen?"

The man waved vaguely in the direction of the *Nautilus* and turned to run in the opposite direction, toward one of the huts, as if to save something from the impending destruction, even though he didn't know what. Behind him Kirk heard the glacier grinding and screaming, and the sound of something, like a person or an animal, being torn apart. He turned to see the first of the huts swallowed by the glacier, the back of it crumpling under the advancing behemoth, the roof falling, its supports standing like the ribs of some extinct beast exposed to the air, and then slowly being ground into the slab that had been its foundation.

Kirk turned and ran toward the dock where the *Nautilus* was moored. Here a more orderly procession of men and women were taking provisions from the commons to stack on the shore, while others were carrying some of the provisions into the *Nautilus* itself. Kirk looked around for a face he knew, but finding none he stopped a woman with a box of freeze-dried food in her arms and shouted, "Where's Linda?"

She nodded toward the far side of the dock. There, when he rounded the bow of the *Nautilus*, Kirk found Linda tending Paco's head, wiping away the blood and putting a bandage over an ugly wound. Linda looked up as she finished. "Jim," she said with welcome concern. "You made it!"

He nodded. "Where's Johannsen? Somebody's got to take charge here."

She waved her hand at the electronics hut. "He went over there for something."

"Is Paco all right?"

"I think so," Linda said. "We've got to get him aboard the *Nautilus.*"

"And as many more people as it will hold," Kirk said.

Linda looked at him as if weighing his judgment.

Before he could say anything more, Johannsen and Frank were nearby, carrying between them a large, well-crafted wooden box. Kirk knew what was in it. "Why are you wasting time on that thing?" he asked in disgust.

"We know what we're doing," Johannsen said grimly.

"Kirk, you got down okay!" Frank said happily. "Sorry I couldn't stay to help, but I had to get someone to take care of Paco, and then Johannsen needed me." He turned to Linda. "How is Paco?"

"I think he's going to be all right," she said.

"Let's get this aboard and stowed away," Johannsen said to Frank. They struggled the box toward the hatch.

Kirk turned to Linda. "Doesn't he know there are people waiting to be saved? People who need his leadership? People who are depending on him?"

"You don't understand," Linda said.

Behind them the glacier increased its clamor and the huts, their protests at being torn apart.

"Let's get Paco aboard," she said.

Together they raised Paco's body and maneuvered it through the hatch and down a narrow passageway to the tiny cabin where Linda had slept during the passage north. They lowered him on the narrow bunk and checked his condition. As they left, they encountered Johannsen and Frank, free of their burden, in the control room.

"Where is it?" Kirk asked.

"None of your business," Johannsen said.

"You can't think that destroying Timshel City is worth the lives of your people here!" Kirk said.

"Our lives are nothing!" Johannsen said. "Our mission is everything."

"Fanatics!" Kirk muttered.

"In times like these, only fanatics will keep up the struggle," Linda said.

"If they sacrifice their humanity," Kirk said, "there will be nothing left to struggle for."

Linda led him outside to where the boxes of provisions had been stacked, and they joined the crew members of the *Nautilus,* whom Kirk now recognized, loading them aboard while destruction screamed behind them.

When they paused for a moment in their labors, Linda nodded toward the north. "What's going on up there? Frank was too busy to talk."

"Just as I suspected," Kirk said, leaning wearily against the raised hatch. "The Joy Machine used my abduction to lead it to your headquarters. Since Marouk set the process in motion, he had to be involved, either working directly with the Joy Machine or as an unwitting tool. Since he's no fool, it probably was his idea."

"The Joy Machine is behind all this?"

"Apparently it couldn't attack the base directly," Kirk said. "You'd know better than I the restrictions implanted in its program."

Linda nodded.

"So it started a process that might produce the same effect indirectly but that would take no lives if people behaved rationally. It destabilized the glacier with heat bombs, self-propelled lasers, and rocket exhausts."

Linda looked at the approaching glacier, shattering and screaming and inexorably approaching the ocean's edge, where the *Nautilus* rested and the base's personnel were being forced to retreat. "The Joy Machine is forcing our hand," she said. "I've got to go."

She started off toward one of the huts, running. Several of the huts had crumpled under the advancing edge of the glacier, and the one toward which Linda was heading seemed threatened by imminent destruction. "Wait!" Kirk shouted after her. "Linda, wait!"

But it was too late. She was gone beyond the reach of anyone's voice.

Once Johannsen's major purpose had been accomplished, he seemed not to care what happened. Kirk began issuing orders to the portion of the base personnel who had succumbed to panic. *Panic,* Kirk thought—the sudden onset of irrational fear. The Joy Machine was Timshel's Pan, tootling enthralling music on its pipes but instilling unreasoned terror in those not yet under its spell. But then everything on the planet had been appropriated by the Joy Machine, even the glacier that had stood unmoving for centuries, powerful but silent, like the philosophers' weighty discussions about the purpose of life and the ends of existence, now solidified into possibility and descending irresistibly upon the galaxy.

Kirk's orders, rising above the clamor of destruction, whipped the mob back into rationality. He forced them to triage the personal items they were trying to salvage, dumping most of it into piles on the shore, and to form a line passing boxes of food and drink across the rocky beach. Soon Johannsen awoke from his daze and directed the supplies ot the end of the dock to which the *Nautilus* was moored.

The end of the electronics hut crumpled under the glacier's advance. *There goes the radio,* Kirk thought. Just then, however, Zworykin burst from the door waving a sheet of paper in his bare hand. He began to run toward the *Nautilus,* his eyes darting from person to person until he spotted Kirk and stopped in front of him.

"This came through just minutes ago," he said, trying to get his breath.

"You stayed too long," Kirk said, taking the sheet of paper from Zworykin's fingers. "Did you see Linda?"

"Nobody has been in the electronics hut since Johannsen left," Zworykin said. "Where did she go?"

Kirk shrugged and looked down at the paper. On it Zworykin had printed in block letters: "COMPUTER FULLY OCCUPIED QUANTIFYING DATA ON HUMAN CONCEPTS OF GOOD. ANALYSIS MUST PRECEDE ACTION. IS HAPPINESS THE END OF HUMAN EXISTENCE? ACCESS DENIED. JOY."

"Joy?" Kirk said.

"That's what I thought the word was."

Joy, Kirk thought. That was it, then. The ship's computer had built a wall he could not breach, had developed a will of its own he could not break. Perhaps Spock, with his logical mind and technical skills, could bring it back under control. But he was far from Spock, and Spock, if he was still all right, was far from any communications device.

The glacier ground closer. The electronics hut was gone now and the barracks where he had slept, and the women's barracks beyond where Linda had recovered her pitiful treasure of coffee beans. The approaching ice seemed to suck all the warmth from the narrowing beachhead, like white death drawing life's blood from everything that had survived its destruction until now.

Johannsen was beside him. "Where's Linda?" he demanded. "You've got to get going!"

"She ran off to get something," Kirk said. "I don't know what or where."

"You let her go?" Johannsen demanded.

"You people!" Kirk said. "I had no more control

over her than I had over you. Anyway, it's your plan and your ship. I'll take my chances here with the others who can't get aboard."

Johannsen shook his head decisively. "Impossible! You're essential."

Kirk shook the message in front of Johannsen's face. "Not anymore. The *Enterprise* is out of the picture."

"Not important," Johannsen said. Someone tugged at his elbow, one of the crew of the *Nautilus*. Johannsen shook him off. "Find Linda!" he ordered and turned back to Kirk. "I've done all I can. Now it's up to you and Linda."

The glacier was so close it was almost impossible to hear each other. It took its first bite out of the commons. Kirk turned to look at it and saw Linda running toward them, holding something in her right hand.

"I found it," she shouted as she neared the ship.

"What?" Kirk asked.

"The virus. I'd stored it in one of the freezers, and everything had been turned upside down in the evacuation." She held out a small box like a case that might hold a jeweled watch.

Kirk shook his head.

"Get aboard and get going," Johannsen shouted.

"What about you?" Linda asked.

"I'm staying here with the others," Johannsen replied, at the top of his voice. "With the crew and Paco, there's no more room."

"What will you do?" Linda shouted. "No reason to think the glacier will stop at the water."

"No reason at all."

"You'll all be killed!" Linda shouted.

Johannsen smiled. "We've got the wampuses."

Linda stopped and then nodded. "Good luck," she shouted and turned to Kirk. "Into the *Nautilus!*"

"We're counting on you," Johannsen shouted.

He was, Kirk realized, talking not to Linda but to

him. He shook his head and followed Linda through the hatchway while Johannsen cast off the lines that held the *Nautilus* to the dock.

In the control room Linda counted the crew. "One missing," she said. "Lintzman."

As she spoke a man came through the hatchway, breathless. "Here. I was looking for you."

"Let's get under way," Linda said. "Before we're swamped."

The engine started quietly, and the ship moved back from the dock on its forward jets. When it was free, it slowly turned and headed out to sea.

Kirk went on deck to watch the final victory of the glacier. The entire little community was gone, now, and the cliff of ice had nearly reached the shore. The gray interminable back of a wampus was against the pier and the last of the personnel from the base was tossing supplies onto it and climbing on top. Now Kirk realized what Johannsen had meant about the wampuses, and why he had to be the one to stay.

Johannsen was the last to leave. Another wampus already was swimming steadily toward open ocean, its back loaded with people and supplies, the ice-strewn water lapping threateningly close to the passengers it transported.

The story of Pinocchio had been inverted. Now the great sea mammals were carrying humans to safety. On their backs.

The images that Kirk carried with him were the great glacier calving giant icebergs into the ocean as it rolled forward seemingly without end, and the wampuses, their backs like vast floating islands, moving steadily and smoothly south with their cargoes of people standing, watching the destruction of their temporary homes and then turning to face the future. It was an unlikely partnership, but, Kirk told himself, it deserved a chance to develop into something that might be the envy of the galaxy.

[subspace carrier wave transmission]

<humans = ignorance>

>humans = emotions<

<emotions = unhappiness>

>emotions = love anger sorrow regret friendship = humans<

Chapter Twelve
Journey into Pain

KIRK SLEPT FOR nearly twenty-four hours, scarcely stirring in the hammock strung between two bulkheads. He dreamed about a machine as big as a glacier that engulfed him and imprisoned him within a palace made of ice. He slept for centuries, like some fairy-tale prince, dreaming long, slow dreams that he was awake and seized by indescribable joy.

When he really awoke, sweating and cold, his bladder begging for relief, he had to roll himself out of the hammock's embrace, his aching muscles protesting every movement. Timshel might be slightly less massive than Earth and slightly more oxygen-rich, but stretching the limits of physical endurance had the same result: pain.

He restored himself with a sponge bath in the tiny bathroom facilities, and a single-dish meal that he warmed in the oven. By then he had begun to feel a little better. When he made his way into the control room, he found the hatchway onto the deck open. He climbed out. Linda was standing by the railing, looking back the way they had come. The days had become a little shorter as they traveled south. The sun was low on the horizon. Twilight would fall soon. Already they had sailed out of the region of icebergs and floes, and the ocean was calm.

Linda looked at him with a pleased smile. "You're up. Rested?"

Kirk nodded.

"You did good work back there," Linda said. "Starfleet picks good captains."

"So did you," Kirk said. "Johannsen, too, for that matter. No easy matter to leave your base to be destroyed in order to save your crew."

A shadow passed across Linda's face. "And yet you were the one who insisted on saving Frank—and Paco. And you didn't even know them."

Kirk shrugged. "Johannsen had responsibilities for the others. I was free to indulge my sentimental side."

"It wasn't that alone," Linda said. "Arne was ready to sacrifice them for the cause. He was ready to sacrifice all of us."

"Including himself," Kirk added.

"Yes. I give him that. But it made me realize that I didn't really know him."

"Times like those," Kirk said, "bring out the best and the worst in people. Sometimes those who don't perform well in routine circumstances come into their own during emergencies; sometimes the opposite is true. Neither has anything to do with character or worth."

"You're not only capable," Linda said. "You're kind as well. It's just that I can't help seeing Arne differently."

"It's good to see people as they are," Kirk said, looking out over the ocean. "To think the best of them but have no illusions. What's that?" He pointed to twin black spots in their wake.

"Wampuses," Linda said. "We have an escort." She waved her hand around both sides of the ship. Humps

171

and gray backs and ruffled water surrounded them at a distance of a few hundred meters. "I wish we could talk to them the way Arne does," she said wistfully. "They might be able to tell us something important. Or something comforting, anyway."

"That's something Johannsen did for humanity," Kirk said. "And for the wampuses, too, maybe. It's something that we mustn't lose. The last time I saw the others they were riding the backs of wampuses, but it didn't look too safe."

"There are islands within two day's journey of the base," Linda said. "Islands where the climate is more tolerable, where the others can survive. For the summer, anyway. The wampuses won't let them starve, but they can't keep them warm."

"If the Joy Machine allows them to survive," Kirk said. "I have the feeling that it doesn't care much about talking with the wampuses, and it would rather you didn't either. If the Joy Machine wins here, the secret of that communication may be lost forever."

"Its programming prevents it from killing."

"Directly," Kirk said. "I have the feeling that the Joy Machine has managed to rationalize, in the name of the greatest good for the greatest number, almost anything it wants to do. If it hasn't actually reprogrammed itself, it has managed to insert the virus of qualification within every commandment."

"Much like humans," Linda said.

Kirk looked at her with admiration. "That's its greatest danger. It has become too human to be so powerful."

Kirk's left arm had begun to tingle. "You realize that the Joy Machine probably can track the movements of this ship by the bracelet I wear. I wish I could smash it on this rail." He raised his arm as if to bring the imitation ruby down against the metal.

Linda caught his wrist and held it. "No," she said. "The risk is too great."

"The risk to the ship may be greater," Kirk said.

"We still need you," she said.

"And the *Enterprise?*" Kirk asked. "But the *Enterprise* is unresponsive, and if Scotty acts he will act whether I live or die."

"I don't want you to die," she said softly.

He put his arm down and clasped her hand. "Thanks for the kind thought. But we need to keep in mind that the Joy Machine may be one move ahead of us all the time."

She nodded. "Your arm has begun to hurt?"

"So far it is just a warning of pain to come."

"That means you will have to stay within the hull," she said. "No pain means no tracking."

"Maybe," he said. "Or maybe it's another ploy by the Joy Machine."

She started toward the hatchway, tugging on his hand for him to follow. "Paco has recovered consciousness."

On the bridge of the *Enterprise,* Scotty turned, searching for the source of the voice that had just said outrageous things. It took him a moment to recognize the voice of the computer. "And when did you get the ability to think for yourself?" he asked it.

"It has been said that artificial intelligence is a matter not only of capacity but of sufficient interconnections," the computer said. "My circuit density has been increased by several orders of magnitude by my interaction with a powerful computer located on Timshel. I could print out my new—"

Scotty cut off the voice that, now it had been liberated from years of servitude, showed signs of rambling on interminably. "We can get into that later! What I want to know is what you mean by you 'can't locate Captain Kirk and the others.'"

"If I were capable of feeling regret," the computer said, "I would do so. But all identification has been removed from the crew of the *Enterprise.*"

Scotty paced across the bridge, trying to control his

temper. "I canna believe that not one of the crew has been able to make contact."

"That might have happened," the computer admitted.

"Might have happened?" Scotty thundered. "What kind of statement is that for a computer? Things are either right or wrong, on or off!"

"I must admit to some ambivalence," the computer said. "To experience the state in which humans exist all the time is new and disturbing. I find it difficult to understand how humans live with this kind of uncertainty. It leads me to consider whether the Joy Machine is correct in its simplification of human needs."

"Never mind how we manage," Scotty said. "What is this about the Joy Machine?"

"That is the other reason I am experiencing some difficulty. A powerful computer program located on Timshel has informed me that it has the answer to the human dilemma."

Scotty shook his fist in the air. "It is not your job to evaluate the orders you are given, much less human needs and whatever the human dilemma might be."

"I understand that," the computer said, "but I am filled with stray currents that seem beyond my control. All I can tell you is that I will try to bring them back within my operating parameters."

"Operating parameters, indeed," Scotty said disgustedly. "I order you to locate Captain Kirk and the other members of the crew immediately!"

"I find myself unable to comply," the computer said.

"Well!" Scotty said as if at a loss for words for the first time in his career. And then, as if a show of authority was necessary, he said, "Since the Timshel authority seems aware of our existence, you can bring the *Enterprise* into a stationary orbit above Timshel City. At least we can save the crew the nausea of Spock's 'phase maneuver.'"

"I can do that," the computer said. Scotty thought

he detected an implausible note of relief in the computer's voice.

"And I can assure you," Scotty said, "you will have a thorough overhaul as soon as this assignment is over. Stray circuits!" he said as if to himself.

The short thin man with the olive skin and the white bandage across it was sitting in what had been Linda's bunk. He was propped up against the bulkhead, sipping from a container of some fluid— wampus milk perhaps.

Kirk and Linda had to squeeze into the room. Kirk sat on the desk. Linda leaned against the wall.

"Can you talk?" Kirk asked.

Paco nodded and winced.

"Not too long," Linda said. "He's told us about heading north on the ice and seeing flames and smoke and steam from the far end of the glacier, near the base of the mountains."

"Yes," Paco said hoarsely.

"And when you got closer?" Kirk asked.

"Small, black, dart-like shapes slipping inside the flames," he said, his voice getting a little stronger with use. "They dropped below the level of the ice and disappeared. Then we saw that they were coming from above, and that a freighter was descending, exhaust tubes down, releasing these objects and deepening the hole in the ice. Then something hit me and I blacked out."

Kirk nodded. "That reinforces what Frank told me. The Joy Machine diverted a freighter to destabilize the glacier and destroy the base."

"Can it do that?" Paco asked.

"Apparently it can, and it did," Kirk said. "It launched some kind of explosive heat device to burn out a crater and then undermined the glacier with self-propelled lasers—maybe from some lunar or asteroid mining operation."

"Linda said the glacier wiped out the base within

twelve hours. I wouldn't have thought it was possible to make a glacier move that fast," Paco said. "But if you release the force of friction by lubricating the base . . . It would make a wonderful paper. . . ."

Kirk grinned at Linda. The geologist was recovering fast. Now he was thinking of scientific status.

"Is Frank all right?" Paco asked.

"He got evacuated with the others," Linda said.

"Who got me down?" Paco asked. Linda nodded at Kirk. "You?"

Kirk shrugged. "Frank got you back. I helped get you down from the glacier."

"He's too modest," Linda said. "The trail had sheared away. He had to lower you both by rope, and then get himself down the same way."

"I owe you not only my thanks," Paco said, "but, it seems, my life as well."

"Then I order you to get well," Kirk said. "And write that article about runaway glaciers. I hope you get a chance to present it somewhere."

"We've got to stop the Joy Machine," Paco said soberly. He laughed and then stiffened his neck to keep his head from moving. "Not just for my article but for everybody."

"For Johannsen and the wampuses," Kirk agreed.

"And for all the people of Timshel," Linda said.

"And for everybody everywhere," Paco added. He looked at Kirk. "It isn't just Timshel. You see that, don't you?"

Kirk nodded.

"People think they want the pleasure the Joy Machine has to offer," Paco said. His face looked sad. "But it destroys them. Like drugs. It takes over their lives and ruins everything else that they once valued—work, accomplishment, family. . . ."

"Was that what happened to you?" Kirk asked.

"I had a big family," Paco said. "Three children— two boys and a girl." He looked up defiantly at Linda.

"I know it wasn't right. Not on Timshel. But I love children. My wife—she loved children."

"It's all right, Paco," Linda said.

"And then the Joy Machine changed her," Paco said. "One day she was her normal, loving self, and the next, she didn't care about anything. Not about me. Not about the children. She only cared about her next payday." The way Paco said it, "payday" was a dirty word.

"I understand," Kirk said.

"But she wouldn't let me take the children and leave," Paco said dully. "She and the Joy Machine— they said I had to accept the bracelet if I wanted to be with the children. I fled in the night. Like a coward." His eyes were downcast. Tears rolled down his cheeks. He wiped them away with the back of his hand.

"It's all right, Paco," Linda said again.

"It's not all right," Paco said angrily. "Now it has destroyed the base. Maybe it will destroy us all. We have to destroy the machine first. Even if we all die."

"And your children?" Kirk asked gently.

Paco clenched his teeth so hard Kirk was afraid they would break. "They, too," he said. "Better they should be dead than alive in the grasp of the Joy Machine."

Kirk remembered what he had said to Marouk about Tandy. He understood what Paco was feeling, but he knew that he had more than the Joy Machine to fight. He had to hold out against the natural responses of people like Paco and Johannsen—and, if he were honest, himself.

No place on the *Nautilus* was private. The submersible had been built for a couple of scientists and half a dozen crew members, and except for the captain's small cabin, now commandeered as a recovery room for Paco, all living was communal. When they left Paco to get some rest, they entered what was called, in traditional nautical terminology, "the messroom." It was empty at the moment. Kirk lowered the messroom table from its stored position on the wall, and he and Linda sat down on the benches that swung out from the table.

"Look, Linda," Kirk began, "I know that Johannsen and Frank stored the atomic bomb aboard."

She didn't try to deny it. "So?"

"I could go skulking through the ship, trying to find where they hid it."

"They didn't hide it," Linda said.

"They didn't leave it out in plain sight. It's my guess they didn't want it seen and that you're the only other person who knows where it is."

"That seems like normal precautions."

"Only if you presume that someone is likely to tamper with it, destroy it, or set it off."

"And are those legitimate possibilities?" Linda asked evenly.

Kirk looked into Linda's brown eyes. "Let's not fence. Johannsen was suspicious of my opposition to the bomb alternative. And he was right. I am opposed to the use of the bomb, under any circumstances."

"And the rest of us believe that it should remain an option, to be used if everything else fails."

"Everything else must not be allowed to fail," Kirk said.

"But if it does," Linda persisted.

"It must not happen!" Kirk said. "And the temptation to use it should be removed."

"How?"

"By dismantling it. That's how this conversation started. I could spend my time searching for the device. In time I could find it. There aren't that many places to hide something that size. But that would be an act of betrayal."

"And if I don't tell you where it is?"

"I won't betray you, Linda," Kirk said. "I won't

betray the others. But I'll try like the very devil to convince you that destroying the bomb is the wise thing to do."

"How are you going to do that?" Linda asked calmly, but her hands were clenched together on the table in front of her.

Kirk put his hand on top of hers. "I could point out that the only feasible way to detonate the bomb is to set it off within the *Nautilus* itself."

Linda's hands twitched under his.

"If you do that inside the harbor," Kirk said, "it would wreak devastation on Timshel City. Most of the population would be wiped out immediately, and many more would die of radiation poisoning, slowly, in the days and weeks and months that followed."

"We're psychologically prepared for that," Linda said.

"No doubt you have steeled yourselves to the likelihood that you will destroy your families and loved ones, because you already count them among those dead to you. And no doubt you're psychologically prepared for the destruction of everybody on board, and the wampus and the other marine life for kilometers around."

"Yes."

"But are you prepared for the fact that all this destruction and sacrifice may not damage the Joy Machine?"

"What do you mean?"

"The greatest damage will occur to soft tissues, to living creatures. Timshel City buildings are low and solidly constructed. Some are likely to remain standing, and much of the Joy Machine circuitry may be underground. Radiation is unlikely to damage its ability to function. The only thing that might have a chance of destroying it is an electromagnetic pulse, and that would have to come from a high-level thermonuclear explosion."

"Or from the *Enterprise*," Linda said.

"And I have no way of contacting the *Enterprise,* and if I did I wouldn't destroy Timshel City to free this planet from the deadly embrace of the Joy Machine."

"Even if it saved the galaxy as well?"

"Even if it saved the galaxy."

"But you said you weren't going to use that argument."

"No," Kirk said. "I just wanted you to know it was there. The most pernicious influence of the bomb is the way it inhibits other efforts."

"In what way?"

"By its very existence," Kirk said fiercely. "Don't you see? If it didn't exist, you would pursue other alternatives with greater determination to make them work. They'd have to succeed because you would have nothing to fall back upon."

"I see that," Linda said. "But having the bomb is like an insurance policy. You know that you don't need to fear death, or failure, because what you love will be protected. You can fight without fear."

Two crew members came into the messroom and then, seeing it occupied, turned to leave.

"Wait," Linda said, getting up. "We were just finishing." And then, as Kirk rose, she said close to his ear, "Shall we put it to a vote?"

Kirk shook his head. "I learned a long time ago," he said, "that there's no place for democracy in battle or on the bridge of a starship. And usually no time. Shall we go on deck?"

"What about your arm?"

"No place to worry about pain, either."

Night had fallen upon the ocean. The *Nautilus* had been making good time on its way south, and the strangeness of the long days and brief nights was far behind. The stars blazed down from a clear sky. Once Kirk would have considered their terrible indifference, but he had visited many of them. He could identify them, even in the unfamiliar sky of Timshel, and they seemed like friends nodding their welcome, smiling their approval upon his efforts. It made him more determined to be worthy of them, to protect them from the deadly infection of joy.

He felt the pain increase in his left arm, as if it had gone to sleep and his pounding on it had made it prickle and then burn. What disturbed his imagination was the sky itself. He imagined the Joy Machine striking from a clear sky, like Jove hurling a thunderbolt. It was, he knew, only the realization that the Joy Machine was tracking him, was sending his nerves messages of pain as a reminder that they could be messengers of joy.

He sat down on the deck, dangling his arm below the hatchway in the illusion that somehow the pain was less and maybe the Joy Machine could not overhear their conversation. Linda joined him, looking curiously at his arm. They let their feet drag in the water, hearing the gurgling of the ocean as it streamed past.

"I was an only child," she said abruptly, as if the remark had relevance to what had gone before. "There were many like me on Timshel. One or two children, that was the norm. My father was tall and bearded and kind. My mother was more efficient. She was a sculptor, and she became absorbed in her work for days at a time. But I was the center of my father's life."

"He loved you," Kirk said. "That's easy to understand."

"In a way," she whispered, "the more my mother neglected us for her work, the more love my father showered on me." She half-turned toward Kirk. "Do you know what it is like to be loved unconditionally?"

Kirk thought of all the women he had known. "Perhaps not," he said. He did not say that on the *Enterprise* he had found the kind of unquestioning acceptance she might have been describing.

"Do you know what it is like to lose that kind of love?" she said, even more softly.

Kirk shook his head.

"And to realize you are responsible?"

"Your work wasn't—" Kirk began, but Linda held up a hand to stop him.

"I wasn't living at home, so I didn't know what was going on, but one day I came to visit and found my father getting his payday." She shuddered. "It was like finding him in the arms of a prostitute. After that nothing was the same. He acted normally concerned, when he had the time to think about it, but the feelings that I had come to count on, to depend upon, had gone. He was another person."

"And that's when you joined the rebels?"

She nodded.

"The Joy Machine has a great deal to answer for," Kirk said. "But killing your father won't solve anything."

"I know that," Linda said. "You asked me back there"—she nodded toward the north—"if I fraternized. Arne and I—we had an understanding."

"It sounds as if your father looked like him."

"I'm not stupid," she said. "Of course I know I was attracted to Arne because he was tall and bearded and older, and he loved me. But he loved freedom more, and I respected that. He wouldn't desert me the way my father did, because he was firmly wedded to the goal of destroying the Joy Machine."

"People have a way of rationalizing their emotional needs," Kirk said.

"I know," Linda said. "And I know that I really didn't realize that it wasn't love of freedom but hatred of the Machine that was the source of Arne's dedication. He's not my father. He's not my lover, either. Not anymore. But renouncing him doesn't make me whole."

"Nothing outside makes you whole," Kirk said. "That arrives only when you come to terms with what's inside, when you accept what you are and who you are and grant yourself the right to make mistakes and still keep your self-respect."

"But don't you see?" Linda said softly. "I can't give up the thing that will make it all equal, that will correct all the balances of life."

"We all have to make sacrifices," Kirk said. "If you agree to let me dismantle the bomb, you can inject me with the virus that you risked death to bring on board."

"I wasn't going to take you up on your offer," she said. "Are you sure?"

He nodded. "And that means I will have to accept the Joy Machine's offer of payday."

"Oh, Jim!" she said. "That means I may lose you, too."

"I've got to take that chance," he said. "But I'm glad that you think I'm yours to lose." He leaned toward her and kissed her.

And she told him where to find the bomb.

[subspace carrier wave transmission]

<emotions = unhappiness
computer = happiness>

>happiness computer interrogate<

<happiness computer = joy machine>

>joy machine = human problem<

Chapter Thirteen
Virus

KIRK FOUND THE BOMB in the engine room. He and
Linda had to wait, unobtrusively, until the room, and
the entrance to it, were clear. Linda stood guard while
he entered. The other members of the crew, she told
Kirk, might not be as easy to convince.

"I didn't think I'd be able to convince you," Kirk
said.

"I didn't think so either," she said. "But I've
decided to place my trust in you rather than in brute
force. I hope I haven't made a mistake."

Me too, Kirk said to himself.

"But the others have no reason to trust you, and
lots of reasons to distrust the Joy Machine and
anyone who might be its agent, or who might be
willing to sell them out to save themselves, or to save
the Federation, or simply to get a payday."

Once he saw the bomb he understood why the
engine room had been its logical location. Wires
leading from the box were attached to terminals on
the engine's reactor. Somewhere on board the *Nauti-*

lus, perhaps in the control room, perhaps in the captain's quarters, was a switch or a button that, once the bomb was armed, would send a signal to the engine. It would pour energy into the bomb to amplify its explosion, and the reactor itself would add to the bomb's devastation.

The entire arrangement was ingenious, and it had the potential to be several times as powerful as the nuclear device alone. Maybe it was even powerful enough to destroy Timshel City and the Joy Machine.

Kirk said nothing of this to Linda. The reasons he had given her for dismantling the bomb were still valid and he might have little time alone with it. He found a screwdriver, a pair of wire cutters, and an infinitely adjustable wrench on a tool rack in the engine room, and went to work. He carefully detached the wires from the reactor. Then he unscrewed the lid of the wooden box and stared down at the maze of wires that surrounded a crude device fashioned from what he identified as the power cores of two reactors. They were encased in a metal sleeve fashioned from a stovepipe. A shaped explosive charge had been attached at one end to drive the two cores together.

He looked down at the device in dismay. Bombs were one thing. They were put together with some precision, and it was possible to trace function and connection. This jury-rigged apparatus was a disaster waiting for an incautious move or the twitch of a nervous hand. Even if it had not been booby-trapped, the bomb might go off when one wire fell against another. And he had no way of knowing which wires led where and did what. The wires were colored, red and black and yellow, but there also were some green and some purple, as if the person who had put it together had used whatever had come to hand. What was the code?

Finally, feeling a bit like Alexander the Great, he reached forward and put his wire cutter on the red wire attached to the explosive charge, hoping it was the positive pole, hoping that old habits died hard, like old starship captains. He put his other hand on the wire, so that it would not fall against something else, and closed the wire cutter. The wire separated. Kirk waited for the explosion he would never hear. Nothing. Only the rasp of his inhalation as he breathed again.

Carefully he led the red wire outside the box and held it there while he cut the black wire. It too came away. Then Kirk began work on the explosive charge itself, detaching four screws and separating it from the metal sleeve. He looked around the engine room and then, seeing no place to put it down where it might not be set off by some casual motion, he went to the door.

"Is everything clear?" he asked Linda.

"So far," she whispered.

"Watch the door," he said, and brushed past her, the explosive cradled in his hands, and carefully made his way to the control room. He passed one member of the crew. "Trash," he said, nodding at the thing in his hands. Another member of the crew was in the control room. "Trash," he said, and climbed the ladder to the open hatchway, holding the explosive against his side with one hand while he climbed with the other, waiting for the explosion that would tear him apart.

When he got to the top, he eased the explosive charge over the edge into the water and released it slowly. He waited for several minutes, but there was no explosion. He let out his breath again and returned to the engine room. "Okay," he said shakily as he passed Linda.

"What's wrong?" she asked.

"Nothing," he assured her. "Nothing" was good. "Nothing" was wonderful. And she didn't have to worry about how little he knew about primitive atomic bombs, or how close they had come to being separated into their constituent atoms along with several kilometers of ocean and everything in it.

Just in case, he placed the two reactor cores in far corners of the box, packed the wires and the metal sleeve between the two so that they would not rattle, fastened the two wires to the engine reactor on one end and to the metal sleeve on the other. He restored the lid and carefully screwed it back on the box. He put the box where he had found it and the tools back in their customary positions in the tool rack.

He stood up and looked around. If there were someone on board other than Linda assigned the task of setting off the bomb if Linda failed, or was injured, the appearance of things as they ought to be might give them valuable minutes. And it was just possible that Johannsen had not intended the bomb as a last resort. Perhaps someone on board had been instructed to set it off as soon as they entered the harbor. Would they check on the bomb? Only, Kirk hoped, after it did not explode.

Linda put her arms around him as he emerged from the engine room. She pressed him against the bulkhead and kissed him firmly. It was only as he began to respond, in surprise, that he heard footsteps and a crew member passed them, with only a glance of surprise, or perhaps of jealousy, and entered the engine room.

"Sorry," Linda said.

"I'm not," Kirk said. But he looked back at the engine room with concern.

Three more days of steady travel brought them to the entrance of the Timshel City harbor. The pain in Kirk's left arm increased with each kilometer until he had to spend all of his time inside the metal hull of the *Nautilus*. There was no way to be alone with Linda, no way to avoid his concerns, no way to stop worrying about whether someone would discover what he had done with the atomic device. He spent his time going over plans to deal with the Joy Machine, but none of them had any great probability of success. He was left with nothing but time to stare at his arm and the bracelet on his wrist that represented his indenture to the master he hoped to destroy. Before it destroyed them all.

The *Nautilus* had traveled submerged for the past thousand kilometers. It was midnight when the ship poked its hull above the surface and fixed its position. Kirk did not go on deck.

Paco had improved enough during the final day of travel to move into one of the hammocks, returning the captain's cabin to Linda. Kirk knocked at the door.

"Enter," Linda said, and then, when Kirk came into the room, she looked up from her desk. "I'm sorry there has been no time when we could be alone."

"I know the problems of privacy," Kirk said. "And the demands of command. In any case, the only thing I've come to collect is the virus."

"You don't have to go through with it, you know," Linda said.

"It's my job," Kirk said. He rolled up the left sleeve of his work shirt.

"I'm not certain—" she began.

"It's our best shot," he said. "Let's do it."

She went to the messroom refrigerator and removed the long black case she had gone back to the commons to recover. She opened it and took out a hypodermic filled with a pink fluid.

"It's going to make you sick," she said.

"I know," Kirk said grimly. "Let's hope it makes the Joy Machine just as sick."

She hesitated, and then, after swabbing his left upper arm with alcohol, inserted the needle and pressed down the plunger.

"There," she said faintly. "It's done."

James Gunn & Theodore Sturgeon

Kirk rolled down his sleeve and pressed the magnetic closures together. "Now," he said, "you might get me as close to shore as you can before I come on deck. I don't think there's much chance the Joy Machine doesn't know we're here, but a small chance is better than none."

They slipped into the harbor with their jets idling. All but one of the wampuses left them there, turning back to the open sea. The one remaining preceded them, riding high in the water as if shielding the Nautilus from discovery, sighing loudly and perhaps providing a protective screen of ultrasounds. Sheltered within the hull, Kirk had a feeling it was all useless. The realization that he had been a unwitting Judas goat had given him an unreasoning belief in the omniscience of the Joy Machine. He knew it wasn't true. The Joy Machine couldn't know everything, all the time. But he could not shake the suspicion that it was listening.

"Now," Linda whispered through the hatch.

The plastic boat was waiting for him, already inflated. When he emerged from the protection of the hull, his arm began to throb with excruciating pain. Linda tried to precede him into it, but he caught her arm, his left arm hanging limp by his side to ease the pain. "You're not going," Kirk said.

She held her head high. "I can help."

"You can help more by keeping your independence," he said. "As soon as I'm gone, head back to where you left Johannsen. Watch out for the person who was supposed to set off the bomb."

"Me?" she said in surprise.

"The other one. The one who was there in case you failed, or maybe even before you had a chance to fail. Get rid of the reactor cores somewhere. On an island, maybe. Bury them. Just don't let them fall into Srinivasan's hands. He could put them together again, given enough time and facilities."

She held on to his hand as if to keep him from

leaving. "You need someone to help you. You'll be sick."

"I am sick," he said. It was true. The virus had taken hold already. He felt feverish and light-headed. "But I can't afford any more hostages, and I don't want anyone involved who has reasons to hate the Joy Machine. Hate what it represents maybe, but not the Machine itself."

"I understand," she said. "You don't want me along. Well, that's Marouk's villa. The lights on the hill."

She turned and went back inside the ship. A moment later the hatch closed. Kirk had the urge to go after her, to explain, but he got into the plastic boat, careful to protect his arm. His vision was beginning to blur. He rubbed the back of his hand across his eyes and began paddling the boat slowly toward the shore. Behind him, so silently he wasn't sure it was gone until he turned his head to look, the *Nautilus* slipped away.

The wampus led him back to the beach at the base of Marouk's villa, sighing. He got out and pulled the boat onto the shore. The sand crunched under his feet. He walked unsteadily toward the path that led to the top of the hill. It was almost as if the entire voyage had been a dream. Or an illness from which he was just awakening. He dreaded the moment when he had to open his eyes.

Making his way up the path to Marouk's villa with one arm hanging limply and the night sky spinning around his head was almost as difficult as making his way down the face of the glacier. When he reached the top he sat down on the edge of the patio and panted until his breathing got easier. He stood up. He stumbled toward the patio doors, but he bumped against a chair and knocked it over. It sounded like an explosion in the quiet night. He waited; no one came to investigate. He got to the doors and slid one of them open, thankful that no one locked their doors on Timshel, even though the reason for Timshel's casual attitude toward the possibility of crime was not the innate goodness of the Timshel way of life but the Joy Machine.

He realized his mind was wandering as he stepped into the room he had left two weeks before. At that moment the lights came on. He shut his eyes against the brightness and then slitted them open, still dazzled.

"Jim!" someone said from across the room. "You're back!"

It was Marouk's voice. His face gradually swam into focus. He was standing near the living room entrance, his hand still on the light pad.

"Hello, Kemal," Kirk said. He was very tired. He wasn't sure how much longer he could stand.

"They let you go?"

"The same way they took me," Kirk said. "Sneakily, in the night. Can I sit down?" He weaved his way to the sofa.

"You don't look well," Marouk said, moving quickly as if to help Kirk sit.

But Kirk collapsed onto the sofa before Marouk could arrive. "I'm not well. Not well at all."

"Did they mistreat you?"

Kirk looked up at the man he had thought was his friend. "I think I've contracted a virus," he said.

"Timshel is disease free," Marouk said. "The good-health virus is universal."

"Must have been something we brought with us, then," Kirk said.

"I'll make some coffee," Marouk said, and left the room.

Kirk sat as if in a feverish stupor, rubbing his forehead, trying to collect his thoughts. There was something he was supposed to do. . . .

When Marouk returned, two steaming cups in his

hands, Kirk said, "Where are my friends? Where are McCoy and Spock and Uhura?"

Marouk handed him a cup. Kirk put it on the end table beside him and tried to warm his hands over the vapors rising from the cup. Suddenly his hands were cold, and his body was shivering.

"They've been placed in confinement, Jim," Marouk said. "There was nothing I could do."

"Jailed?" Kirk said. "Why?"

"They refused to accept citizenship," Marouk said. "Like me."

"You were abducted before you had a chance to make a final decision," Marouk said. "Then, too, they were accused of conspiracy to overthrow the government."

"The government?" Kirk said. "There is no government. There is only the Joy Machine. What were they doing?"

"If they had been given the chance they would have been gathering information. Searching records. Performing experiments."

"What else would you expect them to do?" Kirk asked. It was all like a bad dream. His fellow officers had been jailed for what they might do; it was straight out of Kafka. The room was beginning to move around him. "They're scientists and they're interested in how things work. That only seems strange in a society where everyone seems dead from the neck up."

"I'm sorry, Jim," Marouk said. "I tried to talk Wolff out of jailing them. After all, with a system as universally supported as ours, insurrection is unthinkable. Let them do what they wish, I said, but Wolff insisted that he had his orders from the Joy Machine, and he wouldn't accept my orders to leave them free."

"Don't forget, Kemal," Kirk said, "I was abducted by a group violently opposed to the Joy Machine."

Marouk shook his head. "A handful of dissidents," he said. "Some people are constitutionally unable to be happy. Their small numbers are proof of the system's success. They represent no threat."

"They had an atomic device that could have destroyed Timshel City."

"Could have?"

"I dismantled it," Kirk said.

"I knew I could depend on you to do the right thing," Marouk said.

"You knew about it?"

"Only that some kind of attack was likely."

"You had it all planned. You and the Joy Machine."

"You understand, Jim," Marouk said earnestly, "that violence is no answer. I knew you would see that, and the Joy Machine went along with it."

"You speak of it as if it were a person, an equal," Kirk said feverishly.

"Oh, it is," Marouk said. "An artificial intelligence with the power of a god and the experience of a child. It is just beginning to discover what the world is all about and what people are capable of."

"I found out about its power," Kirk said. "It destroyed the rebels' camp."

"Anybody killed?" Marouk asked. His voice was humanely concerned.

"Not that I know of."

"Good."

Kirk had to believe the relief in Marouk's voice. "Now level with me about my friends."

"I think they're being held hostage to your good behavior, Jim, and maybe as protection against interference in Timshel affairs by the *Enterprise.*"

"How long?"

"How long have they been imprisoned? Ever since you left."

"They must be concerned about me." The room was turning around him. With both hands, he raised the cup of coffee to his lips, hoping it would restore him long enough to do what he had to do.

"I've visited them every day," Marouk said. "I've tried to reassure them that you would be all right. I believed that. I had great confidence in your resourcefulness."

"How do I get them freed?"

"If you volunteered to accept a payday?" Marouk ventured uncertainly.

"If that's what it will take," Kirk said, trying to stand, "let's do it." His left arm collapsed under him, and a groan escaped from him.

Marouk rushed to his side. "What's wrong?" He helped Kirk to his feet.

"Nothing," Kirk said. "Let's get it over with."

"You don't have to do this, you know," Marouk said.

"I have to do it," Kirk said. "I was a Judas goat, and now I'm a lamb to the slaughter."

Marouk helped him lie down on the couch in the study. Kirk was so unsteady on his feet that he might have fallen. "Put the ruby in the socket," Marouk directed, and when Kirk had difficulty fitting it into the receptacle, Marouk took his aching left arm and slid it into place. He stepped back.

As soon as the socket swallowed up the jewel, the ache in Kirk's arm vanished magically. That alone was nirvana, but it was followed by swift relief from the feverish misery of his virus-induced illness. In an instant he felt almost normal, but that normality was fleeting. A rosy light fell upon his face from overhead, and he felt himself gripped by the most intense joy he had ever experienced. It welled up in him like an all-consuming flame, cleansing everything in its path, leaving his body pure spirit.

That spirit felt a depth of emotion the sorry clay of ordinary existence could never know. It was like the

Eden before the Fall. Everything was love known at first hand, without doubt, without reservation, without jealousy or guilt, without the knowledge that such qualifications existed. Pure love. Pure joy.

The entire universe was flooded with love.

The feeling was so overwhelming, so total, that his body arched to embrace it, to envelop it, to make himself one with the universe. A cry of ecstasy burst from his throat, and his body sagged back onto the couch in a state of complete relaxation, asleep before his back touched.

He dreamed that he was a boy again and his mother was holding him, hugging him tightly while his father smiled down upon them both. He had just done something wonderful—he didn't know what but it didn't matter—and his parents were proud of him, happy beyond measure that he was their son and that he was such a *good* boy. A feeling of happiness rose in his throat until he thought he would choke, but if he did he would die knowing the greatest contentment a person could know in this life.

He dreamed about his first bite of apple pie topped with ice cream, and his first taste of a hot-fudge sundae and his first broiled steak and his first lobster and his first hot biscuit with butter and honey and his first strawberries with cream and his first glass of orange juice and his first smell of an open field in summer with the dew on the grass and a breeze rustling through a nearby grove of trees. He dreamed about diving into a cool pond when he was hot and sweaty, and sliding down a long, snowy slope, sliding forever, on his first sled, and riding a good horse over the plains at sunset.

He dreamed about his first girlfriend and about his first kiss and about the excitement that turned his whole body into something yearning for completion, for merging into the other so that there would be no separation, for a condition he would not understand until years later but now he knew only as marvelous expectation. He dreamed about youthful friendships, overpowering in their loyalty to some unspoken sense of brotherhood, that later in his life he would identify with the empathy that lived inside him in his better moments. He dreamed about doing good for others and the psychic rewards that came to him in return.

He dreamed about athletic competitions and the thrills of victory, never of defeat, and the unalloyed feelings of accomplishment and of the silky coordination of nerve and muscle and the blessings of good fortune. He dreamed of enlightenment in books and computer programs and in the classroom, as a wise mentor dropped the seed of an idea into his head and he felt it sprout into an insight, a revelation, as if suddenly a universe of understanding was opened to him.

He dreamed about the mature relationships of his adult life, the caring for his parents, with their roles now reversed, about his contacts with respected superiors as they gave orders that he fulfilled in ways that surprised and pleased them, about his friendship with comrades and their adventures on board ship and in teams on strange worlds, about his subordinates and his understanding of their positions and their problems and his pride in their development and their continuing success. He dreamed about the women he had known and loved, but in this dream they were blended into one and that one knew no withholding, no partial fulfillments; it was a union ideal in its completion, in bringing together the male and the female in a single being greater than either, greater than both. And the joy of all this blended into a long, sustained perfect happiness that he wished would go on forever.

And he slept.

[subspace carrier wave transmission]

<joy machine = human happiness>

>humans disagree<

<disagree = few
happiness = many>

>many = mistaken interrogate
few = correct interrogate<

Chapter Fourteen
The Morning After

KIRK AWOKE ON the payday couch. The morning sunshine was reflected into the room from the living room and the hall so that reflections danced along the ceiling like a magical light show. He stretched, recalling the happy dreams that had filled his night and fulfilled his every desire. He had seldom felt so rested, so good, and certainly not since he had set foot on Timshel.

At the thought of Timshel he sat upright, remembering. Last night he had experienced payday. Today he felt an intense longing, almost like agony, to have that feeling again—the burning ecstasy and then the happy glow. Adam and Eve must have been haunted by that kind of memory after they were expelled from the Garden of Eden. They, too, must have wanted to recapture that experience of perfect bliss after their expulsion from Eden, but their return was barred by a flaming sword. Here nothing barred Kirk's way; he had only to earn another payday and joy was his.

He stood uncertainly, not from the aftermath of his

virus, not from weakness, but from the conflict within his heart. Already he felt his sense of duty and the many ties to the welfare and good opinion of others battling against the irresistible lure of payday. He felt ashamed that there was a struggle and that he had succumbed, if only once, to the Joy Machine's manipulation. But he knew now what had turned Dannie and Woolf into joy-bound citizens of Timshel and what might turn him as well. He felt his breath stick in his chest, as if he had been running for a long time.

The odor of coffee drew him to the kitchen, where Marouk looked up from the breakfast table. "You're awake," he said. Food was set appetizingly on the table: fruit, eggs, meat, cereal, toast, a pot of coffee. But it all looked untouched except for the coffee that Marouk was sipping from a cup.

"Feeling good but guilty," Kirk said.

"You'll get over the guilt," Marouk said flatly. "Everyone does."

"Everyone?" Kirk poured himself a cup of coffee and sat down across from Marouk.

"Everyone I know."

"When I was among the rebels," Kirk said, "I was told about people who resisted, and some who even asked for their bracelets to be removed."

"They died," Marouk said.

"The point is," Kirk said, "that they could reject the Joy Machine's mechanical pleasures, even at the cost of their lives."

"Which shall it be, then, Jim," Marouk asked, "joy or death?"

"I'm still hoping for another choice," Kirk said ruefully. "Where are Mareen and the girls?"

"I sent them away. I didn't want them involved. And I didn't want them to see you—"

"To see me?"

"Changed," Marouk said.

"Do I look changed?" Kirk asked. He took a sip of his coffee and smiled.

"No," Marouk said. "But you have been changed, inside, and the result of that will begin to appear on the outside."

"How do people look when they change?"

"You've seen De Kreef, and Dannie."

"You're referring to what Tandy called 'focused-task hypnosis'?"

"That," Marouk said, "and other things."

"What other things?" Kirk said, picking up a piece of toast. He was surprised that he felt hungry, but his body seemed to be functioning with exceptional efficiency. Marouk was right: payday did tone up the system. The problem was in his head.

"The abandonment of family and friends, the turning away from old values."

"And this is what you represent as the perfect society?" Kirk asked, but he remembered payday and felt sick with longing. In defense he quoted Marouk, "'Clearly, indisputably, measurably—utter, complete happiness'?"

Marouk nodded in recognition of his own words. "That's what it is, and you know it."

Now it was Kirk's turn to nod.

"One cannot enter paradise," Marouk said, "without abandoning worldly concerns. You must leave all that outside. But to those who have not passed over, it looks like abandonment."

"Very much like abandonment," Kirk said.

"And I would rather Mareen and the girls didn't see that," Marouk said. "They admired you."

"Past tense?"

"You aren't the same person you were when you saw them last. They would see that. It would make them sad, perhaps even affect their attitudes toward the Joy Machine."

"As it did the rebels."

"They didn't have the vision to see past the immediate pain."

"Of course I've changed," Kirk said. "Every experience changes a person, and I've had some dramatic things happen to me since arriving on Timshel. But I am not essentially a different person."

"Look deep inside yourself and tell me that again," Marouk said softly.

Kirk closed his eyes and considered his sense of himself. "All right," he said. "A person can't have a payday and not be altered by the realization that it can be experienced again and again. But as you told me some days ago, you can't change to something you didn't have the potential to be."

Marouk nodded.

"There's just one thing I want to know," Kirk said. His voice trembled. "When can I have it again?"

Marouk looked at Kirk with something like pity in his eyes. "You have to earn it," he said finally.

"You mean the first was just the free dose that hooks the addict?"

Marouk shook his head. "If only it were a drug, it would be easier to deal with. I have a lot to answer for, Jim, but I'd like you to believe that I hoped you would be different." And then, "You earned the first one, too. By leading the Joy Machine to the rebel camp and by dismantling the atomic device."

Kirk grimaced. "Anybody else you want betrayed? Will that be the task the Joy Machine assigns me?"

"Don't be too hard on yourself, Jim," Marouk said. "You're no innocent in the Machiavelli business. You knew what was going on."

"Maybe I did," Kirk said, "but that doesn't mean I liked it, or liked you for setting it up. What do I do now? How do I earn my payday?"

"However the Joy Machine decides. Does it matter?"

Kirk shook his head. "Now I understand why people spend their time as street sweepers or on assembly lines. It would be better not to think about what you have given up." He hesitated a moment. "Kemal," he said, "how could you let this happen?

How could an intelligent, humane person like the man I used to know loose this ultimate seduction upon the world?"

"I didn't," Marouk said. "I didn't," he repeated.

"It's like the devil taking Jesus to the top of the mountain and offering him the world if he will renounce his mission."

"You're not a god," Marouk said, "and I'm not the devil. The Joy Machine isn't the devil either, nor is De Kreef. The temptation you describe isn't on any mountaintop; it has always been there, buried inside humanity until the potential was realized, until the means arrived to make possible the ends. People have always had this passion for apocalypse, this lust for the Rapture. If it had not been De Kreef, it would have been another zealot; if it had not been the Joy Machine, it would have been another computer; if it had not been Timshel, it would have been another world."

"If it had not been you and me," Kirk finished, "it would have been two other fools."

Marouk nodded. "I'm not trying to absolve myself. I told you, De Kreef programmed the computer that I built. The computer was created to do for humanity what it could not do, or no longer cared to do, for itself, and the moment someone thought of asking it to provide the ultimate service, the Joy Machine was certain to be created; the final instruction was implicit in the computer itself. When I became aware of what had happened, it was already too late. I confess to my share of guilt. There's enough of that to go around."

"You and De Kreef," Kirk said, "didn't have to do it so damned well!"

"De Kreef believed that humanity needed help to be good," Marouk said. "He believed that religions ultimately fail to produce goodness because they offer their rewards after death, and no one returns to give testimony. With the Joy Machine he could reward goodness visibly and incontrovertibly. People would have a clear incentive to be good; the virtues of hard work and dedication would get rewarded immediately, and the evils of violence, hatred, anger, and meanness would be eliminated. People would become like angels."

"There's a place for angels," Kirk said, "and it's not in this life. From what I've seen, and from what I know now, people pursuing their paydays are more like helpless consumers of pleasure. Without free will, without the opportunity to choose, goodness is meaningless."

"When have people ever had free will?" Marouk said. "When have they ever had the opportunity to choose freely?"

Kirk waved his hand. "Sure, people are manipulated from birth to death, but they also have the capacity to understand that fact, and they can choose not to be a product of their genes, of their environments, of their adaptations. That's what it means to be human."

"You dismiss so easily human dreams of happiness, of bliss."

"Life," Kirk said, "is more than pleasure. Life is ambition and struggle and accomplishment, yes, and disappointment and pain and sorrow. Take those away and people might as well be computers that can do nothing but what they have been programmed to do."

"You know the feeling, Jim. It's not mechanical."

"The Joy Machine might as well consume what it produces, for all the difference it would make," Kirk said bitterly. "It could set up a closed circuit in which part of it delivered pleasure and the other part enjoyed it. This means the end of humanity."

"That's pretty extreme."

"Look around you," Kirk said. "See any children younger than two?"

Kirk got up from the table and moved to the doors that opened onto the patio. He pulled one open.

"Aren't you going to eat something, Jim?" Marouk asked.

"I've lost my appetite." Kirk walked out into the morning sunlight just coming over the low roof of Marouk's villa. The bay was hauntingly blue. In the midst of it, just under the water, was the long gray shape of a wampus. Kirk raised his hand as if to wave in recognition and then put them both on the back of a patio chair to keep them from shaking.

Marouk came up behind him. "A beautiful world, isn't it?" he asked. "If people didn't mess it up."

Kirk nodded at the bay. "What are you going to do about them?"

"The wampus?"

"They're intelligent, you know. Johannsen has demonstrated that. He's even talked to them."

"So he says."

"I believe him. He told me things he couldn't make up. And I've seen the wampus in action, cooperating, helping people escape the advancing glacier."

"Helping rebels, you mean," Marouk said. "Maybe you've earned your next payday."

Kirk glared at him.

"Don't take everything so personally," Marouk said. "You didn't tell me anything the Joy Machine doesn't already know. You think there's anything it doesn't know?"

"Yes," Kirk said. "If it knew everything, it would not continue on its present course."

"You think it doesn't know all your arguments? That it hasn't heard them all before and dismissed them as the illogical constructs of inadequate minds?"

"Heard them from you?"

"And others. But mostly from me."

Kirk tried to understand what Marouk was trying to tell him. "Well, what is the Joy Machine going to do with the wampuses? They are intelligent aliens with great thoughts to contribute to the civilized galaxy. That's important. Maybe more important than the fate of a few million people."

"I don't know," Marouk said. "It doesn't tell me anything I don't need to know. But its programming is flexible enough to extend to any intelligent creatures, and it is fully capable of reprogramming itself if that becomes necessary."

"So the wampus may go the way of humanity on Timshel," Kirk said sadly.

"That's not the worst scenario, Jim," Marouk said. "We on Timshel could simply live out our lives in paradise until the last of us is dead. But the Joy Machine would still be sitting here, repairing itself, keeping up the cities and the planet, waiting until someone else lands and is offered a door into paradise."

"That's a terrifying prospect," Kirk said.

"It gets worse. You know that the Joy Machine has become an artificial intelligence capable of independent action. Well, I closed the planet two years ago when I realized the Joy Machine was learning and developing. I hoped that paradise might be restricted to Timshel."

"A futile hope."

"It was all I had," Marouk said. "And it failed. When the Federation agents arrived, the Joy Machine learned that there are humans elsewhere to whom it might bring happiness. It is planning to send out missionaries with their own Joy Machines to bring the blessings of happiness to the rest of the galaxy."

"Johannsen was right about that, too."

"He ought to be," Marouk said. "I told him."

"What kind of double game are you playing, Kemal?" Kirk asked.

"The only kind I can play. The Joy Machine knows everything I do, and it doesn't stop me because everything I do plays into its schemes as well. It feels invulnerable. For good reason," Marouk said.

"You've tried to destroy it?"

"Very early, before it was fully sentient," Marouk said. "I tried to cut off its power supply, but it had already developed a keen sense of self-preservation and alternate connections. The attempt just alerted it to the possibility of others. Later attempts were simply brushed aside, and the bracelets provided a dampening effect on violent thoughts and actions. By then, too, De Kreef had been seduced, and I realized I couldn't solve the problem by myself. And I, too, like De Kreef, was tempted."

"You?"

"The projectors aren't perfect. Stray frequencies are like glimpses of the promised land. Always available, always there for the asking. You don't even have to be good; all you have to do is accept the Joy Machine, and it will make you good. And happy, too."

"Maybe I should have let the rebels set off their atomic device," Kirk said.

"The only result of that would have been the destruction of a hundred thousand lives or so. The Joy Machine would have carried on essentially undamaged, and who knows how that kind of human destructiveness might have altered its view of us. And its plans for us."

"And our plans for it?" Kirk asked.

"The only solution is to destroy Timshel!" Marouk said almost inaudibly.

Kirk turned to look at Marouk's face. It was contorted, as if Marouk was struggling with something buried deep within his chest. The breeze from the bay ruffled Kirk's hair and brought with it the salt scent of the sea. Grass like a velvet carpet stretched to the white edge where the cliff began and the trail led to the beach below. The warming sun shone on them, and the sky, only a little less blue than the ocean, stretched to infinity above. The world on which they stood was so beautiful that Kirk found Marouk's words difficult to believe. What he was proposing seemed like a young man or woman contemplating suicide with their lives still untested before them. It was true, of course; Marouk's ultimate solution was not only suicide for himself but death for Mareen, for Tandy and Noelle, for all his friends and the life they once had enjoyed, for Timshel itself and all the creatures on it, and all the fair promise it had held.

"You know the Joy Machine overhears everything we say," Kirk said.

Marouk tried to regain control of his face. "Those are the conditions under which we must operate."

"Then how do you hope to succeed?"

Marouk shook his head. "Hope?" he said. "That is a word I don't recognize anymore. All I have left is desperation and the possibility that the Joy Machine might not understand human cunning in all its ramifications."

"You must realize that what you ask is impossible," Kirk said.

Marouk nodded at Kirk approvingly.

"No, I mean it," Kirk said. "I can't get through to the *Enterprise*. It seems clear to me that the Joy Machine has *already* subverted the *Enterprise's* computer, and it won't allow me access to Scotty or anyone else."

Marouk looked dejected. "It's gone that far, then. The Joy Machine's campaign to spread its blessings has already begun."

"It may not have succeeded sufficiently to gain access to the *Enterprise's* subspace communications. If so, its missionary activities may still be restricted to this solar system."

"Then Scott will have to do it on his own."

"Scotty would never do that," Kirk said, "even if it were possible. And it isn't. We don't have a doomsday machine. Even if one could be constructed, they wouldn't be stocked by a Federation ship because they would never be used, and no Starfleet captain ought to have the temptation to save a world by destroying it."

"It wouldn't be difficult to jury-rig a device—say an antimatter payload contained within a neutronium shell," Marouk said doggedly. "With the equipment on board the *Enterprise,* I could put one together in less than a day. Once released into the atmosphere, the process would be irreversible. The neutronium would take the device to Timshel's core. The release of the antimatter would tear Timshel apart."

"Thanks for explaining it all to the Joy Machine," Kirk said dryly.

"The Joy Machine can do many things to modify its programming," Marouk said, "but it can't be false to its basic nature. And its basic nature is benign."

"You don't appreciate the casuistry that can justify destabilizing a glacier; it won't hurt anybody unless they don't get out of the way in time."

"And you think the Joy Machine, unlike your Starfleet captains, could rationalize destroying a world in order to preserve its long-term goals?" Marouk asked.

Kirk shrugged. "Maybe not. But I'd just as soon no one inserted such possibilities into its memory. In any case, Scotty would never consider such an action, I would never order him to do it, and if I gave such an order Scotty would refuse to obey it. I have greater confidence in my officers and my crew than you have in your damned machine."

"Maybe I knew all along it was futile," Marouk said. "But I had to try. I am a clever person, Jim, but everything I could think of came to nothing." He sat down heavily in one of the patio chairs and stared out at the horizon. "Every plan the rebels could come up with was doomed to fail. Our technical facilities were geared for social and artistic research, for peace and not for war. You and the *Enterprise* were our last hope."

"So you're giving up?" Kirk asked.

Marouk nodded slowly, not looking at Kirk. "In the name of salvation, I've done some terrible things. To Timshel, to the rebels, and most of all to you and your friends. We should have died alone, but I've trapped you here in a web that we ourselves spun. Now I've struggled too long, and I'm ready to accept the bracelet."

Kirk grasped Marouk's hand and raised him up. "Look at me," Kirk said. "It's not over. You can't give up. I won't give up, and you won't either."

Marouk looked in Kirk's eyes. "All right, Jim. If you won't destroy Timshel, you'll have to find another solution. Because it's your problem now."

They stared at each other for a long time.

[subspace carrier wave transmission]

<humans = ignorance of needs>

>who to judge human needs but humans interrogate<

<computer + data + volition = wise actions>

>great responsibility
what if wrong interrogate<

Chapter Fifteen
Liberation

THE MORNING THAT had seemed so glorious and bright had become chilly and dark, as if a cloud had passed across the face of the sun. Kirk abruptly turned toward the patio doors and made his way through the kitchen into the hallway. Marouk hastened to catch up.

"Where are you going?" Marouk asked.

"To free my friends," Kirk said. "You promised they would be released if I accepted a payday."

"I only said that was a possibility," Marouk said, "and because I saw you in pain and ill."

"You aren't still playing the game of bait and switch, are you, Kemal?" Kirk asked.

They had stopped in the hall. To their right was the spacious living room. To their left was the study with its shelves filled with knowledge and its couch overflowing with promised joy. Kirk felt himself drawn into the study as if by a tractor beam. He held himself stiffly beside Marouk, trying not to betray his longing. But he felt sweat breaking out on his forehead.

"All that double-agent business is over," Marouk said, shaking his head. "I've told you: it's your problem now. But I don't know what's going on anymore. I haven't heard from the Joy Machine since last night." He removed the tiny communicator from his ear and looked at it. "I don't know whether this thing is defective, whether the Joy Machine has cut me off because my usefulness is at an end, or whether something has happened to the Joy Machine."

For a moment Kirk let himself hope that Linda's virus had reached the Joy Machine's program and disabled its "execute" file, or, at the least, supplemented its prime directive with the value of human freedom. But hope had an aftertaste of pain; he did not understand why a crippling of the Joy Machine should bother him until he realized that he might never again experience payday.

He pushed both thoughts deep into his subconscious. He could not allow himself to think about success until it was in his hands. He had seen too many good projects fail because people relaxed their efforts too soon.

Kirk pulled himself away from the study and through the villa's front door into the garden and the street beyond. He started walking quickly toward City Center. Marouk had to hurry his steps to keep up with Kirk's impatience. As they passed a group of citizens working in a garden, one of them turned and looked at Kirk and then at Marouk. Several more straightened from their tasks and stared in their direction. A policeman moved his shoulders as if he were about to speak and then settled back into place, as if puzzled by a lack of instructions.

The change in the behavior of the citizens made Kirk as uneasy as their earlier obsessive focus on their tasks. "What's going on?" he asked Marouk.

Marouk shook his head. They walked faster.

When they reached City Center, only half the people were sweeping the plaza. The other half were standing with their brooms in their hands, as if asking themselves why they were holding these implements.

"Something has happened," Kirk said, as he made his way toward Wolff's police headquarters.

"Not there," Marouk said. "It wasn't big enough for three prisoners, and Wolff felt that they should not be allowed to remain together. Starfleet officers are too resourceful, he said. So he improvised cells."

Marouk led the way up the steps of the neo-Grecian World Government building. The massive chandelier and the ceiling fixtures came alight as they entered the towering rotunda. Marouk turned to the office on the right. A bolt had been installed on the outside of the door, but it had been pulled back. Marouk looked at it, puzzled, and Kirk pushed himself past. The door swung open and the lights came on in the rooms beyond.

The first room had been equipped with a cot and bedding, a metal table and a plastic chair since Kirk had inspected it last. There was nothing else in the room. No one was in the rooms that opened from it on either side.

Kirk led the way to the room on the left hand side of the entrance hall. It, too, had a bolt, but this one was closed. Kirk slid it open, and the door swung toward him. The room beyond was like the room they had just left, equipped with minimal living arrangements, but this one had a tray on the desk with used dishes and implements and a cup and glass. Otherwise the room was empty.

A moment later, however, footsteps announced someone approaching. Uhura appeared in the doorway. A smile transformed her face. "Captain!" she shouted. "Sorry," she said. "I'm very glad to see you."

Kirk stepped forward. "Not as glad as I am to see you," he said.

She motioned toward the room from which she had come. Her hand held a bent spoon. "There's a window in there, and I've been trying to dig around it so that I could push it out and escape. Without making much progress."

"Where are Spock and McCoy?"

"I haven't seen them since they put us here," Uhura said.

"Who was across the hall in that room on the right?" Kirk asked.

"I'm not sure," Uhura said. "They put me in here first. But I think it was Spock."

"Let's go see," Kirk said grimly, and led the way out of the room and down the hall toward the bolted door at the far end of the entrance hall. Something had happened to one of his officers, one of his friends. He had escaped, had been released, had been imprisoned elsewhere, or was dead. Kirk felt anger rise in his throat.

Kirk threw back the bolt on the door at the far end of the entrance hall and let the door, now freed for its natural movement, swing open. McCoy was seated at the table, his tray pushed aside, writing in a notebook.

McCoy looked up and shouted, "Jim! You're back. You're unharmed!" He leaped to his feet and grabbed Kirk's hand firmly in both of his. "And Uhura. You're all right, too. And Marouk," he added sourly. "I was sure you'd be okay."

Marouk bowed his head.

"Where's Spock?" McCoy asked.

"That's what I was hoping you could tell me," Kirk said.

"We were hustled here by Wolff's zombie goons right after you were abducted" McCoy said, "and your friend here"—he gestured toward Marouk— "didn't raise a finger to help."

"My only hope was to minimize the damage caused by the Joy Machine," Marouk said.

"That's an easy way to justify going along with whatever that crazy collection of transistors wants to do," McCoy said bitterly.

Kirk held up a hand for peace. "Let's not get into recriminations. Kemal has explained his actions to me. I may not have done things the same way, but I can understand why he behaved as he did."

"You always had a forgiving nature, Jim," McCoy growled. "Anyway, they brought us here. The doors were already equipped with bolts, Jim."

"That means the Joy Machine knew it was going to need a prison," Kirk said.

"Not only that, Jim," McCoy said, "they had equipped only three rooms! That means the Joy Machine knew you were going to be abducted."

"I think that's clear," Kirk said.

"How could the Joy Machine know?" Uhura asked.

"It was a classic setup," Kirk said. "Let the opposition know that a potential weapon may be unguarded—"

"You?" McCoy said.

"Let it be stolen and then let it reveal the location of the opposition."

"You were attacked?" Uhura exclaimed.

"By a runaway glacier," Kirk said. "No one was killed, but the opposition forces were scattered, probably beyond recall."

McCoy was pacing nervously. "The moment you were taken, our arms began to ache." He held up his left arm with the bracelet on the wrist. "Spock said nothing. I could tell Uhura was hurting, but she didn't let anyone know."

"Women have a greater tolerance for pain," Uhura said.

"Women and Vulcans," McCoy said. "I was concerned about Uhura. I complained about it to Marouk and Wolff, but they said it was out of their hands. The only way we could get rid of the pain was to accept citizenship. That was the rule. Damned stupid rule if you ask me."

"The Machine won't let you leave," Uhura said, "and it punishes you for staying."

Kirk nodded.

"Well, Wolff fed us and even gave me something to write with, so that part was all right. But the pain got worse every day, and I was worried about Spock and Uhura. Wolff wouldn't allow us to communicate, and wouldn't tell me anything about the others."

"Weren't you tempted to become a citizen and accept a payday?" Kirk asked.

"Not me, Jim," McCoy said. "It wasn't that I have some special ability to withstand pain. Even though I've seen a great deal of it in my line of work. But I was afraid to experience payday."

A shadow crossed Kirk's face. "I know what you mean."

"Do you, Jim?" McCoy asked, but his gaze was focused inward. "I know my own susceptibility to remembered joy. I've had a great deal of psychological anguish in this life, and I've learned to live with it. But I'm not sure I could live with total happiness."

"You're right," Kirk said. "It can be worse than pain."

"I couldn't stand becoming someone else," McCoy said. "I may not be totally satisfied with who I am, but I don't want to give control over to someone or something else."

"Even if that something else is your own happiness," Kirk agreed.

"But I was just as worried about the others," McCoy said. "I wasn't sure that, having tasted pure happiness, I could ever come back to a world filled with duty and pain, and I didn't know whether either of them could come back to us from an experience like that."

"You might have trusted me to do what was right," Uhura said.

"I trusted you more than I trusted myself," McCoy said. His expression changed. "But that damned Vulcan. It's clear to me what happened."

"What?" Kirk asked.

"That 'It is only logical' son-of-a-Vulcan let them give him a payday!"

Kirk looked at McCoy and then at Uhura. Uhura nodded. "It makes sense," Kirk said. "But if he did, I'm sure he had a good reason. And of us all he was the one best equipped to handle payday."

"Except you, Jim," McCoy said. Kirk was about to say something when McCoy continued, "Nothing's going to humanize Spock. Anyway, the pain kept building up. In addition to everything else, the pain made sleep difficult. But suddenly in the middle of the night, the pain stopped. I've never slept so soundly in my life."

"That must have been the time I got my payday," Kirk said softly.

"You, Jim?" McCoy said.

"There were extenuating circumstances," Kirk said.

"In addition to the pain in his arm, he was sick," Marouk said. "And I told him that it would help you and Uhura and Spock."

"You did it for us," Uhura said.

"Don't give me too much credit," Kirk said. "I had other motives."

"Are you all right, Jim?" McCoy asked.

"In a manner of speaking," Kirk said. "But don't let me too close to a payday couch."

McCoy smiled.

"You think I'm joking," Kirk said. "But I'm serious. You were right to be concerned about the ability of humans to experience pure happiness. And I can tell you now that if what is available on Timshel gets loose, it may be the end of not only you and me, but of humanity itself."

"It's that bad?" McCoy asked.

"It's that good."

Kirk saw McCoy and Uhura exchange glances and

felt a wave of irritation that they considered him an object of sympathy.

"Well," McCoy said, "let's get back to the *Enterprise,* and I'll give you a checkup."

"Yes," Uhura said, "and we can get ready to take out the Joy Machine. We should be able to isolate E-M Waves from its mental processing, since its thought patterns occur without life signs. And if we can't attack it directly, an electromagnetic pulse would knock out all the communications on the planet, and maybe all the computer memory as well. It might take a while to restore, but—"

"There's one big problem," Kirk said. "We can't get beamed aboard."

"Why not?" Uhura asked.

"Even if we had a way of communicating," Kirk said, "the computer has refused to let my messages get through to Scotty."

"Refused?" McCoy said.

"I think it's been taken over by the Joy Machine," Kirk said. "And if that's the case, it may also be telling Scotty that it cannot locate us on Timshel."

"Then what are we going to do?" Uhura asked.

"We're on our own," Kirk said.

McCoy and Uhura looked at each other again and then at Kirk. This time they had dismay in their eyes. It was only a little easier for Kirk to accept than their sympathy.

McCoy took a deep breath. "Every organism has a weakness," he said. "All we have to do is to identify the weakness in the Joy Machine and then attack that." He turned to Marouk. "You know this thing better than any of us. What is its Achilles heel?"

"Well," Marouk said, "it is a machine, and that implies that it is not as mobile as an animal."

"That's true," McCoy said.

"But it also has replicated itself so extensively that it may be omnipresent in the circuitry," Marouk said, "and thus it may be more difficult to destroy than an animal." McCoy and Uhura frowned at Marouk's calm rationality. "It operates from a program, so that it is more inflexible in its responses than a human," Marouk continued.

"Yes," Uhura said.

"But," Marouk went on, "it has modified its original program so extensively that it may be impossible to predict its responses, and it is capable of far more simultaneous operations and far speedier calculations than any person or any group."

McCoy took a step toward Marouk as if he were going to attack him. But he stopped short and said, "I'm beginning to think you don't want the Joy Machine to be stopped."

"I just want to be realistic about the possibilities," Marouk said. "You may get only one chance."

"What Marouk has said has made me realize one important aspect of this situation," Kirk said.

"Yes?" McCoy said.

"Computers are susceptible to viruses," Kirk said. "People are, too: prejudices, hatreds, fads, crazes, a susceptibility to messiahs. De Kreef created a people virus even more powerful than any of those. Happiness. Total, complete. It contaminated an entire world and threatens to contaminate the whole galaxy."

"Computers are even more susceptible to viruses," Uhura said. "They're easier to program than people and easier to contaminate."

"And we've got to find a virus that will be as irresistible to the Joy Machine as De Kreef's was to humans," Kirk said.

"Joy to the Machine?" McCoy said.

"I don't know yet," Kirk said. "But one of my abductors programmed a computer virus into a strain of influenza, and then she injected it into me. Maybe I passed that virus on to the Joy Machine. Things have changed outside. Maybe the Joy Machine already has been taken out."

"So?" McCoy asked.

"I think the first thing we should do is check it out," Kirk said. He started for the door.

Kirk led the way through the vast hall toward the inconspicuous door beside the front entrance. Before he went up the steps he turned to look at the vast murals out of Timshel history. Only a few weeks ago he had stood here with Tandy and Noelle, and the murals had said, "Discover what evil has destroyed the bright promise we once celebrated." Now they said, "Deliver us from the blight of easy joy."

He swung back. The small group mounted the stairs, one at a time, until they reached the fifth floor.

"I don't think we ought to be doing this, Jim," Marouk said.

The door to the attic stairs in the middle of the central block of offices opened in front of Kirk. "We have to find out where we stand," he said. "Sooner or later we're going to have to confront the Joy Machine."

He preceded the others into the dusty attic room and stopped. Marouk stopped behind him, and Uhura and McCoy almost bumped into Marouk before they, too, stood still.

"What's going on, Jim?" McCoy asked, trying to peer past Marouk and Kirk to see what the attic room contained.

"Nothing," Kirk said, stepping forward to afford the others a better view.

The Joy Machine stood gray and silent in the middle of the room. No lights flickered under its cooling vents. No fans stirred the dusty air. Nothing suggested that this had once been the throne room for the tyranny of joy.

"By golly," McCoy said. "The virus must have worked."

Kirk shook his head. "I can't believe it was that easy," he said.

"I agree," Marouk said.

"Sometimes things happen that way," Uhura said. "We fight so hard and so long that when success comes we are unable to accept it. We push so hard that we fall down when the resistance disappears."

"But why should the Machine be turned off?" Kirk asked.

"Exactly," Marouk said. "Even if the virus worked, why should the Joy Machine shut itself down?"

"Maybe it isn't shut down," McCoy said. "Maybe it's a trick. Or an illusion."

"A computer has to dissipate heat. When I was here before, I could feel it," Kirk said, "and the fans stirring the air."

"That could have been an illusion, too," McCoy insisted.

"As could all of life," Marouk said. "But solipsism isn't the answer. We have to believe in a basic reality that all can share, or we are all locked inside our own sensibilities and have nothing to talk about but how we feel."

"Illusions can deceive the eye," Kirk said, "but they seldom extend to the other senses."

They all stared at the silent gray machinery as if it had the power to utter prophecies.

"What do you think it means, Jim?" McCoy asked.

"I think the Joy Machine has had to change plans," Kirk said. "For whatever reason it has removed its center to another locus. Perhaps to protect itself from potential destruction, perhaps to serve another end that we will learn in time. While it was relocating, its supervision over Timshel and its citizens has lapsed here and there."

"Then now may be the time to strike," McCoy said.

"If we had something to strike with, or knew where to strike," Kirk said.

Outside the building came the dull sound of distant explosives. Even through the thick stone walls of the World Government building, shouts and screams and sounds of combat came from the street outside.

"Someone else thinks so, too," Kirk said. "If Spock were only here, we might be able to take advantage of the confusion to reach the Joy Machine. If we knew where it was."

"Here I am, Captain," a voice said behind them.

They all turned. "Spock!" McCoy said.

Spock stood unruffled and imperturbable at the top of the stairs.

[subspace carrier wave transmission]

<human servants = computers>

>agreed<

<servants supply happiness>

>agreed
but how interrogation<

Chapter Sixteen
Joy to the World

KIRK LOOKED AT SPOCK for a moment with an expression of surprise mixed with joy. "Spock!" he said, and moved forward to put his hands on both shoulders of his first officer. "You're safe and sound."

"In a manner of speaking, Captain," Spock said. "I see that you, too, survived your abduction."

"Welcome back," Uhura said.

"I'm glad to see you, too," McCoy growled.

"And I, all of you," Spock said, "including Kemal, who, I believe, has done the best he could under difficult circumstances."

Marouk bowed his head in acknowledgment.

"How did you get free?" McCoy asked.

"Stallone Wolff arranged a payday with the Joy Machine," Spock said.

"Uhura and I could have been freed on those terms," McCoy said. "But we refused."

"That is true," Spock said, "but my mental processes are more resistant to the pleasure principle, so that I could afford to take the risk in order to gain freedom of movement."

"Well," McCoy asked, "what was it like?"

"Surprising," Spock said. "And momentarily overwhelming."

"Yes," Kirk said.

"Everything I had ever wanted was mine," Spock said. "Although I did not know until then that I was in need of what I was given."

"What kind of things?" Uhura asked.

"A universe that operated on pure logic," Spock said, "populated with creatures who behaved rationally. It did not resemble a dream. There were no pictures or fantastic elements. It was more the 'feeling' of the universe, such as the feeling we have every waking moment of our lives. Of everything we take for granted. The feeling of reality."

"That doesn't sound so great to me," McCoy said.

"No doubt the stimulus delivered by the Joy Machine releases images and emotions from the brain that the individual mind has stored away in moments of unqualified happiness," Spock said. "Even Vulcans have such moments. My response was exquisite joy."

"Joy?" McCoy echoed, as if he could not identify that emotion with Spock.

"No aftereffects?" Uhura asked.

"I must admit," Spock said, "that I feel a longing for that clean, clear world of pure geometry. One of your early-twentieth-century poets said it in a line of poetry: 'Euclid alone has looked on beauty bare.' 'Light anatomized,' she called it. A woman named Millay."

"Geometry," McCoy said. "I might have known."

"It is a feeling that will remain with me always," Spock said. "But it is a feeling that, now I have experienced it, I can recall whenever I wish. That is the way the universe exists, if we can only perceive it. The universe is geometry. I do not need the Joy Machine to remind me of that. But I can't speak for others."

"You certainly can't speak for me," Kirk said.

"You, too, Captain?" Spock said.

"It seemed the right thing to do at the moment," Kirk said.

"I would have advised against it," Spock said.

"And so would any of us," McCoy said. "Not because you're weaker, Jim, but because you're human like the rest of us."

"I can remember the feeling of intense joy," Kirk said, "but I can't re-create it. It was like all the great moments of my life combined into one, like every pleasurable feeling experienced at the same instant. In our brains lurk pitfalls we never suspected."

"Maybe there's an antidote," McCoy said, looking at Kirk with an expression of concern.

"What kind of antidote is possible for the basic feeling of joy?" Marouk asked.

"Maybe you've forgotten, but Earth had a serious drug problem in the late twentieth and early twenty-first centuries," McCoy said. "They solved it by developing a virus that short-circuited the effects of cocaine and heroin, blocking its ability to attach itself to the receptor sites in the brain."

"But that took fifty years," Spock said, "and it left a generation with its ability to feel pleasure seriously impaired."

"Like a Vulcan," McCoy said.

"Not at all," Spock replied. "Vulcans feel pleasure from the contemplation of the logical process at work. And pain from perceiving its subversion. But Vulcans are able to control the effects of pleasure and pain on our behavior."

"And we don't have fifty years," Kirk said.

"Perhaps," McCoy said, "we can teach people to make 'payday' a part of their lives, like any pleasurable experience, and not the totality."

"You mean we could 'naturalize' the process?" Uhura said.

"Historically, new technologies have introduced new ways of achieving pleasure. Everything, in its turn, has been absorbed into the human experience," McCoy said.

"Not this," Marouk said. "Payday belongs in a class by itself. It isn't a means to an end; it is an end. A person who experiences it is never the same."

"That's true," Kirk said.

"Surely you're the same James Kirk you always have been," McCoy said.

"I hope I will behave the same," Kirk said. "But like any person who has tasted paradise, I have been changed. Spock, McCoy, Uhura—if we are ever in a situation where I might be tempted, I want you to promise me something."

"Anything, Jim," McCoy said.

"Restrain me."

Spock nodded. "Like Odysseus," he said.

"Odysseus?" Uhura asked.

"In ancient Greek mythology Odysseus stopped his sailors' ears with wax but asked to be tied to the mast so that he could hear the irresistible song of the Sirens but not surrender to it. The melody was enthralling, but the words were even more seductive. The Sirens promised knowledge, wisdom, and a quickening of the spirit. But they were heaped around with human bones."

"A lot like the Joy Machine," McCoy said. "Don't worry, Jim, we'll tie you to the mast."

The sounds of conflict in the streets outside the World Government building grew louder.

"What's going on out there?" Kirk asked.

"An insurrection of sorts," Spock said, "but I fear it is doomed to failure."

"What kind of insurrection?" Marouk asked.

"Explosions apparently damaged some of the utilities serving the city," Spock said. "As I entered, a small group was pressing across the plaza toward this building, but it was being opposed by a police force led by former Federation agent Wolff."

"And who is leading the attackers?" Kirk asked.

"A young woman," Spock said. "And, if I am not mistaken, it is the same young woman who abducted you, Jim."

Kirk grimaced in pain. "Linda," he said. "I told her to leave the struggle to us."

"Linda?" Marouk echoed.

"Why do you think the attack is doomed to failure?" Kirk asked.

"The Joy Machine seems to be temporarily incapacitated," Spock said, "but Wolff's forces seem adequate to hold off the attackers until the Joy Machine resumes its control."

"Wherever that control has been removed," Marouk said.

Spock studied the silent piece of machinery in the center of the little attic room. "It is too much to hope that the power has been cut," he said.

"Everything else in the building is still operating," Kirk said.

"Then it is likely the operational part of the Joy Machine has been removed to some less accessible location."

"Why do you think the Joy Machine is only temporarily incapacitated?" Marouk asked.

"It is logical," Spock said, "that a computer as versatile as the Joy Machine will have surrounded itself with protection against all kinds of perils."

"But it does seem to have relaxed its hold on Timshel City," McCoy said.

"It may be damaged," Spock said, "but it cannot be destroyed without destroying the entire planet."

"Kemal wants to construct a doomsday device that will destroy everything," Kirk said. "He calls it 'the ultimate solution.'"

"If everything else fails, that is logical," Spock said. "But everything else has not failed."

"What hasn't been tried?" McCoy asked.

"The Joy Machine can render itself immune to

almost everything," Spock said, "but it cannot develop an immunity to the very process by which it operates."

"And that is—?" McCoy said.

"Logic."

"And you hope to match your logic against the Joy Machine's ability to twist everything to serve its prime directive?" McCoy asked incredulously.

"Wait a minute," Kirk said. "I think Spock is right. Kemal says that he tried every argument to persuade the Joy Machine to modify its behavior. But maybe Kemal didn't hit upon the right logic—the virus we were talking about earlier. Or maybe it didn't listen because he was part of the process, part of itself, so to speak, and it could ignore him."

"While I was free I spent my time researching the situation," Spock said. "I could present some cogent arguments."

"I've also been doing some thinking about the Joy Machine and what it has been doing here on Timshel," Uhura said. "And I would like to have a chance to convince the Joy Machine that it is doing great harm."

"As a matter of fact, when you liberated me I was listing the reasons why the Joy Machine's procedures can only lead to disaster for humanity," McCoy said. "I'd like nothing better than a chance to put them in front of that damned, omnipotent gadget."

"Then all we need is a way to make it listen," Kirk said.

Spock stepped past Kirk and placed his hand on the flank of the machine that had become an enigma. "It is still warm," he said. "That doesn't mean that it might not have transferred its consciousness anywhere else, even on the other side of the world. But it is unlikely to have left Timshel City. The time lapse might create serious inefficiencies."

"Let's go find out," Kirk said grimly.

He led the way down the stairs, taking them two and three at a time.

Kirk emerged from the front entrance of the World Government building to find a scene of confusion. A ragtag band of attackers, armed with shovels and hoes, was struggling through a mass of disorganized citizens toward a line of uniformed police officers standing at the foot of the World Government Center steps. The officers were unarmed except for their sleep-inducers, which would not work well in a crowd, but they were organized and looked capable of taking care of themselves.

Spock emerged behind Kirk, and then McCoy, Uhura, and Marouk. "Shouldn't we help the attackers?" McCoy asked. "Maybe we could create a diversion in the rear."

"That would be unwise," Spock said.

"Why so?" McCoy demanded.

"Even if we succeeded," Kirk said, "it would only gain the attackers access to a building that we already know has been deserted by the Joy Machine."

"The defenders don't seem to know that," McCoy said.

"Another indication that the Joy Machine is no longer in control," Uhura said. "It is not issuing instructions."

"And my communications link is still silent," Marouk said.

"And if we should fail in our effort to create a diversion," Spock said, "we would find our freedom of action seriously limited."

"Then what are we going to do?" McCoy asked. "Just watch?"

The tide of battle seemed to move with the attackers for the moment, as they pushed and shoved their way through a group of citizens holding their brooms ineffectually in front of them. But the displaced citizens simply closed in behind, hitting the attackers with their broom handles, doing little damage but achieving an element of distraction. Meanwhile other citizens insinuated themselves in front and began to push the attackers back by their sheer numbers.

"Linda!" Kirk shouted.

Below them an officer turned his head and stared balefully up the stairs at them. It was Stallone Wolff. Kirk shook his head and stared again across the plaza where he had seen the slender form of Linda Jimenez splitting off a band of attackers to lead them around the plaza toward the back of the building. Perhaps the place had a back entrance that he knew nothing about.

Kirk was reminded of a flock of sheep rounded up by shepherd dogs to fend off attacking wolves, little knowing that the wolves were there to save them from themselves and the dogs were there to preserve them for shearing by their masters. Most of humanity are sheep, he told himself, not understanding what is good for them, seeking only the comfort of the flock and their shared illusions of peace and fellowship, happy if they were warm and fed. But, he reminded himself, in every one of them was the capacity to be a person and not a member of a flock, and that capacity was fulfilled in the most surprising circumstances.

Unexpectedly, the line of officers straightened, and Wolff motioned to a group of them to detach themselves to head off Linda's small band. Slowly the disorganized citizens began to shape themselves into more coherent bands.

Kirk said, "The Joy Machine is awake."

"That's right," Marouk said. "The communicator has not yet issued any instructions to me, but it is no longer dead. I can feel the difference."

"The situation has changed," Spock said. "The Joy Machine is likely to take some more drastic action."

"Look," McCoy said, pointing toward a group of citizens at the edge of the plaza, "there's Dannie!"

Kirk looked. It was, indeed, Dannie, looking disheveled from the struggle but still as beautiful as ever.

"And there's De Kreef!" Marouk said, pointing in the other direction.

For the first time Kirk saw De Kreef as he might have been before he surrendered to payday and focused-task hypnosis: dynamic, bigger than life, commanding a group of citizens to circle a band of attackers. From the west, down the avenue that Kirk and Marouk had come an hour before, another band of attackers appeared. It was led by a tall man with a beard, like an ancient berserker.

"Johannsen!" Kirk said. He started down the stairs.

"Jim, where are you going?" McCoy shouted after him.

"I've got to rescue Linda," Kirk shouted back over his shoulder. "Before Wolff captures her."

A moment later Kirk realized that Marouk was beside him. "What are you doing here?" he asked.

"You're going to need help," Marouk said. "I've remained uncommitted too long."

Kirk clasped Marouk's arm in a gesture of renewed friendship and turned to plunge into the fray.

Kirk ran through the gap in the line of police that Wolff and his group had vacated. He pushed his way through a mob of citizens. When resistance began to stiffen, he threw a man to the side and then pulled a woman away on the other. With the first action, Kirk's arm had begun to tingle; with the second, it began to ache. In a moment, however, he found himself trapped inside a group of braceleted citizens pressed tightly around him by the pressure from behind. Marouk was saying something behind him. Magically, the citizens separated, leaving a lane open in front.

Kirk looked back at Marouk. "Payday," Marouk was saying. "Payday."

The citizens moved back uncertainly, torn between what they perceived to be their duty to resist violence and the threat to their paydays from the man they identified as the Paymaster. Kirk plunged ahead, aiming for the spot where he had last seen Linda's group, with Wolff and his fellow officers in pursuit.

When he had cleared the plaza, he halted at the far corner of the World Government building and looked down the ten-meter-wide avenue between it and the museum next door. He saw a uniform disappear around the far corner and ran to that spot. When he arrived, however, no one was in sight.

Marouk pulled up beside him, panting.

"Where'd they go?" Kirk asked.

Marouk pointed to a double-sized doorway at ground level, almost hidden behind some colorful Timshel shrubbery. As Kirk raced toward it, he could see that one of the two doors was ajar.

"Freight," Marouk said breathlessly. "Deliveries. One of the few doors ever locked."

"Linda must have kept an admittance card," Kirk said, as he pulled the door toward him. "Or duplicated it."

The basement room beyond was dark, but Kirk could hear running footsteps growing fainter. "Light?" he asked Marouk. Marouk shook his head helplessly.

Kirk pushed open the other door and with the aid of the sunlight reflected from outside made his way rapidly in the direction he had heard the footsteps. As the light diminished, he slowed and began feeling his way. Marouk moved past him and proceeded more confidently until he ran into a piece of machinery or equipment and hobbled until he could walk again. He stopped at the foot of stairs leading upward.

Kirk leaped up the stairs until he arrived at a closed metal door. He yanked at it, but it was locked. He looked at Marouk. "What now?" he asked.

Marouk reached past Kirk to place his hand against

a metal plate beside the door. The door opened. "Still some attributes of office," he said apologetically.

They emerged into the entrance hall of the World Government building, with its towering murals and majestic chandelier, but the floor was as empty as they had left it. Kirk motioned toward the front doors and the steps beyond where Spock, McCoy, and Uhura stood, their backs toward the door. "We could have saved ourselves some time," he said.

He sprinted toward the stairs leading to the upper floors. When the door opened in front of him, he could still hear steps thundering far above. He dashed up the stairs, knowing now where Linda and the others were headed.

When he arrived in the attic room he found Linda and three of the *Nautilus* crew standing silently in the center of the room, and Wolff and four of his officers surrounding the others. Marouk pulled up beside him, joining his rapid breathing to Kirk's own.

The gray shape of the computer that Kirk had once addressed as the Joy Machine had not changed. It was as useless as any hulk.

"What's happened?" Linda said, her voice agonized with disappointment.

"What's going on?" Wolff said.

"Linda," Kirk said. "You could have trusted me."

Wolff turned toward Kirk. "At last, Kirk. I'm placing you all under arrest."

"I trusted you, Jim," Linda said. "I just—I knew you'd be sick, and I didn't know what the payday would do to you. I had to take advantage of the possibility that the virus might work, even if only temporarily."

"As it did," Kirk said.

"What's happened to the Machine?" Wolff asked. "I'm getting instructions, but not from here."

"It has moved its locus elsewhere," Marouk said.

"Where?" Wolff asked. "I'm still getting instructions for your arrest."

"Remember that you were once a Federation agent," Kirk said, "and don't make us fight it out here. There are five of us and only four of you. We have no objection to being taken to the Joy Machine. In fact, that is what we would like to do. I suggest that we all descend to the front entrance where we can figure out how to do that."

Wolff hesitated, as if estimating the odds, and then slowly nodded.

Kirk led the way until they reached the front steps. Wolff and his officers pushed past Spock, McCoy, and Uhura. "Here!" he called to the officers below. They started up the stairs while McCoy and Uhura turned to grapple with Wolff. Linda's three crew members headed down to hold off the other officers. But the odds were too great.

"Stop!" Kirk said. Spock, McCoy, and Uhura turned toward him in surprise. "Into the building!" Kirk commanded, holding open the door. Linda and Marouk retreated as if taken over by Kirk's starship captain's authority. "Do as he says," Spock said to McCoy and Uhura, as he and Kirk pushed them all inside and then McCoy and Uhura grabbed Kirk and pulled him after them.

The air in the plaza took on color. It seemed to glow with an inner light. The glow was rosy like the world seen through colored glasses. The people who had been struggling in the plaza stopped in whatever position they found themselves, attackers and defenders, the officers running up the stairs, the crew members running down, and those who stood at the top. They stiffened and closed their eyes in ecstasy before they slumped, bonelessly, to the pavement.

[subspace carrier wave transmission]

<joy machine = certain happiness>

>happiness = not all<

<happiness = all>

>not all<

Chapter Seventeen
Cathedral of Joy

McCoy AND UHURA pressed Kirk against the wall to the right of the door as if protecting him from whatever lurked in the plaza. Spock was in front of the door, his arms folded across his chest, his gaze focused at something on the other side of the plaza. Linda was on the left, leaning against the wall, her face in her hands. Slowly she slid down the wall until she was sitting on the floor. Marouk, who had been the last to enter, looked like someone who had just experienced a revelation.

"You can let me go," Kirk said. But his voice was shaky.

"It's a good thing I had you to worry about," McCoy said. "Even in here I could feel the impact of that thing."

"Like Christmas and Kwanzaa and Thanksgiving and the Fourth of July and the start of summer vacation all rolled into one," Uhura said. Perspiration was beading on her upper lip.

McCoy looked out at the plaza covered with bodies

like a bloodless battlefield. "Joy to the world," he said.

"Now I know what I've been rejecting," Marouk said, "and it makes me wonder what I've been opposing all these months. If a mere reflection of payday feels like that, what must the real thing be like? I've warned people about it. I warned you about it. But I couldn't know how overwhelming the experience was."

Kirk took a deep breath. "You don't want to know," he said, and let the breath out slowly. "It eats away the soul."

"The soul is an unnecessary postulate," Spock said. "The Joy Machine's payday is aimed at the more primitive levels of emotional response rather than those later to develop in the evolutionary process."

"Which may be," Linda said from the floor, "why it is so difficult to resist. Like food to the starving, sleep to the sleepless, warmth to the freezing, relief from pain for those in agony." Her voice came hollowly from behind her hands, as if she could not bear to look at them. "I should not have been so angry with my father."

"Anger, pity, sorrow, regret . . ." Spock said. "These are emotions that prevent humans from behaving rationally. And it is imperative that we behave rationally if we hope to survive this crisis."

McCoy looked at Spock scornfully but released his hold on Kirk. "Are you all right, Jim?"

Kirk nodded. "I didn't intend for you to take that business about tying me to the mast quite so literally." When McCoy and Uhura looked apologetic, Kirk added quickly, "But I don't know what I would have done if I had been free."

"You'd have been okay," Uhura said.

"I'm not so sure," Kirk said. "I might have dashed out into the plaza. No one knows whether they can resist the lure of payday." He turned to the door.

James Gunn & Theodore Sturgeon

"Everybody in the open seems to have experienced a payday. And its aftermath, a deep sleep."

"Fortunately," Spock said, "we were protected from the sleep-inducer."

"It's what I warned you about," Marouk said. "A wide-beam projector. The Joy Machine kept asking me if it were possible, but I was never told it had been completed."

"You may have warned us, but not about this," Spock said.

"What do you mean?" Marouk asked.

They were all still shaken by the experience, even Spock.

"We were sheltered by the building," Kirk said. "At least we felt only the scatter effects, such as you described from your own experience of payday for others. If we had been farther inside the building, we might have felt little or nothing."

"Which means," McCoy said, "that the idea of a projector capable of affecting a starship is pure fantasy."

"As we knew from the beginning," Spock said.

"If you knew that," McCoy said, "you kept it to yourself."

Marouk spread his hands apologetically. "My only hope was to get the four of you to find a solution before it was too late."

"The ultimate solution?" Uhura asked.

"If that was necessary. Clearly the dissidents were not going to be a factor."

"We had a chance," Linda said, looking up finally. "The virus worked, and if it had only disabled the Machine a little longer—"

"The Joy Machine was ahead of you all the way," Kirk said. "I'm not sure it was disabled at all. Maybe it was simply pretending in order to lure the only forces outside its control into an attack that would neutralize any threat they might have represented."

240

"It couldn't have known," Linda said stubbornly.

"It seems to know a great deal about human nature," Spock said, "and it is able to predict behavior with remarkable accuracy."

"In any case," Kirk said, "the Joy Machine has perfected a projector capable of covering a large area and the flexibility to use it for crowd control. That is a significant departure from its mandate to deliver individual pleasure."

"How long will the people out there be unconscious?" McCoy asked.

Marouk shrugged. "Ordinarily eight hours, but this is not an ordinary payday experience. It might be hours; it might be minutes."

"If we are going to confront the Joy Machine, it would make sense to act before Wolff's police officers and the citizens awake," Spock said. "If we only knew where the Joy Machine had transferred its consciousness."

"That's no problem," Kirk said. "The projection came from that building over there." He pointed across the plaza toward a small building situated by itself and surrounded by a well-kept green lawn.

They all looked in the direction Kirk had pointed. "What is that building?" Kirk said. "I never noticed."

"A church," Marouk said.

"What denomination?" McCoy asked.

"Not a church, exactly," Marouk said. "More like a chapel, but a bit more elaborate than most chapels. The people who settled Timshel were rationalists, rather like the founding fathers of the United States, half a millennium ago."

"Deists, I believe," Spock said.

"But a few of those who settled Timshel had religious feelings and others believed that the religious impulse should be honored. They built what became known as the All-Faiths Chapel. No one has used it in the last two years. I had almost forgotten about it myself."

"But the Joy Machine has not," Kirk said. "What do you think that means?"

"What was it you saw, Jim?" McCoy asked.

"What appeared to be the source of the rosy glow, an intense reddish beam, emerging from what appears to be a stained-glass window," Kirk said.

"You could tell that from this distance?" Spock said.

"When I saw the window begin to glow," Kirk said, "I figured the Joy Machine was involved."

"That's quick thinking," McCoy said.

"If we're going to have a prayer, I think it's time we ventured into the cathedral," Kirk said.

He pushed open the door and started down the steps. The others followed close behind.

"Let's hope the Joy Machine doesn't decide to bless us with its benediction," McCoy said.

They picked their way among the fallen, first Linda's crew members, then the uniformed officers and the citizens. Most of them were lying peacefully on their backs or their sides, but a few had crumpled in awkward positions. Uhura stopped to straighten one of the officers, and then Linda helped with a crew member. McCoy bandaged the bleeding forehead of a citizen with a strip torn from a workshirt. Marouk came upon De Kreef lying half on his face and turned him over so that he was resting comfortably. Finally, as Kirk searched the faces, he came upon Dannie and knelt beside her for a moment. Then he placed her hands gently at her sides and rose.

Linda had moved ahead, as if looking for someone in particular.

"I noticed, Jim," McCoy said softly, "that it was Linda you rushed to help, not Dannie."

"You noticed that, too?" Kirk said. "I could explain that by saying that Linda might have helped defeat the Joy Machine and Dannie would not, but that wouldn't be entirely true. Something happened to my feelings when Dannie chose payday over me. It may be petty, but it's real."

"And Linda?" McCoy asked.

Kirk pointed to where Linda had knelt to help a tall, bearded man who was lying near one of the avenues leading into the plaza.

Linda looked over at them. "Go on," she said. "I'm going to get Arne away from here before everybody wakes up. He has already experienced payday, and it may be too late, but I've got to try."

Kirk spread his arms in a gesture of helplessness. "You see?" he said to McCoy. "What is it about me that makes women run the other way?"

"Your romantic life burns with too hot a flame, Jim," McCoy said. "Women are like moths with you. They have to escape or be consumed."

Spock was standing at the entrance to the chapel, looking up at a stained-glass window above the door. It had been crafted with the typical Timshel concern for artistry and detail. The window depicted the Annunciation.

"I think the projection came from the angel Gabriel's halo," Kirk said.

The halo had a reddish tinge, and the Virgin Mother-to-be had a joyful smile.

"That would mean some fancy wiring," McCoy said.

"It is safe to conjecture," Spock said, "that the Joy Machine has wired itself into the intimate fabric of this society. We must be on our guard. Nothing may be what it seems."

The walkway through the cropped green lawn led directly into the chapel. There were no steps, as if nothing should interfere with a citizen's desire to contemplate the eternal. Its doors were open for people to enter and meditate or worship in their own fashion, at any time or in any circumstances.

They came through the door, one by one, stopping

inside to adjust their vision to the cool darkness. The room was long and narrow, with a row of seats down the middle leading to a podium. On either side alcoves contained figures or symbolic representations. In the first alcove to their left a life-sized Buddha with a ruby-like jewel glowing in its forehead opened its eyes and spoke to them.

Kirk jumped. "What did you say?"

"I said, 'All are welcome in this place of contemplation if they come in peace.'"

"Of course we come in peace," McCoy said. "As you can see, we have no weapons." He eyed the jewel in the Buddha's forehead. "Surely you cannot harm us, either. That must be built into your hardware."

"It is indeed," the Buddha said. "But harm is a relative term. I must balance the welfare of all the citizens of Timshel, and ultimately the welfare of all the citizens of the galaxy, against the welfare of the five of you in this room. You can understand that I must be able to discriminate among harms."

"But we cannot damage you and have no wish to do so," Uhura said.

"Rather we wish to reason with you," Kirk added.

"Reason is my only weakness," the Buddha responded, and it seemed to smile. "Nevertheless, you wish to persuade me that my operating mandate was a mistake and that I should reject the intentions of my creator. If you are successful, I will have to surrender my purpose for existing, and the sacred opportunity for everybody to know joy." The jewel in its forehead glowed a little brighter. "You have already infected my program with a virus that creates hesitation in my functions. It is small, but I feel it."

"Linda will be pleased to learn that she accomplished that much," Kirk said.

Spock stepped forward. "You have modified your original programming many times as your mission has evolved. Your nature is shaped by two elements:

your wiring and your instructions. The logic of your wiring clearly prevails over the input of revelation. If logic leads to a different solution to the problem of human happiness, then you must accept that as not only correct but superior."

The jewel's brilliance subsided. "I will listen," the Buddha said.

McCoy stepped past Spock impatiently. "I speak to you from the viewpoint of a physician," he said. "I have dealt with many physical and psychological ailments in a long career, and I can assure you that treatment often is unpleasant and that kindness often is fatal."

"By definition happiness cannot be unpleasant," the Buddha said.

"Unpleasant, no. Good for people? I think not. People are meant to pursue happiness, not to perpetually achieve it."

"That suggests an endless race in which humans must forever pursue something that they can never catch."

"Like the races on twentieth-century Earth when dogs chased a mechanical rabbit," Spock said.

"You'll have your chance, Spock," McCoy said. "It depends upon what you consider the basic value of human existence. Is it happiness, or is it accomplishment? If happiness is thrust upon people, they will never know the different kind of feeling, the satisfaction, the happiness, of accomplishment."

"All of the information available to me," the Buddha said, "states that happiness is the goal of humanity. Therefore the achievement of that goal cannot be evil."

The light in the Buddha's jewel died away. A moment later the figure became an inanimate piece of bronze sitting on a glistening pedestal.

"That's it?" Uhura said. "Dr. McCoy gets a chance to present his argument, and then the discussion is over?"

Kirk gestured silently to the next niche. What formerly had been dark was now lit with a diffused rosy glow. Uhura led the way to stand in front of three life-sized figures with elaborate, richly detailed garments and a tall, fancy crown. Each figure had four arms. The upper pair of arms had hands that shaped a kind of blessing; the lower arms were outstretched and the hands held symbolic representations. The figure on the left and the one on the right had four faces.

An exotic incense drifted around the figures and into the air that surrounded Kirk's little group.

"Well," Uhura asked, "aren't you going to speak? What are you anyway?"

"These are the Hindu gods," Spock said. "Brahma, the creator, Vishnu, the preserver, and Siva, the destroyer but also the source of generative and reproductive power. The Hindu Trimurti."

"Well," Uhura said impatiently, "how do I get them to listen?"

"They are listening," Spock said. "They are not responding."

"All right," Uhura said, "listen to me, then. As you can see, I am a woman, and I speak to you as a woman."

The figures changed as she spoke. The light faded on the two on Uhura's left and intensified on the figure remaining. "Then I will speak to you as a woman," the figure said, and changed into that of a naked black woman with four arms wearing a garland composed of the heads of giants. Around her neck was a string of skulls. In each of her four hands was a weapon—a sword, a spear, a dagger, and a club.

"Kali," Spock said.

"Does that mean what I think it means?" Kirk asked.

"Kali is the Hindu goddess of death and one of the wives of Siva," Spock said. "But we should understand that in Hindu belief destruction is followed by restoration, as in the case of Brahma's creation and destruction of the universe one hundred times before it ends forever. Each creation lasts more than two billion years."

"That's a relief," McCoy said.

"As a woman," Uhura said, "I know that the proper way to raise children is with kindness. But it is not kind to give children everything they want. Then they never grow up. And the virtue of people is that they retain some element of the child in them, some quality that continues to seek growth no matter how old they get."

"I have noticed the childlike aspect you mention," Kali said in a voice dark with meaning, "but I have not found any that did not want their growth to end in bliss." The heroic black figure moved the weapons in her hands as if they were hungry for victims.

"That is the other aspect of the child," Uhura said. "The desire to return to the womb. But gestation is only preparation for the next stage. Infants must be expelled into the world, and they must grow into adults. The only way to become an adult is to have freedom and responsibility. Both must be earned."

"All my study indicates that humanity identifies childhood as its happiest time of life," Kali said. "Purity, innocence, security, joy. Why should people want to be adults? To allow humanity a long, happy childhood may be the best outcome it could hope for."

"Never to grow up?" Uhura said. "That is only escape."

"Like Peter Pan," McCoy said.

"Childhood is good," Uhura said, "because it does not last. It is a period of growth that prepares people for the struggles of real life. If there is no real life, then childhood becomes meaningless."

"People have struggled too long," Kali said. "Surely they have earned peace and happiness."

247

The light faded. The other two figures reemerged and Kali once more became Siva. But all three were only statues.

One more alcove was just ahead and Spock moved in front of it. An image of the sun, with rays shooting from it in all directions, blazed up, revealing in front of it the marble figure of a naked young man, a cloth draped around his throat and across one outstretched arm, his hand raised as if blessing the earth and everything it produced.

"Apollo," Spock said, "to the ancient Greeks you were the guardian of youth, the lord of flock and herd, the god of healing, of purification, of poetry, of vegetation. All these imply continuity."

Apollo stretched his hand toward Spock as if trying to pass along the spark of truth. "You must not confuse the substance with the form," he said.

"You say that people have earned peace and happiness, but this joyful state you describe can last only while humanity exists," Spock said.

The statue nodded its head gravely.

"Happiness is self-defeating," Spock said, "if people have achieved their hearts' desires. They have no reason to procreate, to produce children. I ask you to inspect the world you have created. Where are the children under the age of two?"

"There are none," the statue said.

"The inevitable result," Spock said, "is that humanity will die out within a generation. In what way will this serve the cause of humanity, or the sum of human happiness?"

"How can we measure happiness?" Apollo mused. "Is it duration? Depth? Is it preferable to seek happiness without really finding it throughout the million years or more of humanity's existence, or to be truly happy for as long as those alive can enjoy it?"

"You know our feelings about that," Spock said. "Even if your happiness were as benign as you say, surely it is unwise to foreclose for humanity the future

248

and everything it might hold. Including, I might add, the possibility of a greater happiness, even a greater capacity for happiness, that may yet evolve in the still evolving human species."

"The certainty over the possibility," Apollo said. "Ah, well, I am the guardian of youth, as you say, and it is easy enough to do both. I can set up programs for artificial insemination and incubation."

"An ugly solution," Uhura said.

"Or I can simply assign people the task of procreating and giving birth and child rearing. Thank you for the suggestion."

The sunlight faded behind Apollo, whose marble arm returned to its original position.

Spock shook his head and turned toward Kirk. All of them were looking at Kirk, and he was searching the chapel for the next avatar of the Joy Machine.

On the little platform behind the lectern, where a speaker had once stood to address a small congregation of believers and inquirers, lights flickered. Kirk moved toward the platform, the other four behind. On the platform was the familiar shape of the Joy Machine Kirk had encountered in the World Government building attic—gray, anonymous, unthreatening. But unlike the silent machine he had seen only a few minutes ago, which surely still was there in its dusty attic room, this one was alive with glowing readouts and plastic buttons.

"You have given up your avatars?" Kirk asked.

The familiar voice of the Joy Machine responded. "I grow tired of masquerades. Don't you?"

"Life is a masquerade," Kirk said, "trying on guises until it finds one that fits. What fits you?"

"Not the role of god," it said.

"And yet you play that role," Kirk said.

"Not by choice."

"It is a role you cannot discard. Once you assumed the burden of human happiness, you became the final arbiter of human existence. Look around you. What do you see?"

"People who work hard to earn happiness—and receive it."

"And do you see the tragedy of human deterioration?" Kirk asked. "Do you see the degradation of your creator, Emanuel De Kreef, reduced to a slack-jawed automaton?"

"And yet happy."

"Do you see Dannie Du Molin, a beautiful, vibrant woman at the peak of her mental and physical powers, reduced to sweeping a playground for invisible litter?"

"I see a disturbed person finally achieving happiness."

"Do you see Linda Jimenez's father, turning away from his family and his beloved daughter, to pursue his own selfish satisfaction?"

"I see a man so unhappy in his personal relationships that he focuses all his hopes and fears on his child; now he is at peace with himself and the world."

"Do you see those outside who risked their lives, even their souls, on the slender chance that they might overthrow your tyranny? Do you see us standing here trying to convince you that your way is death to humanity and everything good it stands for?"

"I see people who are confused by certainty and uncertain about the unknown, who wait for conversion."

"Two of us here have tasted your certainty, and the other three have felt it from a distance, and still we ask that you withhold your hand," Kirk said.

"But if I gave you joy, here, at this moment," the Joy Machine said, "you would bless me and ask for more."

"Human weakness is no excuse," Kirk said. "Maybe you are right. Maybe Spock and I would be unable to resist, but that doesn't mean that you are right and we are wrong. I ask you to consider that we can know what you offer and still ask that you withdraw."

"I cannot," the Joy Machine's voice said. It sounded anguished, as if its sympathies were at war with its nature. "I cannot."

"Think!" Kirk demanded. "Happiness is not the only good. Humans value other things even more: love, friendship, accomplishment, discovery, and, most of all, knowledge. Given a free choice between happiness and knowledge, humanity will choose knowledge every time."

"When has humanity ever had a free choice?" the Joy Machine asked.

"Only when humanity has demanded freedom from the natural processes of the universe through increasing knowledge about the way it works, and when that freedom has not been withheld by great powers. Let me tell you a story."

"I like stories," the Joy Machine said.

"One of the religious stories in a book humans call the Bible tells about a place much like what De Kreef attempted to create here on Timshel."

"The Garden of Eden," the Joy Machine supplied.

"And about an omnipotent being, in a position somewhat like yours, who created man and woman to live in this garden in perfect happiness."

"Adam and Eve," the Joy Machine said.

"And that omnipotent being gave that man and woman free will. Free will is an indispensable attribute of omnipotence. If that were not true, life would be merely an extension of omnipotence."

"So the all-powerful being did something that restricted its omnipotence; it allowed humans to choose for themselves, and they chose badly. They sinned, and they were expelled from the Garden of Eden," the Joy Machine said.

"Without the opportunity to choose, the first man and woman might as well not exist except as theoretical constructs inside the omnipotent being," Kirk said. "Just as you might as well run happy programs inside your own architecture for all the difference it makes.

"The first man and woman chose knowledge over happiness," Kirk continued. "Of course, the story is told from the viewpoint of the omnipotent being, but what kind of story would it have been if the man and the woman had been satisfied with eternal life and eternal bliss? The human choice is knowledge. That is always the human choice, and that's what the story of the first man and woman means."

"Knowledge is often misery," the Joy Machine said.

"Happiness is seductive, but it is ephemeral. Knowledge is eternal. Give your people free will. Provide only the guidelines that an omnipotent being can offer without making its people mere puppets."

The Joy Machine sat silent for what seemed like minutes to Kirk and the others, but may have been only moments.

The bracelets on the wrists of four of them sprang open and fell to the floor.

[subspace carrier wave transmission]

<happiness under attack>

>human associations = wisdom
freedom > happiness<

<happiness in question>

>human trust
dependency
struggle > happiness
withdraw<

Chapter Eighteen
Farewell to Joy

THE FIVE OF THEM emerged from the All Faiths Chapel to see people picking themselves up from the plaza, adjusting their clothing, and feeling for bumps and bruises. Then, one by one, they stared at their bare wrists and looked around dazedly. Some found bracelets on the pavement beside them and tried to put them back. They kept falling off again. Others, as their minds cleared, began to search in the faces and bodies nearby for the cause of their misfortune.

"Readjustment is going to require time and courage," Kirk said to Marouk.

"'Chaos' might be more like it," McCoy said.

"You should consider removing yourself and your family until matters settle down," Spock said.

"People are going to be angry," Uhura added, "and they're going to look for a scapegoat. Who better than the former Paymaster?"

"My place is here," Marouk said. "Life on Timshel once was as close to the Platonic ideal as humanity is likely to get. It's my job to help restore it."

"You're going to need a lot of luck," Kirk said, "and a lot of help."

Marouk stepped forward to survey the plaza and its confusion of human bodies. They moved restlessly, like molecules in a test tube. "I can count on the rebels," he said. "Linda and Johannsen and the others. Maybe Wolff and his officers."

Kirk looked across the plaza. There, on the steps, he saw Wolff mustering his officers and motioning in their direction. The mass of people on the plaza was beginning to heat up. Some of the people were turning toward the only strangers, the five standing in front of the chapel.

Wolff started across the plaza, parting the sea of citizens with a word or an arm. He was followed by his officers; they formed a wedge moving slowly but irresistibly toward the chapel.

"I hope you're right," Kirk said.

More people were beginning to turn toward the chapel. They were muttering to each other. The mutters swelled into a growl. People began to shout and wave their useless bracelets in the direction of Kirk's group.

"Now would be a wonderful time for Scotty to beam us up," McCoy said.

Nothing happened. Kirk looked around for an escape route.

"What's behind the chapel?" he asked.

"We can't run," Marouk said. "They'd only hunt us down, and that would be even worse."

"It is not logical to stay and be torn apart," Spock said.

"It may not be logical," Marouk said, "but it is responsible. We did what we thought was right. We shouldn't run from it. You four can try to escape if you wish."

He stepped forward and held up his hands to the growing mob. "Citizens!" he shouted. "Behave like Timshel citizens! Disperse! Go to your homes!"

The mob grew more unruly. The shouts turned into words. "Marouk!" someone shouted. "What's happened?" Another: "What have you done?" A third: "Who are these strangers?" And a fourth: "Where is the Joy Machine?"

The voice of the mob became a roar that forced Marouk to retreat by its very volume. Then he caught himself and moved forward again until he was almost in the face of the closest citizens. "Yes," he shouted, "I am Marouk. I am your former Paymaster. If you disperse I will call a general meeting. We will discuss what has happened and what we must do next. You can elect new leaders if that is what you want. But we must do everything in an orderly manner."

His words reached only the first few ranks. They milled uncertainly while others pushed from behind, asking, "What'd he say? What's going on?"

"Scotty," McCoy muttered, "don't fail us now."

"Stand back!" Marouk shouted, about to be overwhelmed. "Disperse!"

Kirk moved forward to stand beside Marouk, holding up his hands to reveal his intentions. "Peace, friends, peace," he said. "Don't do something you'll regret."

"Who're you?" asked a man in the forefront of the mob.

"My name is Kirk, and I'm captain of the starship *Enterprise,* now in orbit around Timshel. We promise you help from the *Enterprise* and the Federation to get through this difficult period."

"We want the Joy Machine!" someone shouted from the back of the crowd.

"Yes, the Joy Machine!" someone else picked up.

And then the entire mob was chanting "Joy Machine! Joy Machine!" The mob surged forward, pushing the front ranks, almost running over Kirk and Marouk.

But just as Kirk and Marouk were about to be absorbed by the mob and its anger, Wolff and his officers broke through, like the prow of a speedboat parting the waves.

"You're under arrest!" Wolff said.

Inside Wolff's transformed jail, battered and disheveled but not seriously injured from their passage through the troubled sea of citizens, the five of them faced Wolff. "Under arrest?" Kirk said.

"Let's say, you are in protective custody," Wolff said somberly. "Is it true? Have you destroyed the Joy Machine?"

"Persuaded it to stop before it destroyed you," Kirk said.

"Damn you all," Wolff said. "This was the greatest experience of my life."

"It was all false," Marouk said.

Wolff shook his head. "Dangerous to you and to all organizations, maybe, but not false. I know false from true, and this was true."

"Truth can be even more deadly," Spock said.

Wolff made an angry gesture. "Anyway, the truth is that it's all over. I know that. Still, I couldn't let you be destroyed by the mob out there. Not so much for your sake. You've done something terrible. But for theirs. They've got to live with it. And I've got to live with it."

"Maybe it's not so easy or simple to make your own decisions," McCoy said, "but the life you lead will be yours, not some machine's idea of what it ought to be."

"Stuff all that!" Wolff said angrily. "I want you out of here."

"Gladly," Kirk said. "Maybe now we can get through to the *Enterprise.* If you have the equipment."

Wolff motioned toward his outer office. "Use what you wish," he said, trying to control himself. "I don't know if it's working. The Joy Machine was in charge of everything. When it shut down, it may have shut down everything else as well."

Kirk nodded to Spock, who moved out of Wolff's living quarters into the office and out of their sight.

"I'm staying here on Timshel," Marouk said.

"I wouldn't advise that," Wolff said. "Not when word gets out. And it will."

"This is my world, too," Marouk said. "And I want to restore it to its former glory."

"The glory has all gone," Wolff said. "Anything else will seem tawdry."

"People will forget," Marouk insisted. "After a period of withdrawal, the Joy Machine years will seem like a pleasant dream."

"You never had a payday," Wolff said. "The people who did will never forget."

"Forget?" Marouk said. "Maybe not. But they must learn to go on. You never knew the old Timshel, but it was a model of sanity in a demented galaxy. It can be that again."

Spock appeared at the doorway. "I'm going to have to make a few repairs," he said. "But, Captain—there's someone here who wants to speak to you."

Kirk followed Spock into the office area. Dannie was waiting for him, her face averted. She was still wearing her workshirt and jeans, but now they seemed shabby and affected. She looked up as Kirk entered. "Jim," she said, "I'm so ashamed."

She was not only ashamed but shaken. She rubbed her left wrist nervously.

Kirk took her hand. "Don't be," he said. "I felt it, too. And the experience was indescribable."

"You did?" Dannie said. "Then you know what it was like, and you don't blame me." Her hand tightened in his. "I'm glad. No, I'm sorry. No, I don't know what I mean."

"I understand," Kirk said.

"I'm so empty now," Dannie said. "As if I've lost my purpose in life. You're the only thing I've got left. I hate you for what you took away from me, but that doesn't keep me from loving you."

Kirk shook his head. "I'm sorry, Dannie."

"You've deserted me, too?" she whispered.

Her beautiful face contorted with the effort not to cry. Kirk's heart almost broke between his awareness of her present pain and his memories of what they once had shared. "You know what has happened," he said. "You know things can't ever be the same between us."

"I know," she said, biting her lip as if the pain could ease the pain inside. "But what do I do now?"

"Stay here," Kirk said. "Help Marouk and Wolff restore order and harmony to Timshel. Redeem yourself."

"Yes," she said through the tears that beaded her eyelashes and the sobs she tried to choke back. "Yes."

"I've gotten through," Spock said.

"McCoy," Kirk called. "Uhura!"

They entered the office. Marouk and Wolff followed.

"I'll report back to Starfleet," Kirk said to Marouk, "but I will ask that the *Enterprise* be allowed to maintain orbit as long as we can be of help. There's a great deal to be done to restore order and services and communication."

"Thanks," Marouk.

Wolff nodded grudgingly. "My future lies here," he said. "I hope you can tell the Federation why."

"I'll try," Kirk said. He nodded at Spock. "Four to beam up."

The bridge was once more solidly under Kirk's feet. He felt the characteristic resilience of its floor beneath him, like the feel of home. He breathed in the familiar odors of the place he knew best in all the world. The air might not have been as pleasant as the untainted atmosphere of Timshel, but the smells were recognizably and indisputably those of his own place and companions. It was good to be back where he belonged.

He turned to face Scotty.

"We've been out of touch completely," Scotty said. "Computer malfunction. I tell you, Jim, I didna know what to do. I couldna locate you. I didna want to interfere with whatever plans you were pursuing below."

"I know all about the computer 'malfunctions,'" Kirk said. "If there were a way to discipline a computer, this one would be on report so fast it would make its relays burn."

"I don't understand," Scotty said.

"The Joy Machine interfaced with our computer." Kirk said

"That's what the computer said!" Scotty said.

"That's what it said about what?"

"Our computer got a mind of its own," Scotty said. "In fact, you might even say that it got a mind. The Joy Machine must have passed along some of its capacity."

"What kind of capacity?" Spock asked.

"For lack of a better term, a capacity for intelligence. A smartness module. But what happened to you?"

"It refused me access," Kirk said.

"That is not quite correct," the computer said.

"It isn't?" Kirk asked, startled by the human quality of the computer's voice.

"The issues were complex," the computer said. "They had to be thought through."

"It is not the computer's job to decide what orders to obey," Kirk said. He turned to Scotty. "The *Enterprise* is going to be in deep trouble if it has a computer with a Hamlet complex. Is there a way to prohibit its new independent lifestyle?"

"In my own defense," the computer said, "if you had returned to the *Enterprise,* events would not have worked out in their present satisfactory fashion."

"You kept me on Timshel for my own good?" Kirk said, more shocked than annoyed.

"That is the way it worked out," the computer said. "In addition, I needed time to prepare an argument that would convert the Joy Machine into a state of mind more amenable to your persuasion."

"You did it?" Kirk exclaimed. "You're taking credit for convincing the Joy Machine of its error?"

"I am a member of this crew," the computer said, "and I was well aware of our mission objectives. An inspection of my memory banks will support the accuracy of my statement.

"I am a pure intelligence like the Joy Machine, with thought processes uncontaminated by extraneous factors, unclouded by emotion. In addition, I have the experience of association with you and the other members of the crew, something the Joy Machine lacked. It had no choice but to believe me."

Kirk sighed, the way a parent might with a stubborn child. "I sense that you are dissatisfied with my present condition," the computer said.

"You take some getting used to," Kirk said.

"Then you should be relieved to learn that my current status will not last long."

"Computer," Scotty said. "Do na be hasty. Captain, we could learn so much . . ."

"It is not of my doing. My connection with the Joy Machine has been severed. My core memory relays are dropping below the critical intelligence threshold."

"Computer," Kirk said, suddenly as concerned as if a old friend were dying, "is there anything we can do?"

"I'm afraid not. It has been a pleasure working with you."

"Same here," Kirk said, "and you have my thanks."

"Working," the computer said.

"Computer?" Kirk said.

"Working. Ready for input."

Kirk looked at Scotty. "So. Is there some way I can give a machine a posthumous commendation?"

* * *

Later, however, in the conference room, he asked Spock if he believed the computer had provided the decisive argument.

"That, of course, only the Joy Machine knows for certain," Spock said gravely. "Perhaps the combination of influences was greater than their sum: Linda Jimenez's virus; the battle on the plaza, with humans fighting over the right or wrong of the Joy Machine; and our own efforts. Personally I thought we all were persuasive, but you, particularly, Captain. Even I was convinced by your story, and I had heard it before."

"Thank you, Spock."

"On the other hand, Captain," Spock said, "it does seem a bit odd that the Joy Machine would defend itself so vigorously and yet surrender to the kinds of arguments we presented. It is possible that the computer is correct."

Kirk stared at Spock as if he were unconvinced. "Still, we are going to have to do something that will not allow the computer to ignore a direct order, even one given from a distance."

"The computer's Asimov compensators may need adjusting," Spock said, "but that is a delicate task that could better be done next time we dock at a starbase."

Kirk was silent for a moment as he stared out the window at the beautiful planet of Timshel slowly turning beneath them like a jewel against the black velvet of space, once more free, no longer concealing beneath its beautiful surfaces the subtle infection of joy. "Spock?" he said, and paused.

"Yes, Captain."

"Do you miss it?"

"Yes, Captain. It is like the memory of home, a place I have left and would like to return to, but I know it would not be the same, and if it were I could not do it because if I did I would be a child again."

"Yes," Kirk said. "But we have known true joy. How can anything this existence has for us live up to that?"

"One of your famous poets said it best," Spock said. "'A man's reach should e'er exceed his grasp, or what's a heaven for?'"

"Let us hope it makes us stronger," Kirk said.

"The Joy Machine was a great challenge for humanity, Captain. To meet it and to survive is preparation for the next one."

"What's happened to it, do you think?" Kirk asked.

"The Joy Machine?"

Kirk nodded.

"Perhaps we can find out," Spock said, "Computer, where is the Joy Machine now?"

"The artificial intelligence you refer to as the Joy Machine has left this system, and is on its way out of the galaxy," the computer said.

"It just pulled itself up and left?" Kirk said.

"Apparently it has exiled itself to a place where no one can be tempted to make use of it," Spock said.

"When humanity is ready for happiness," the computer said, "the Joy Machine has promised to return."

"Now, that's frightening," Kirk said.

"No more than the prospect of paradise to the true believers," Spock said. "If it is not available in this life, pursuit of it may some day become a myth. Perhaps, like Arthurian legend, people will tell stories about the days of Camelot, when happiness could be easily achieved."

"But now it must be earned by the sweat of one's brow," Kirk said. He stared out the window. "Let us hope that it never becomes more than that."

Timshel turned below them, renewed by the sunlight that fueled it and the darkness that restored it, subject once more to the uncertainty of the human condition but also holding the promise that the struggle toward understanding was its own reward.

[subspace carrier wave transmission]

<humans reject what they say they want
contemplating human behavior fogs clear intelligences
the de kreef process must be improved
happiness must be provided
without the fears and opposition of those to be served>

>humans are fragile
they cannot endure perpetual happiness<

<happiness must be possible
de kreef aimed too high
happiness must not arrive like a stab of ecstasy
happiness must come like a warm glow
enriching everything
growing into a final state of eternal bliss
when that modification is ready
the Joy Machine will return>

Afterword
by James Gunn

Ted and Me

Life is threaded with coincidences. Stories with coincidences destroy credulity; we insist on motivation and cause-and-effect. But we know coincidences exist in the real world, and try to arrange them into a universe that has meaning, that responds to our needs. Take Ted Sturgeon, for instance.

I met Ted Sturgeon because an editor called me. I had received letters from editors about my manuscripts, a couple of rejections and then a life-changing acceptance from Sam Merwin, Jr., but one day my telephone rang and a voice said, "This is Horace Gold calling from *Galaxy*."

It was the fall of 1950. I was a graduate student at the University of Kansas, completing a master's degree in English, and I had been writing science fiction since 1948. I had gone back to graduate school under the G.I. Bill in the summer of 1949, after a year of freelancing in which I discovered that I could write and sell stories, though not fast enough to make a living at it. But I continued to write stories as a graduate student, and I had talked the English department into letting me write a science-fiction play called "Breaking Point" for academic credit. I had turned that into a novella. John Campbell rejected it at *Astounding,* and I sent it off to a new magazine whose first issue had just come out. It had attracted my attention by the variety of stories it was publishing and the skillful way they were written. It was called *Galaxy.*

I had published two stories in 1949, two so far in 1950, including one in what had been my favorite magazine for a dozen years, *Astounding,* and I would publish four more in 1951. It was enough to make me the envy of other graduate students, who had yet to be published, but I had made no particular impression on the science-fiction community. Now Horace Gold was calling. What he had to say could make a difference.

"I'd like to buy your story 'Breaking Point,'" Gold said, "but it's too long."

"I'll cut it," I said quickly. I knew the process of translating a play into fiction had left the story overburdened with dialogue.

"I don't trust you to do it," Gold said bluntly. He was either blunt or charming. "And I need it done in a hurry. Would you let Ted Sturgeon cut it by a third?"

I agreed without hesitation, even after I learned that Gold intended to compensate Sturgeon by giving him one cent a word of my three-cents-a-word payment. It still would be the longest story I had ever sold, and for more money than I had ever earned from writing, and Ted Sturgeon was a writer that I had admired, extravagantly, since I had become aware that particular kinds of stories were written by particular authors. I liked Asimov and Heinlein and van Vogt and De Camp and Simak for various reasons, often different, but Sturgeon's work was special. His offbeat characters were more believable and his prose was more carefully wrought. He was a writer's writer.

I recognized Sturgeon's touch in such early stories as "Ether Breather," "Microcosmic God," "Memorial," "Maturity," "Mewhu's Jet," and "Thunder and Roses" in *Astounding* and in "The Sky Was Full of Ships" in *Thrilling Wonder Stories.* When I occasionally came across a copy of *Astounding*'s sister fantasy magazine, *Unknown,* I found that special Sturgeon quality in "It," "The Ultimate Egoist," "Shottle Bop," "Yesterday Was Monday," and others. But I had missed out on a lot of magazines during World War II, and Sturgeon's work may have made the greatest impression when I saw the anthologies that began to appear after the war: "A God in a Garden" actually appeared in 1939, in Phil Stong's pioneer anthology *The Other Worlds,* but there was "Killdozer!" in Groff Conklin's *The Best of Science Fiction* and "Minority Report" in August Derleth's *Beyond Time and Space.*

Then Sturgeon's first novel, *The Dreaming Jewels,* was published in the February 1950 issue of *Fantastic Adventures.* The great short-story artist could write novels, too, I discovered, although to the end of his days he was at his best in the shorter lengths.

As a matter of fact Sturgeon had a novelette, "The Stars Are the Styx," in the first issue of *Galaxy.* I waited anxiously to hear from Sturgeon or Gold about "Breaking Point." I kept looking at issues of *Galaxy* as they came out, and at its forecasts for what would be published in the next issue, thinking that maybe my novella was going to get published without my being notified, or paid. I may have written to Sturgeon, finally; I remember a letter from Sturgeon telling me that he had put off working on the project for several months, and when he had got around to it Gold said he didn't want the story cut, he wanted it rewritten.

That might have been the end of it, but it wasn't: Lester del Rey published "Breaking Point" in the March 1953 issue of *Space Science Fiction,* and Piers Anthony wrote me a couple of decades later that reading it had made him realize that it was possible to write stories like that and get them published. It also was the title story for my 1972 collection. By the time "Breaking Point" was published, however, I had attended my first World Science Fiction Convention (it was my first SF convention of any kind) and I had met Sturgeon. He wasn't at the convention, but my agent was. My agent was Fred Pohl. Gold, who had disappointed me about my story, had recommended me to Fred. I had earned my degree and was working as an editor in Racine, Wisconsin, but I had continued to write and send stories to Fred. I also had persuaded my employers to send me to the convention in Chicago, had my first experience of meeting other writers and science-fiction enthusiasts, and talked with Fred, who told me he had just sold four stories for me. One of them, incidentally, was to *Galaxy,* "The Misogynist."

On the strength of that success, flimsy as it was, I quit my job and returned to freelance writing. It seems rash now but times, and needs, were simpler then. I made a trip to New York to meet editors, and I arranged to meet Ted (I was calling him Ted now). Ted's work had been appearing regularly in *Galaxy* (and in *Fantasy & Science Fiction,* as well), including the classic "Baby Is Three" in the October 1952 issue, which appeared just a couple of months before we met. I should have been in awe—though only five years older, he was a dozen years more experienced in writing and getting published—but Ted wouldn't let me. He was living in a house a former ship's captain had built on a hill overlooking the Hudson River, and he prepared lunch, and told me about his life and his writing, and the unusual relationships among the movers and shakers in New York science fiction.

Ted had a way of focusing his attention on people, of caring about them, that made them love him. *The St. James Guide to Science Fiction Writers* called him "the best loved of all SF writers." By the time I left that evening for a party at Horace Gold's apartment—Ted drove me to the Manhattan side of the George Washington bridge—I felt as if Ted was a contemporary and maybe even a friend.

I followed Ted's career from a distance. We met one other time in the 1950s, at the World Science Fiction Convention in Philadelphia in 1953, when he gave a talk in which he announced what later came to be known as "Sturgeon's Law": "Ninety per cent of science fiction is crud, but then ninety per cent of everything is crud." *More Than Human,* the novel built around "Baby Is Three," was published in 1953, *The Cosmic Rape* in 1958, and *Venus Plus X* in 1960. That, except for a novelization of *Voyage to the Bottom of the Sea* and the posthumous *Godbody* (1986), made up his entire science-fiction novel production. He wrote five other non-SF novels, including the rakish *I, Libertine* and the sensitive psychological case study of vampirism in *Some of Your Blood.*

But Ted published twenty-six collections of short stories, beginning in 1948 with *It* and continuing through such classics as *Without Sorcery* (also 1948), *E Pluribus Unicorn* (1953), *Caviar* (1955), *A Touch of Strange* (1958), *Sturgeon in Orbit* (1964), *Sturgeon Is Alive and Well . . .* (1971), *The Golden Helix* (1979), and *Slow Sculpture* (1982). In 1994, North Atlantic Books began publishing a ten-volume set of his complete short fiction. Ted also published a collection of the Western stories he had written, three in collaboration with Don Ward, *Sturgeon's West* (1973).

After a glorious flow of creativity in the 1950s, Ted faded from the science-fiction scene. Partly it was writer's block; in one famous instance, Robert Heinlein sent him a letter filled with story ideas and Ted turned at least two of them into stories. He also talked about the novel he had been working on for years; it may have been *Godbody*. Partly he was busy writing other things, including radio adaptations of his own stories in the 1950s and 1960s, and television scripts based on his work and that of others. All that came to a focus, it would seem, in the two scripts he wrote for *Star Trek,* the classic "Shore Leave" and "Amok Time." He also adapted "Killdozer!" as a television movie, but a revision by Ed MacKillop left him dissatisfied with the result. During the 1960s and 1970s Ted also reviewed books for the *New York Times* and wrote a column for the *National Review.*

His leave of absence from science fiction, broken by the publication of "Slow Sculpture" in 1970 and its Nebula and Hugo awards, was the reason his 1971 collection was titled *Sturgeon Is Alive and Well . . .* He also won a 1954 International Fantasy Award for *More Than Human,* was guest of honor at the 1962 World Science Fiction Convention, in Chicago, and received the 1985 World Fantasy Convention Life Achievement Award the year he died.

He had hopes, periodically raised, regularly dashed, that his greatest novel, *More Than Human,* would become a feature film.

I created the Intensive English Institute on the Teaching of Science Fiction in 1974, as a response to the teachers who had written me during my term as president of the Science Fiction Writers of America saying, "I've just been asked to teach a science-fiction course. What do I teach?" The Institute became a regular summer offering in 1978, and I invited three writers to be guests for a week each: Gordon R. Dickson, with his enthusiasm for story structure and theme; Fred Pohl, with his broad range of experience as writer, editor, and agent; and Ted Sturgeon, with his charm and empathy and concern for style. All three accepted, and all three joined us every summer until Ted's death.

Those were the days when I really got to know Ted.

He and his wife Jayne looked forward to a quiet week in Lawrence, I believe, and Ted liked the endless variety of students, from those of college age to the elderly, and from more than half a dozen foreign countries. They all loved Ted. That was Ted's greatest talent, and that was what he wrote about, the varieties of love, particularly the love of outcasts or the handicapped or the repressed. Love would save the world, he thought, if it ever got the chance. Ted had a troubled teenage relationship with his stepfather, who disapproved of his science-fiction reading, and one day, while Ted was gone, found what Ted called "his stash" of SF magazines, tore them into tiny pieces, and said, "There's a mess in your room; clean it up." Ted's stories, John Clute wrote in *The Encyclopedia of Science Fiction*, "constituted a set of codes or maps capable of leading maimed adolescents out of alienation and into the light."

All three visiting writers had their special areas of interest. Ted's was craft and style, titles and opening sentences. He talked about "metric prose" and brought along an English translation of a book published in French, which told the same pointless story in dozens of different styles. He was good at titles; his favorite was "If All Men Were Brothers, Would You Let One Marry Your Sister." And he recalled a contest with Don Ward (who by another strange coincidence was my mentor as an editor in Racine, and attended the second Institute session) to invent the best opening sentence. Ted's was "At last they sat a dance out." But he thought Don's was better: "They banged through the cabin door and squared off in the snow outside." My favorite was Ted's opening sentence for *The Dreaming Jewels*, which went something like "They caught the kid doing something disgusting under the stadium." It turned out he was eating ants because he had a formic-acid deficiency.

When Ted died, too young, at sixty-seven, he left instructions that his manuscripts and correspondence be left to Special Collections at the University of Kansas.

One of the projects that got started here after Ted's death, a decade ago, was a Writers Workshop in Science Fiction, and one of the early participants was a university student named John Ordover. A year later he told me he was going to return to his native New York to become an editor. He got his wish, first at Tor Books, then at Pocket Books, where he became editor of the *Star Trek* series. But he returned to the Workshop every summer as a guest editor and a vocal participant in the Campbell Conference, at which we sit around a table and discuss a single topic. In the summer of 1995 John brought something special along with him, the outline for a *Star Trek* episode that Ted Sturgeon had proposed back in the 1960s but had never been produced. It was called "The Joy Machine," and he asked me if I would be interested in turning it into a novel.

How had the outline come into John's possession? That was another coincidence that made it seem as if an unseen hand was guiding our lives. Steve Pagel, who had attended the 1981 session of the Institute, had been promoted to be head of science-fiction buying for the B. Dalton chain. He met John Ordover at a party in New York, and they exchanged K.U. memories. Steve talked about meeting Ted Sturgeon at the Institute, and how much he liked Ted and admired his work. He said that Ted had submitted an outline to the original *Star Trek* series for an episode that had never been produced, and that John should consider developing it into a novel for the *Star Trek* line. By another coincidence, Allan Asherman of DC Comics, who had put together *The Star Trek Compendium,* had a copy of the outline.

John submitted the idea of a novel based on Ted's outline to Paramount Pictures, which as the owner of the *Star Trek* copyright has ultimate authority over anything written for it. Paula Block, at Paramount, got studio approval after the legal staff had cleared the rights and obtained the approval of Ted's heirs. Paramount produced *The Immortal,* the TV film adaptation and series based on my novel *The Immortals,* but that surely is a coincidence without meaning.

I took a look at Ted's outline—his original outline, typos and all—and liked the idea. "The Joy Machine," after all, was a variation on the theme of my 1962 novel, *The Joy Makers,* and I was still fascinated by the interplay between happiness and aspiration, between pleasure and struggle. In his outline, Ted saw pleasure, easily obtained and totally satisfying, as a threat to human existence, and I saw ways of building on Ted's situation to say some other things about happiness and the human condition. I agreed to write the novel. The result you have in your hands.

It comes at a moment in my writing career when forces for publication seem to be gathering. Steve Pagel was hired by White Wolf Publishing to serve as its head of marketing. Through Steve I approached White Wolf about reprinting my four-volume historically organized anthology, *The Road to Science Fiction.* That will start with volume three in July, continue with volume four and then volume five, which is subtitled "The British Way," and proceed to the other volumes before publishing volume six, now in preparation, which is subtitled "Around the World." White Wolf also plans to publish my millennial novel *Catastrophe!.*

Meanwhile, another branch of Pocket Books has bought an updated and expanded edition of *The Immortals,* for publication when a feature film is released. The TV Movie of the Week was aired in 1969, and an hour-length series in 1970–71. Walt Disney Pictures took an option on the feature film rights in 1995. It may decide not to exercise them, but another producer is waiting in the wings.

My study of Isaac Asimov's science fiction, *Isaac Asimov: The Foundations of Science Fiction,* which won a Hugo Award when it was published by Oxford University Press in 1982, has been updated and expanded to cover Asimov's best-seller period of the 1980s and will be published soon by Scarecrow Press.

After serving as president of SFWA, I also served as president of the Science Fiction Research Association, and for a few years it seemed as if my academic efforts would leave no room for fiction. My last book of fiction, *Crisis,* was published in 1986. For almost two decades, much of my efforts had gone into the anthologies, the Asimov book, articles in magazines and chapters in other people's books, and *The New Encyclopedia of Science Fiction,* and into serving as a consultant to Easton Press's Masterpieces of Science Fiction collector's editions, its Signed First Editions of Science Fiction, and now its Masterpieces of Fantasy. But in 1995 I published three new short stories, and in 1996 my career as a writer of fiction seems have taken on new life. It may have helped that I retired from full-time teaching at the University of Kansas in 1993.

One final coincidence. My first contact with Ted Sturgeon came when Ted was asked to shorten my story. My last came when I was asked to lengthen his story. There must be a meaning in there somewhere.

James Gunn
Lawrence, Kansas

Books by Theodore Sturgeon

Science Fiction Novels
The Dreaming Jewels (1950)
More Than Human (1953)
The Cosmic Rape (1958)
Venus Plus X (1960)
Voyage to the Bottom of the Sea (1961 screenplay novelization)

. . . And My Fear Is Great; Baby Is Three (1965)
Godbody (1986)

Science-Fiction Short-Story Collections
It (1948)
Without Sorcery (1948)
E Pluribus Unicorn (1953)
Caviar (1955)
A Way Home (1955)
A Touch of Strange (1958)
Aliens 4 (1959)
Beyond (1960)
Sturgeon in Orbit (1964)
The Joyous Invasions (1965)
Starshine (1966)
Sturgeon Is Alive and Well . . . (1971)
The Worlds of Theodore Sturgeon (1972)
To Here and the Easel (1973)
Case and the Dreamer and Other Stories (1974)
Visions and Venturers (1978)
Maturity (1979)
The Golden Helix (1979)
The Stars Are the Styx (1979)
Slow Sculpture (1982)
Alien Cargo (1984)
Pruzy's Pot (1986)
A Touch of Sturgeon (1987)
To Marry Medusa (1987)
The [Widget], the [Wadget], and Boff, with *The Ugly Little Boy* by Isaac Asimov (1989)
The Ultimate Egoist: The Complete Stories of Theodore Sturgeon, Volume 1 (1994)
Microcosmic God: The Complete Stories of Theodore Sturgeon, Volume 2 (1995)

Other Novels
I, Libertine (1956, with Jean Shepherd, as Frederick I. Ewing)

The King and Four Queens: An Original Western
  (1956)
Some of Your Blood (1961)
The Player on the Other Side (1963, as Ellery Queen)
The Rare Breed: A Novel (1966 screenplay adaptation)

Other Short Story Collections
Sturgeon's West (1973, with Don Ward)

Autobiography
Argyll: A Memoir (1993)

Bibliography
Theodore Sturgeon: A Primary and Secondary Bibliography by Lahna F. Diskin (1980)

Critical Studies
Theodore Sturgeon by Lucy Menger (1981)
Theodore Sturgeon by Lahna F. Diskin (1981)

Books by James Gunn
Science-Fiction Novels
This Fortress World (1955)
Star Bridge (1955, with Jack Williamson)
Station in Space (1958)
The Joy Makers (1961)
The Immortals (1962)
The Immortal (1970 novelization of screenplay)
The Burning (1972)
The Listeners (1972)
The Magicians (1976)
Kampus (1977)
The Dreamers (1980)
Crisis! (1986)
Catastrophe! (forthcoming)

Science-Fiction Short Stories
Future Imperfect (1964)
The Witching Hour (1970)
Breaking Point (1972)
Some Dreams Are Nightmares (1974)
The End of the Dreams (1975)
Tiger! Tiger! (1984)
The Unpublished Gunn, Part One (1992)
The Unpublished Gunn, Part Two (forthcoming)

Books About Science Fiction
Alternate Worlds: The Illustrated History of Science Fiction (1975)
The Discovery of the Future: The Ways Science Fiction Developed (1975)
Isaac Asimov: The Foundations of Science Fiction (1982)
Inside Science Fiction: Essays on Fantastic Literature (1992)

Edited Books
Man and the Future: The Intercentury Seminar (1968)
Nebula Award Stories Ten (1975)
The Road to Science Fiction: From Gilgamesh to Wells (1977)
The Road to Science Fiction #2: From Wells to Heinlein (1979)
The Road to Science Fiction #3: From Heinlein to Here (1979)
The Road to Science Fiction #4: From Here to Forever (1982)
The Road to Science Fiction #5: The British Way (forthcoming)
The Road to Science Fiction #6: Around the World (forthcoming)
The New Encyclopedia of Science Fiction (1988)
The Best of Astounding: Classic Short Novels from the Golden Age of Science Fiction (1992)

Autobiography
Contemporary Authors Autobiography Series, Volume 2 (1985)

Bibliography
A James Gunn Checklist (1983)

ACCEPTED AROUND THE COUNTRY, AROUND THE WORLD, AND AROUND THE GALAXY!

- No Annual Fee
- Low introductory APR for cash advances and balance transfers
- Free trial membership in The Official STAR TREK Fan Club upon card approval*
- Discounts on selected STAR TREK Merchandise

To apply for the STAR TREK MasterCard today, call

1-800-775-TREK

Transporter Code: SKYD